CONNED

A ONE NIGHT STAND IS THE ONE, BODYGUARD ROMANCE

ALIAS PRIVATE WITNESS SECURITY ROMANCE

LISA HUGHEY

SALTY KISSES PRESS, LLC

To my mom who was an amazing role model. RIP, Mom. I miss you every day.

PROLOGUE

Zara Cooper rolled over in the luxurious sheets of the hotel room. The exorbitantly high-thread-count cotton tangled between her legs, and she stretched sore muscles from last night's strenuous workout.

Jake, first name only—because getting personal information hadn't been the point of last night's adventure—was gone. Not a surprise. She'd expected it. His absence made this morning easier. No awkward post-hookup interactions where she would pretend she'd call and he'd pretend he wanted her to. Or vice versa.

Last night hadn't been about forging new connections. More like forging ahead with her new life.

She'd taken back her power, approached him under her own steam, and initiated the best sex of her life.

She'd managed to keep her cool and take what she needed.

She hadn't intended to pick him up. But when she watched him reject the bartender in a kind way, she decided to go for it.

Her radar was clearly back on track after a really bad stretch when she'd trusted the wrong man. David Trask had fooled her. But she'd gotten out of a bad situation and reclaimed herself.

Jake had been a good guy and amazing in bed. She smiled.

Now she could focus on her future. She glanced at the clock on the nightstand. She needed to get up and get dressed. She had a meeting with her new boss in two hours. Just enough time to wash away the smell of a night well spent and get her head on straight before having breakfast with Jillian Larsen.

A few hours later, she shut the door on the suite with a tinge of regret. Jake, first name only, was now part of her past.

Time to look toward the future.

In the ornate lobby, marble floors, Persian rugs, low-slung settees, and round coffee tables gave the hotel an art deco vibe.

The company had put her up in this lovely hotel. It wasn't too far from her new rowhouse. The movers should be here later today.

She sauntered past the scene of last night's triumph at the hotel bar, and a tiny smile quirked her mouth. She'd chosen wisely.

Jillian Larsen strode toward her in no-nonsense manner. Her focus was laser tight on Zara, completely oblivious to the appreciative looks she garnered from the people loitering around the hotel lobby.

Jillian smiled with a warmth that reached her ice gray eyes. "Zara. Great to see you again."

They shook hands, Jillian's grip firm and assertive.

Zara liked her. She didn't think they'd be besties or anything, but she was hopeful that Jillian would be a fair and open boss.

"Nice to see you, too."

"How are the accommodations?" Jillian walked toward the small restaurant off the lobby as if she owned the place.

"Stellar." She thought about Jake, and her smile widened.

After they were seated at the restaurant, Zara decided to get this out of the way first. "Thank you for taking a chance on me."

Her background wasn't quite what Adams-Larsen had been looking for, but she'd had a feeling when she applied that their firm would be a good fit. The bonus was that Washington, D.C. was a long way from California. It didn't hurt that her parents knew one of the founder's parents. They were friends with Judge Bobby Adams. Zara had met the judge at a holiday party one year. He had put in a good word for her which helped as well.

"Your references are impeccable." Jillian brushed aside her thanks. "And I am an excellent judge of character."

Zara's pride grew. "I'm excited to get started."

"Let's go over the logistics." Jillian handed her a set of keys. "These open the front and back door. We've also got security cameras which are monitored from our other location in Georgetown."

Zara accepted the keys. The moment felt fraught with an unexpected tension. The hefty metal keys solid and heavy in her hand gave the moment weighted importance.

"You will run the office in Arlington. The main focus is public relations and some spin. At the moment, we don't have any political clients. However, I'm not opposed to them, and they are hard to avoid in this town."

Zara nodded.

"We handle reputation management out of the Georgetown office. Ours are hush-hush clients. We don't have a list posted anywhere, and we never, ever, disclose their identities."

A trickle of unease filtered through her excitement.

"If you get calls about anyone, refer them to me."

"Done."

"We also keep your office client list private." Jillian worried at one white-blonde eyebrow. "We don't guard those names quite as closely. We work primarily on referrals and word of mouth."

Zara was a little surprised. Most PR firms wanted potential clients to know who they represented. But she supposed in Washington, D.C. there were plenty of movers and shakers who didn't want their need for public relations or spin known.

She and Jillian chatted through breakfast. At the end, Jillian handed her a credit card. "This is a company card. You'll handle the expenses with accounting. Obviously, if it's a very large expenditure, we may need to discuss. Send me monthly reports."

Sounded fine to her.

"You have autonomy to run the business the way you want." Jillian shrugged into her suit jacket. "We can meet once a month to go over clients and programs. Typically, there isn't any crossover, but if you ever have any questions, I will be available for you."

Zara's excitement built. She could take the reins and run with it. "Thank you for entrusting me with it."

"I'm looking forward to seeing what you can do with the agency." Jillian smiled ruefully. "We haven't spent as much time as I would have liked building your side of the business, but we are pleased to expand it now."

"You won't regret it."

"Consider this your official welcome to Adams-Larsen Inc." They shook hands.

Zara was on a new journey, and everything was looking up.

1

———

SEVERAL MONTHS LATER
Zara waited nervously at the bar of her favorite hotel.

She'd confess to no one that she'd come back here a few times to grab a drink with friends, hoping to run into Jake, first name only.

She'd been disappointed. She'd never seen her mystery man again. She wasn't even sure where he lived. It was possible he'd only been here for a trip, although she'd gotten the feeling he lived in D.C. She shoved aside the severe disappointment.

She had bigger things on her mind this morning.

She'd been slowly building the ALI business, and she was thrilled that the agency was getting notice. Their word-of-mouth referrals had tripled since she'd taken over. They'd recently hired another two specialists with excellent experience. Adams-Larsen Inc. paid well.

This morning's meeting could up the cachet of the ALI brand for all involved. At the very least, this client would add another client sector to their portfolio.

The current it-guy in the media, a self-made billionaire and philanthropist from California, and recently elected to his second term in the House of Representatives, walked into the bar with confidence but not arrogance. He scanned the patrons and noticed her sitting at the table in the corner; he smiled and strode toward her. His wife, Carolina, whom he had met in college, followed slightly behind him.

A couple of bodyguards discreetly trailed their boss.

"Zara. It's a pleasure to meet you in person."

They'd had multiple conversations on the phone over the past week.

He shook her hand quickly and then let go. His handshake was firm without trying to wrestle her to the ground but not limp, either. His demeanor was respectful with no suggestive undertones.

"It's nice to meet you, sir."

"No formality needed. Call me Xavier." His voice was deep and filled with an assurance that oozed from his very being.

Xavier Rodriguez was a dream client. He had attended a state school and graduated with honors. Then he'd attended Stanford Law school. He had married his college sweetheart, a woman whose parents had immigrated to the United States to seek asylum. Together, they'd had two adorable daughters. His foundation supported causes that Zara was also passionate about, especially giving opportunities to those who might be overlooked by traditional funding, supporting underserved communities by backing entrepreneurial oppor-tunities, and mentoring young people committed to making a difference at the local level. He was willing to fight for anything he believed in.

His physical appearance only helped his ratings. He was a little under six feet tall, thin, athletic build, square jaw, longish black hair with a bit of a wave, and thick lashes framing his dark brown eyes.

Two years ago, he'd run for the House of Representatives as an Independent and won in a landslide. This last election, he'd run unopposed.

He'd built his empire by diversifying XR Global Innovations into multiple business. Technology, corporate farming, the service industry, and now he'd turned to politics.

"This is my wife, Carolina." He pronounced her name with the Spanish accent, the emphasis on Caro-*lee*-na.

She smiled with kind eyes. Zara wasn't often fanciful, but something about Carolina Rodriguez inspired whimsy. She had delicate features and soulful brown eyes lit with a deep well of kindness.

She was dressed conservatively in what Zara privately referred to as preppy chic. A twinset pale yellow cardigan and shell emphasized her beautiful light brown skin and was paired with a flowy floral skirt and ballet flats in a neutral beige. Exquisite large pearls adorned her ears and her soft pink lipstick matched the skirt.

Xavier pulled out the chair for his wife and then sat next to her. She crossed her hands in her lap. Xavier placed one large hand over hers and squeezed, then rested their loosely joined hands on the tabletop.

Zara had arrived early and ordered an iced tea. "Would you like something to drink?"

"Only ice water for me," Carolina demurred.

"I'll have an orange juice." He smiled. "Did you know that California has surpassed Florida in orange production?"

She loved that he supported his home state in small ways as well as big. She knew that as part of his personal portfolio, he owned several citrus farms in the Central Valley.

The waitress left to get their drinks, and Xavier began.

"I'm sure you're wondering why I want your services."

They hadn't discussed much beyond fee structure and confidentiality. "Would you prefer that we sign nondisclosures first?" Zara had brought pre-printed documents, hopeful that she was going to snag this business. "I have them prepared."

He glanced at his wife and smiled broadly. "See. I knew she was the one. She's already putting us first."

Carolina's lips tilted up. "You were correct."

"I'm always right." Xavier laughed, his teeth white in his tanned face. "I'm going to remind you that you said that."

Carolina's smile lost some of its shine.

Their discussions had been very informal and light on content, but she wondered if her instincts had been on target. Prior to running for office, Xavier had made a name in Washington as a major contributor to lobbyists who advanced his business interests, but he also personally advocated for laws that benefited marginalized communities.

In his first term in Congress, he had co-sponsored bills that had garnered bi-partisan support. He was known for working with all politicians to affect governmental change.

His entrance into politics had been relatively seamless. He'd purchased a house— mansion—in D.C. and split his time between the nation's capital and his ranch in Central California.

He was a household name. Even though he was a billionaire, he came off as a regular guy. No hundred-million-dollar yachts or twenty rare automobiles or sixty-thousand-square-foot mansions. Even his mansion in the D.C. area was modest compared to many billionaires. He lived a fairly low-key life.

People knew who he was. He was featured in the news consistently.

He'd been on the cover of *Forbes, Time* and *Harvard Business*

Review, all touting his business acumen and his civic mindedness.

As a client, he would be a major coup for Zara. She loved that he'd contacted her, but she also wondered why he was interested in Adams-Larsen Inc.

"We want to start positioning for a run for higher office."

Zara's heart thudded hard, then sped up. This could be huge. He didn't say it out loud. But higher office could only mean he wanted to run for president.

She wanted his business. She *really* wanted it. But she also didn't want to misrepresent what they did. She hated to point this out.

"You know I'm not a political strategist." While she had studied spin, reputation management, and image restoration and seen the results in action, it wasn't her area of expertise. She focused more on strategic communications and brand management.

"That's exactly why I want *you*."

He was a flatterer, but his flattery came off as sincere. In no way did he hint at anything other than a business relationship. Xavier Rodriguez was everything he seemed to be.

"You might be better off with our sister business. They are on the reputation management side."

"Ah, I don't believe they will bring the same passion and commitment that you will." Xavier brushed aside her demurral. "Plus, I don't need to be managed. I want to continue to increase my reach in a way that feels organic and authentic."

She knew she could help him.

"These days, it's all about the messaging to sway public influence. With the right message and vehicles, the public will see the image I wish to portray. My scheduler can get me on television news shows, but that isn't what I want. I want to be out there, meeting people and effecting change."

"We believe you are who we need." Carolina didn't come off as politically ambitious, but she'd been top of her class in undergrad. "Xavier has goals that you can help us with."

"What my wife means—" He shot Carolina a tight smile. "—is you are the one."

He had major political support. He had the respect of colleagues on both sides of the aisle. He was young—but not too young. Charismatic. Passionate. And he had broad appeal. He worked hard to get the youth vote out and encourage kids to get politically active. He'd never run any kind of smear campaign. He'd literally refused to do it when he could have highlighted his opponent's misconduct in his first race. A staffer in his campaign leaked the information after Xavier won his seat, and after the leak, the staffer was fired.

The thought of working for him was thrilling.

"We need to find events that cement my brand and align with my values and to garner positive press while doing it. Without advertising that I'm using a PR firm."

She wanted this so badly.

"As long as you know that my background is not in reputation management." As far as she could tell, he didn't have anything negative in his background. He was a dream client and a dream candidate.

"We did extensive research before contacting you," Xavier said.

The way he asserted that made her pause. Did he mean research on Adams-Larsen Inc. or on *her* specifically?

Carolina's next words distracted her. "We love the idea of having a fellow Californian run this next step in Xavier's efforts to open up to broader appeal and gain more positive name recognition."

Zara's heart warmed, a glow of happiness spread through her. They wanted *her*.

Xavier said, "Adams-Larsen has a reputation for being discreet."

"We are."

"Excellent. Our relationship will be confidential."

The little bubble of optimism popped. No one would know she was working on his campaign, except Jillian. At least her boss would know that she had recruited a high profile, well-paying, client.

"Which I require." Xavier's smile disappeared.

"Absolutely. You can expect complete discretion from me."

"Carolina keeps our laundry nice and clean. Don't you, *mi amor*?"

Carolina's smile dimmed. "Absolutely."

Zara thought about what they'd already discussed and knew that she needed to expand her research. If he was making a run for the presidency, she would also need to work on the potential first lady's agenda as well.

"I'd also like to know what kinds of causes you support, Carolina."

Zara had done research on Xavier's wife, but most of the information out there pertained to her impact on Xavier's career. She'd been humanities studies, pre-law in college, but then she'd gone to work as a teacher while Xavier went to law school. Her healthcare and steady income had been instrumental in supporting Xavier's ambitions.

"Let's keep the focus on me."

Zara got a little ping. It wasn't surprising that a guy this successful had an ego. He wouldn't have gotten where he was today if he didn't.

"I am not going to be one of those candidates who gets upstaged by his wife." With that steely tone and rock jaw, Zara didn't believe he was kidding. She might have found his flaw.

She dismissed the fanciful thought, and they got down to business.

"A supportive and accomplished partner is always an asset, not someone who will overshadow." She smiled at Carolina kindly. They could discuss her interests later. She had been a teacher; maybe policy ideas regarding the cost of child-care and paid family leave. "Think about what you want your emphasis to be on. Typically, the First Lady has an issue that she champions."

"You're getting way ahead of the game." Xavier's sharp tone shifted the conversation back to him.

"Just something to keep in mind."

Obtaining Xavier Rodriguez as a client was a major coup even if no one knew about it. While she hadn't specifically targeted politicians as a customer base, the idea that she could help influence lawmakers and policy gave her a thrill.

"I am honored to be working with you."

If only she had someone to share this victory with.

2

---

id-December

"Jill needs to see you in her office."

Jake Brown wondered what that was about. He reviewed the past few weeks. He hadn't done anything that would warrant a call to the boss's office.

Unlike when he'd been a hotheaded kid and in the principal's office a lot, these days he thought before he reacted. Time and life had evened out his temperament.

He smiled at the new receptionist, Hannah. She'd been giving him clear signals that she'd be interested in hooking up, but he didn't mix sex with business. Ever.

Plus, she was coming off a traumatic situation, involving murder, violence, and domestic abuse.

He walked into Jill's office.

The office was divided into two sections, a giant partner desk with wing chairs across from the boss and a sitting area with fancy sofas and a coffee table. The room was walled with bookshelves and a few windows. Jill sat behind the desk.

Jillian Larsen was a stunning woman. She had an ice queen vibe with platinum blonde hair and steely gray eyes, but underneath that forbidding exterior, she hid a kind heart. He used to think the slightly stuffy interior suited her, but since she'd met Hamish, her Scottish boyfriend, she'd lightened up.

The décor and atmosphere of the room reminded him of the wealthy folk in the town where he'd grown up . . . his mother's resentment, his sister's fascination, and how both had imploded his life.

His sister was dead, and his mother rarely talked to him.

"I need you to head over to the Adams-Larsen Inc. office and pick up a promotion plan for me."

He shook off the toxic memories. He couldn't change the past. "We're doing promo?" That seemed…odd.

"We're going to leak a few PR clients to the press."

They'd had bad news coverage recently. There were rumblings around the Capitol that ALIAS was doing shady things. Which, of course, they were. All within the confines of the law, but their client list was confidential, top secret, and under serious lock and key.

Each client file had a number, not a name. They relocated ordinary citizens in danger who didn't qualify for federal witness protection. They took care of people under duress and made sure they were safe. It was an excellent way to make a living.

ALIAS's business was naturally covert. Leaking clients from their affiliated office seemed like a bad precedent. He didn't like it. Of course, he wasn't the boss, so he didn't have a say.

"Why?"

"Throw the press off."

That seemed ill-advised. "You don't want to wait for the next political scandal to hit?"

They had recently helped Dr. Mina Patel, and that scandal had hit the papers this week. It wouldn't be long before there was another. Washington, D.C. was ripe with rumors and coverups.

"Nope. Marsh has a family friend who needs public relations help. We're going to take care of her PR problem, and, hopefully, solve our own at the same time."

That made sense.

"I hired a new managing director a few months back to expand that area of our business." Jillian worried at the edge of a piece of paper on her desk. "She's doing a great job. So it's time to make that branch more public."

She continued to trace the paper on her blotter.

"Okay." She clearly had something else on her mind. "What's up?"

He hated the look on her face, somber and concerned. His heart picked up in rhythm. "What's wrong? You're freaking me out."

"Edward Drayton is up for parole."

The man who had killed his sister, Amancia. Jake stilled, unable to process. That asshole could get out of prison and be free to live his life while his sister never would?

Over his dead body. Jake didn't move a muscle while his brain whirled with rage and unadulterated fear.

"I thought you'd be more upset," Jill commented.

"Oh, I am upset." Feelings weren't his strong suit. He'd worked long and hard to suppress the rage that had gotten him in trouble before he'd learned to master his anger. Jake's brain was pinging around, unable to settle on a subject. He would need to go see his mother. That made him feel things.

"When's the hearing?" He was surprised he hadn't been notified.

"They haven't set it yet. I have an agreement with the warden to notify me ahead of time."

Looking out for him. Jake's heart warmed. "I appreciate it."

The heads up would give him time to refine his plea to the parole board so that fucker only saw the light of day through a fenced prison yard. He didn't deserve his freedom. But Jake had to be smart about how he presented his case.

"Do you…want to talk about it?" Jill's body was stiff, awkward.

Jake laughed. One of the reasons he liked his boss was that she wasn't an over-sharer. She was matter-of-fact and got shit done.

"Man, that looked painful."

"Yeah, this whole sharing thing is still a challenge for me," she said wryly.

Ever since Jill had hooked up with her Scottish guy, she'd been more warm and fuzzy. Warm and fuzzy *for her*. Though subtle, the change was apparent.

"How is Hamish?"

"He's brilliant." Brilliant was said in a Scottish brogue. Her face transformed when she smiled, thawing that ice queen vibe.

"I'm really glad for you." She deserved to be happy.

"So, what are you going to do?" Jill sat behind her desk, looking concerned.

"Talk to the parole board and state my case." Tell them about how Drayton the Fourth was a master manipulator and couldn't be trusted. He presented a charming façade to the world. but beneath that outer layer lurked a predator.

"Good." Jill fidgeted in the wing chair. "Want to talk about whatever else is bothering you?"

Shit. When had she become so perceptive?

"Not really."

"Thank God."

He laughed again.

"But I would, if you needed to talk it out," Jill said earnestly.

"I know." He paused, wondering. "Do you really need me to go pick this thing up?"

"Truth?"

"Yeah."

"I could have one of the others do it, but I thought getting out of the office for a bit might be good for you."

He smiled. "Then I'll do it."

"Great. Head on over. The new managing director who does Media Relations has worked up a comprehensive plan. I need it right away."

"Sure thing, boss."

Jake had suddenly become an errand boy. He'd been picking up the slack while the rest of the group paired off with their new significant others. It was weird. He didn't know how he felt about it.

He knew his friends were happy. They had fallen in love on ops, so their new partners understood their business, understood the need for secrecy.

Love wasn't for him.

He didn't share much whenever he dated, and he couldn't imagine being vulnerable enough to share his feelings with a woman. Having sex was one thing. But opening up was the road to being hurt. History proved that one day they would leave. Permanently like his dad or his sister, or emotionally like his mom.

Being alone was safer.

So, he'd suppressed the longing to go back to that bar and see if his one-night stand showed up again.

That night was his best in recent memory, the sex and the laughter, but also the worst when he woke up and realized that all they were going to have was a fleeting connection in the dark.

He'd thought of Zara from that night more often than he should over the past few months. He'd even been tempted to go back to that hotel bar…just in case. That sense of connection he'd felt with her had to be exaggerated in his mind. Right?

It was awesome. It was over. And he'd left without saying goodbye.

But ever since his hookup, he'd been off.

"Zara is expecting you."

Jake stilled. Zara?

"Zara?" It was an unusual name. What were the odds that his Zara and the new manager were the same person? Pretty fucking high.

He wasn't crazy about his brain tacking *his* onto her name.

"Yes. She moved here from California to take this position, and she's doing a stellar job. She already picked up a few high-profile clients."

"Okay."

He hadn't been able to get Zara out of his mind after their explosive one-night stand. He'd wake up after dreams that left him hard and aching for a woman he couldn't have.

Suddenly, he was going to see her again.

His heart sped up. He shouldn't want to see her. Nothing could happen between them. They worked together. Sort of.

He literally couldn't tell her what he did for ALIAS. His anticipation fizzled like a spent helium balloon. As his pal Viktor said, how do you have a relationship with someone when you can't reveal how you spend seventy percent of your life?

Which meant she was totally off-limits.

3

Zara finished straightening her desk.

She had plenty of work left to do for the night. She'd been preparing to head to her rowhouse, turn on the fireplace, and study her plans for Xavier Rodriguez with a glass of reserve cabernet while tucked underneath a throw.

But Jillian had called and said she was sending someone over to pick up the media plan that she'd had Zara assemble—in a hurry, no less—for one of the other office's clients, an artist.

Zara's stomach gurgled.

It wasn't hunger. It was nerves.

She'd been at Adams-Larsen Inc. for over four months. She'd settled in. She liked her staff. She was slowly building their business, which was far less expansive than she'd expected.

One of the major reasons she'd left California was that there, everyone had expectations of her. Many people in the business assumed she'd gotten her job through nepotism and expected nothing from her. And when she had a successful client project, many assumed she'd gotten the credit while someone else did the work.

She wanted to be judged for what she did, not her family name.

This job had given her that opportunity.

In one area, Jillian had been completely up front. Zara was solely in charge of this office. She sent monthly financial reports and kept Jillian informed when they signed a new client, especially if it was a big one. Otherwise, she didn't interact with the other office at all.

That was not unexpected; plenty of public relations firms had separate offices for their segmented businesses. However, a few unsettling articles in the paper recently and sly queries about the other branch of Adams-Larsen from a few clients, and little things about their business reputation had begun to nag at her.

Her phone rang. Her mother. She sighed and clicked the answer button.

"Hi, Mom."

"Hey, honey."

A genuine warmth flowed through her. She loved her mother. She did. But she had a feeling they were about to have another argument.

"How are your holiday plans coming along?"

"My boss dumped a bunch of work on my plate." *Truth.* "I may not be able to make it." Technically that wasn't a lie. The excuse wasn't the truth, either.

She'd pulled away from her family after the debacle with David. Her parents would be ashamed of her weakness. *She* was ashamed of her weakness. She'd never told a soul what had happened.

"Oh." Her mother sighed dramatically. "Your father and I were hoping you'd be able to come home for Christmas."

So her mom could hound her in person about taking a job all the way across the country. Only because she loved Zara and missed her. She knew that.

"Our annual charity ball won't be the same without you."

Her family's foundation raised a lot of money at the holidays. It was a great event. She'd worked in the office as a teenager and run the promo for it when she'd lived in the Bay Area.

"I'll send a check this year."

She loved her family. She'd grown up in a wealthy family with solid middle-class values. She'd had a fairy tale childhood and life, pretty much getting everything she'd ever wanted. Made the cheerleading squad in high school, got into her first choice for college, got in her first pick sorority in college, president of her sorority, graduated with honors, got a job with the most prestigious public relations firm in San Francisco. All part of the experience of growing up in the Cooper—as in Cooper Winery—family. Not everything she'd accomplished had been because of her family name. But plenty of opportunities had come with her connections.

She hadn't had a contentious relationship or difficulty ever. Her life had been smooth until she'd made a horrible mistake with David.

"I just got a new client. An artist. She does really cool work." Ayesha Brown was an up-and-coming artist. If she'd come to ALI, Zara would have been thrilled to represent her. But the fact that Jillian's branch had taken Ayesha as a client, and then called her to write the media plan, was bothering her on a cellular level. A niggle of doubt as to why the other office was handling Ayesha Brown's account worried in the back of her brain.

The plan Zara had composed was for standard public relations, her specialty, not reputation management. So why was the Georgetown office handling Ayesha Brown?

To top it off, Jill wanted paparazzi notified, which meant a higher profile than they typically arranged. They did have pap contacts. But most of their clients preferred to stay *under* the radar. What the heck was that about?

That jiggly feeling in her stomach wouldn't abate. It felt as if the world was shifting on its axis in a way she couldn't predict.

"Things are up in the air."

The lock on the front door rattled. "I've got to go, Mom. Love you."

"Love you t— ." Zara hung up.

The person in the doorway wasn't Jillian. It was a large man, shadowed and broad. She wasn't afraid, exactly, because she was expecting a visitor from the other office, but a frisson of apprehension sizzled up her spine.

"I'm sorry. We're closed."

He stepped into the light, and her world tilted again. The tall, Black man with broad shoulders, a small waist, black curls short and tight against his scalp, and hypnotic topaz eyes stared back at her.

Jake, no last name.

She didn't know how he'd found her, but he needed to leave. She didn't have the emotional resources to deal with her one-night stand when her coworker was due at any moment.

"I'm sorry, you need to leave."

"I can't."

Zara flinched.

He hadn't struck her as being a crazy stalker. Fuck. Had she been wrong about him, too?

"Can't or won't?" she asked sharply, gripping her phone tightly, because she was in the office alone. She had some self-defense training. A must for every woman. But against a large man, she'd have little chance. How the heck had he gotten in?

"Can't. Our boss sent me."

Our boss. Her world dropped out from underneath her.

"Nice to see you again, Zara."

Dear God, what had she done?

4

W ow, she was *really* unhappy to see him.

The dismay on her face would have been comical if it hadn't been about him. She certainly didn't hide her feelings. Rather than amused, he was disappointed. Apparently, she'd been happy that he hadn't come looking for her. Clearly, she didn't want to see him again.

He hadn't missed her flinch.

As a large man and a Black man, he had garnered more than enough fearful looks over the years. He tried not to let it hurt. He was used to it.

But for once, it would be nice to be judged for his actions rather than his appearance.

"You work for Adams-Larsen?" Her shock coated every word. He guessed that from her perspective, he wasn't public relations employee material. She wouldn't be wrong.

He had had time to digest the fact that their one-night stand wasn't going to stay an anonymous hook up never to be seen again. But still.

"I could say the same." He kept his voice neutral.

She exhaled deeply. "This is … unfortunate."

Ouch. For some reason, her uneasiness rankled. "That's not what you said a few months ago. I distinctly recall—"

"Stop." She held up her palm. "I'm sorry. I'm just… surprised."

Disgusted, irritated. Jake thought he could substitute any of those words, and her meaning would be the same. Annoyance sharpened his words.

"We didn't stop fucking long enough to exchange business cards."

Her face flamed. "True," she said softly.

Shit. He was an asshole. Ever since Jill had told him about his sister's killer, he'd been off-balance.

"Sorry," he muttered.

None of this was her fault. None of the sleepless nights he'd endured recently were her fault. This restlessness that seethed inside him wasn't her fault.

He opened his mouth to apologize again when she thrust out her hand.

"Let's start over. Hi, I'm Zara Cooper, managing director of Adams-Larsen Inc."

Jake held out his hand in response. "Jake Brown, Adams-Larsen Inc and Associates. I'm one of the associates." They called themselves ALIAS as a joke, but it had stuck.

"Nice to meet you." She smiled, but he knew it wasn't her real smile. It was completely different from the smile she'd given him that night as he slid inside her.

Shit. Stop thinking about that!

He clasped her much smaller hand in his and ignored the zing. "Nice to meet you, too." He dropped her fingers as if they were radioactive.

She looked great. Maybe a little thinner than the last time he'd seen her. Her blonde hair with streaks of light brown was perfect in a perky bob that framed her face, accenting her cheekbones and sharp chin. Her blue eyes, reminding him of the wild blue phlox that carpeted meadows in his hometown, were framed by a thick sweep of lashes.

Her suit jacket hung on a hanger on a peg by the door, and her skirt was short but demure. The slate blue silk of her blouse draped over her breasts, drawing his gaze to her petite frame.

She had the physique of a runner.

He remembered those angular hipbones and the sleek perfection of her body. All angles and lines without lush curves that she'd apologized for not having. But she'd fit perfectly in his hands.

"You're here for the promo plan for a client."

"I guess so." Jake blinked, coming back to the conversation. "I'm only the errand boy."

She clutched the sheaf of papers in her hands tightly.

"Are you going to hand them over?"

"Why are you doing media relations for a client?"

Jake knew she had no idea what the "associates" did for a living. According to Jill, it wasn't uncommon to have different branches of a public relations firm. It also wasn't uncommon for the branches to be completely autonomous. The good news was, he could answer truthfully.

"Apparently she's a family friend of Marsh."

She looked blank.

"Adams in Adams-Larsen."

"Oh." She flushed. "Right."

But she hadn't handed it over. "Did you have anything to do with the stuff in the paper?"

"Stuff in the paper?"

"Yes. A Russian shot in the office, an international criminal shootout." She waved her hand vaguely.

Jake hadn't been involved in it all. The past few months

had been crazy. Marsh missing, guilty clients—the company had been in the papers, mostly as a footnote to the stories. But there had been enough mentions recently that he knew that Jill and Marsh were worried about their exposure and had worked hard to minimize the press surrounding ALIAS. Their business depended on secrecy.

Zara had missed crazy stalkers, endangered heiresses, and crooked politicians.

"I don't really know what the papers said." *True.*

"Seriously?"

"Seriously," he repeated emphatically. "I've been busy." Cleaning up messes that should have never made it into the papers that he totally hadn't read.

"Should I be worried?"

He wasn't sure what she was asking him. "About what?"

"Scratch that. You wouldn't tell me even if I should be concerned, would you?"

"Ah...." He didn't want to lie. "Probably not."

"So what do you do as an associate?"

Ugh, he couldn't really tell her that either. "A little bit of this and a little bit of that."

"Errands?" she asked skeptically.

"Sometimes."

"Huh, your errand the night we met must have been a doozy."

He'd been wrecked after that job.

Layla Habib's father, a local private investigator, had inadvertently done work for the Iranian government, spying on a dissident scientist in the D.C. area. After he was arrested, her father had committed suicide in jail. The speculation was that the Iranians had murdered him. Then the Iranians went after Layla because they believed that she had evidence of their guilt. They stalked and harassed her, and when she didn't give them what they wanted, they issued a Fatwa against her and put out a contract on her life.

Jake and ALIAS had relocated Layla to save her life. Jake had bonded with Layla because she reminded him of his sister. He had been determined she would survive.

But the night he had met Zara, he had just left Layla, miserable and alone, pining for the apparent love of her life.

That night he'd been unwilling to go back to his empty apartment and worry about Layla. He'd felt overprotective, and yet also as if he'd failed her too.

A month later, after going against all prior protocols, he had delivered Ben to Layla. He hoped and prayed the guy would stick. Layla deserved to be happy. He thought about Layla and Ben regularly. They were together now. Happy, hopefully. But in the back of his mind, he didn't believe they would last. No one did.

Which meant Ben was a loose end.

Shit, lost in memories of Layla and Ben, he'd been silent for too long.

"Yeah. A doozy." He couldn't tell her more than that. This was why guys like him, with his job, didn't have relationships. He couldn't tell her anything of substance.

Weirdly, he found he wanted to share with her.

"I'm sorry," he said again. Apologizing to her was becoming a habit.

She studied him.

"What's the plan?" Jake prompted when she didn't say anything else.

She held up the sheath of papers. "Um, to give you this then go home and work more."

"I meant, what's in that plan?"

"Oh." She blushed. "Media appearances, articles, and I got her a feature in the Sunday Lifestyle magazine."

That sounded like a foreign language.

Jake nodded as if he was familiar with all the things she'd mentioned when he didn't have a clue.

"Tip offs for the paparazzi for Ayesha Brown."

Paparazzi? He shuddered. Nothing sounded worse than publicity vultures lying in wait for innocent people trying to live their life.

"Oh, Ayesha *Brown*. Is she related to you? Like your sister or something?"

"Nope." His sister was dead. "I don't have a sister anymore."

"I'm sorry."

Him, too.

"Amancia's killer is up for parole," he blurted out. Not sure why he'd thought that was appropriate, but she was easy to talk to. They'd had an instant connection when they'd hooked up. But that was in the past and couldn't really happen again.

"Oh, my God." She tilted her head, her blonde bob brushing her shoulder. "Are you okay? What can I do for you?"

What popped into his head wasn't shareable.

"Uh, nothing." There was nothing to do. Jake had helped put the bastard away for his sister's murder. He'd make sure to testify to the parole board and warden. If Drayton got out, Jake would keep tabs on him. It wasn't justice, but it was what he was going to get. He couldn't kill him. He'd be no better than the asshole if he did.

Unfortunately.

5
___

God, she wanted to give him a hug.

A murdered sister. Her killer up for parole. How terrible. The need to comfort him rolled through her.

Was it too forward to give him a hug? Probably. He'd get the wrong idea. Or she would.

"Are you getting support?"

"Me?" His brow crinkled as if he was confused.

"Yes, you," she shot back. "I feel like you need a hug."

He blinked.

"Never mind." Her ex was always telling her she was too impulsive and too friendly with the opposite sex. "I mean, I'd offer a hug even if you were a woman. It's not because you're a man. Oh my God, stop me before I embarrass myself any further."

He snorted. "That was a lot." His mouth widened into a grin.

She may have embarrassed herself, but she'd wiped that despairing look off his face.

"Extra. That's me."

He stood very still. His head tilted a bit to the side, as if he couldn't quite figure out what to do with her.

"Huh. I would like a hug."

She nodded, now a little uncomfortable. Because shit, she'd been naked with him. But this was totally normal, right? Just one person offering another comfort after a rough day. She stepped toward him. Tentative, not as confident as she used to be. Damn her ex.

Zara stepped closer. The heat of his body enveloped her, seeping into her bones.

Jake sighed, a small puff of breath, as if he'd been holding it. His shoulders relaxed when she wrapped her arms around him.

She'd forgotten how big he was. He was all solid muscles with a small waist and a tight butt. Stop thinking about his ass, girl. But the rest of him was big. His shoulders were wide, his neck thick, his thighs and arms solid like the old oak branches in the front yard of their ancient farmhouse at the vineyard.

He slowly wrapped his arms around her, and she squeezed him tight.

"I'm sorry about your sister."

"Thanks," he replied softly. "Me, too."

"I'm always available to listen if you need a friendly ear." She didn't want to intrude on his privacy unless he wanted to share.

"He hit her." He ground out. His muscles tightened again, as if he were ready to spring into action. "And she let him."

"Oh."

"I'm sure it's hard for a woman as confident as you to understand, but my beautiful soul sister had self-esteem issues. He preyed on that."

"You'd be surprised," she murmured. "I'm so sorry."

"We tried to get her to leave, but she wouldn't. Eventually, one day he hit her too hard because she'd smiled a thank-you at the guy who pumped her gas."

She squeezed him more tightly. She remembered those days. Walking on eggshells, never sure what was going to set David off. "It wouldn't have made any difference. He'd have hit her for another reason."

Jake stiffened against her embrace, as if he heard the subtext beneath her words. As if he understood that she had personal experience with an abuser. Shame rolled through her, her stomach tossing and turning, souring everything around her. How had she, an educated, financially independent woman with plenty of resources, let that happen?

She couldn't pinpoint the exact moment she'd realized that she was trapped. She knew the moment she decided to leave, but it had taken far longer than it should have to make it happen. But she'd done it.

She was free. And she was happy.

"Is that why you moved across the country?"

She smoothed her face and stepped out of the embrace, surprised at the sense of loss that accompanied the move.

"I'm sorry about your sister."

He studied her for a few silent moments and then didn't push, thank God. "Me, too."

The rest of their brief conversation was stilted, and after another few minutes, he left.

Zara sighed as exhaustion rolled over her. It had been a long week. She'd been burning sleep as she worked on the large plan for Xavier Rodriguez and also got her new employees up to speed.

Taking on the extra payroll would be expensive, but the Rodriquez campaign was going to be big and time-consuming.

Zara was feeling a bit adrift. She was used to be part of a

team. But now she was in charge. Her employees respected her, but they didn't hang out together. She was the boss.

The only physical affection she'd had recently was the hug she'd given Jake.

She ran through a gamut of emotions as she thought about her one-night stand. She'd gone back to that hotel bar several times and never seen her mystery man Jake again. She'd finally assumed that he had been passing through when they met.

She couldn't believe they worked for the same company. She'd relived those memories often in the dark of the night. Their connection forged in scented air and heated sighs.

Now that she'd found him again, he was off-limits. He worked for the same company. A branch that had secrets. She hadn't missed that he'd been evasive about the reputation management arm of Adams Larsen.

The last thing she needed was an office affair.

She was in the process of taking back her power and forging a new life with new ambitions and new goals. She wasn't about to complicate this new chapter with a man, even if he had rocked her world one night.

She had no time for a guy who wasn't truthful with her.

All those cautions catalogued, accepted, and regretted—because not renewing her connection with Jake was the logical path forward. Instead, she stared wistfully toward the door and wished he'd stayed longer.

6

A FEW WEEKS LATER
He had threatened a woman with violence.
Acid burned his esophagus, geysering up as his stomach revolted again. Jake was back home and dry heaving in his bathroom as his body rejected his actions.

Images strobed in his brain: the terror on the woman's face, his panic as she'd fainted, restraining her, locking her in the safe room.

Worse than the physical symptoms, a despair gripped him, making it hard to focus.

He'd had to do it. Terrify her. Make her think he was going to kill her. It had been a matter of life and death, literally.

But he was bone-weary with a fatigue that went to the depths of his soul.

Jake and Viktor had gotten the information they needed from the sex worker, but at what cost to his soul? *He* knew he wasn't going to hurt her. But she hadn't known that he was a literally teddy bear. His crusade in life was to protect women, not hurt them. Never hurt them.

He was no better than Edward Drayton if he hurt a woman.

Viktor had needed information, and they hadn't had time to finesse answers from her. He was under a time crunch.

More people were going to die—especially the woman Jake threatened—if they didn't find out what she knew. But it didn't stop Jake from being revolted by the intimidation. After the second interrogation, he'd thrown up violently at the office.

She was secure now. Spirited away to a safe house where the bad guys couldn't get her. ALIAS didn't have any leaks. They were too tightly controlled and tight-knit to let anything happen to their protectees.

But he needed to cleanse the stain from his soul.

He'd been thinking about Zara since the day he'd stopped in the office, lamenting the fact that he'd been both happy to see her and horrified that they worked for the same company.

He'd longed to seek her out again and see if that connection he believed they'd shared the night they met was just his imagination. Maybe love wasn't for him, but he longed for some surcease from the sorrow that dogged him lately.

He had no plans to sleep with a co-worker.

And yet…as soon as he stepped into the shower, his thoughts returned to her. To the softness of her skin, the breathy sighs she'd uttered as he'd slid inside her. The respite she'd given him, if only for the night.

He needed to get out of his own head.

If he stayed home, he'd wallow in the despair and disgust haunting him. Everyone at ALIAS was all loved up these days. Even Viktor was probably tucked away with his mysterious guy.

While Jake couldn't stand his own company right now.

He slipped on a white button-down shirt and khakis. The exact opposite uniform of the thug who threatened that woman and headed out to find a distraction.

No drinking, he was on call for the office. He'd need his ride in case he had to go. Things had been crazy lately.

Without a place in mind, he left. When he got in his truck, of its own volition it turned toward the place that haunted his dreams, the hotel where he'd met Zara the first time.

Coming here wasn't going to help him forget her, so he must be a glutton for punishment. He headed toward the bar and his memories.

Jake paused to let his eyes adjust to the dim lighting. He scanned the interior, jolting when he spied Zara at a table in the corner by the fireplace.

Could she be feeling the same pull as he did?

Anticipation swelled in his chest. His heart thudded in an uneven beat. Maybe she was as haunted by that night as he was. Maybe she'd been longing for that connection again, too. Maybe she felt the same sense of loss.

Maybe he was meant to see her here tonight.

His mood shifted from somber to buoyant. *Zara was here.*

He *should* stay away from her, but he couldn't resist her pull.

When he was only a few feet away, she looked up, her eyes widening. Before he could say anything, a man cut in from his right with a coffee pot in his hand.

"Tracked down the bartender and got her to make a new pot." The smooth man lifted the carafe at Zara, completely oblivious to Jake. "Used to be a waiter in high school."

It was then Jake noticed the two coffee cups on the table and the sheaf of papers between them.

Hope disintegrated into a sick ball in his gut.

Jake stiffened. Guess he was the only one haunted by the memories of their night together. He nearly stumbled, his body leaden, the last few steps as if wading through the swamps where he grew up.

Zara's jaw snapped shut and she smiled tightly.

For whatever reason, he couldn't just walk away. This was probably a business meeting even if it was late and an unusual venue. "Hi, Zara."

"Jake." Her voice sound like she was speaking through broken glass.

He turned to the man, dressed in khakis and a button down, the same as Jake, but his clothes were fancier, and he had that polished veneer of money. People were probably impressed by that polish, but Jake understood that veneers covered up the ugly and the diseased, putting a pretty façade on rot.

"Hello." The guy didn't seem territorial, and yet Jake felt the need to piss in the sand.

Jake thrust out his hand. "Jake Brown."

Two big men one table over stood quickly. One put his hand to his waist as if ready to go for a weapon. Bodyguards?

The guy extended his hand, and they shook, his grip solid, firm with a little squeeze as if he wanted to strangle Jake's fingers but was holding himself back.

"Xavier Rodriguez."

Shit. Everyone knew Rodriguez. He was practically a household name these days. Billionaire businessman-turned-politician.

"How do you know Zara?" Rodriguez asked.

Jake dropped the man's hand.

"We work together," Zara interjected quickly as if she knew he wanted to make it more personal.

"Ah," was all Xavier said. But there was a wealth of understanding in his brown-eyed gaze. "Well, I'd best be getting home. Carolina had a charity thing tonight, and I want to check in and see how she spent my money."

The guy shrugged into his sport coat and picked up the papers. "I like what you've come up with so far. I'll be in touch."

He tapped the papers against his palm. "Night."

The two large men followed their principal.

Zara wanted to leave, too. Jake could see it in her eyes. She stood up.

"Good night, Xavier." Her smile was warm, congenial but not suggestive.

Once Xavier Rodriguez was out of sight, she turned toward Jake.

"What are you doing here?"

He should say he just wanted a drink. He should deflect. "What are *you* doing here?"

She shrugged. "Xavier likes this place."

Jake raised one brow, suspicion simmering in his gut and clear in his voice. "Xavier?"

"Really, Jake?" she hissed. "He's a client."

Jake pulled up a chair from a neighboring table. He couldn't bear to use the other man's chair. He was acting like an ass. He knew it, and he couldn't stop.

His body rejected his behavior, bile rising again.

Zara picked up the rest of her belongings from the table and stuffed them into her bag. "What do you want?"

So many things. "That's a loaded question."

He ached with the desire to hold her in his arms again. But his behavior wasn't going to earn him that right.

She rubbed at her temple with nails tipped with white. "It's been a long day. Can you cut to the chase?"

"Something is off about him." Xavier must be a client of Adams-Larsen Inc. But meeting at a hotel bar late at night was strange. "Why didn't you meet in the office?"

"When a client is going to pay us as much as he is going to pay us, if he wants to meet at the local garbage dump, I will do it."

"Isn't it a little weird?"

He couldn't put his finger on what was bothering him.

"It is unusual. However, since we promo-ed Ayesha Brown, we've had more reporters staking out the office, hoping for a peek at our clients. If the client wants to keep a low profile, we agree to meet offsite."

Offsite. He got that. But that little voice of intuition told him there was more to the location than that.

Jake continued to frown, unable to pinpoint his concerns.

She rolled her eyes. "He's a billionaire."

Xavier emitted a vibe. Too slick. Too assessing. Too calculating.

"There's something off about him."

"He's a genius."

She defended the guy, but Jake trusted his instincts.

She rolled her eyes. "Having money doesn't make you bad."

"It's true that I am not a fan of people with too much money—"

"Not everyone is like Edward Drayton." She bristled. "Plenty of people with money are perfectly nice people."

"How do you know about Drayton?" He hadn't shared anything except that the POS was up for parole. He had only mentioned small details. Not his name or the fact that his family had tons of money.

"I googled him," she muttered.

What? "Why?" he asked blankly.

Her gaze cut to the fire. "I was curious."

About me? My sister?

"Occupational hazard." Zara flushed. "I research everything."

Every*one* was implied.

7

____

*C*ould *the floor please open up and swallow me?*

Good going, Zara. She was tired, or she never would have admitted that she'd googled his sister's murder because she was fascinated with Jake. She'd been a little obsessed with learning more about the man who'd rocked her world. She couldn't forget their night together.

Her obsession had gotten worse since she'd seen him again and discovered they worked for the same, sort of, company. Different office. With very different focuses.

The man who'd murdered his sister was from an old southern family who'd ruled the town for over a hundred years. It was almost a miracle that he'd been convicted.

Jake grimaced.

"I'm sorry." She placed her hand over his. Tingles zinged through her arm. How could this man affect her so completely?

She'd tried to forget him. Her work schedule had been insane. Getting the business ramped up had consumed her. Wanting to make a fresh start and wanting to impress her new boss, she'd spent all her time working and building her team.

She hadn't even set up new online dating profiles with D.C. as her home.

She had a few friends who lived here, and they'd grabbed drinks occasionally, but they were more casual relationships. She'd left her family in California, and her good friends were scattered across the country. She'd wanted a break, and she'd gotten it, but she was lonely.

In Jake, she sensed a kindred spirit.

Like a monolith, cloaked in a cape of loneliness, his solitude gave off serious 'leave me alone' vibes.

He clearly had a chip on his shoulder about rich people. What would he say if he met her family? Why did that even cross her mind? There was literally no reason for Jake Brown to meet the extended Cooper clan.

"You don't have to be rich to be violent and abusive."

He shut down at her words, his face completely wiped of emotion.

"What's wrong?" What had triggered that look?

"Nothing." His voice was flat.

But she knew intuitively that he was thinking of himself. "You wouldn't hurt anyone."

He snorted. "What makes you think that?"

Because of the way he'd treated the bartender the night they met. Because of the way he'd treated her. She used to believe the best of everyone. But David Trask had shaken her faith.

"I have excellent instincts." Or she had. Shit. Hopefully she hadn't let any of her own insecurities leak into that sentence.

"When I was a kid, I had anger issues." He said it almost defiantly as if daring her to argue with him. Clearly, he hadn't noticed her slip-up. Phew.

"When you were a kid." She kept her voice neutral. "What about as an adult?"

"I've done things I'm not proud of." Jake stood abruptly. "I should go."

Wait. What? "What's wrong?" She grabbed his hand and threaded their fingers together. The jolt of attraction startled her all over again.

He stopped moving as if stunned by the same powerful attraction that she felt.

Zara eased to her feet. "Don't go," she requested softly.

The Universe had thrown him into her path again. She wasn't about to waste this opportunity. When she got into bed at night, she relived the night she met Jake. The ease they'd had together and how opening up to him had felt effortless.

She wanted to draw him in and do dirty things to him in the dark. To slake away that sadness and make him smile. Based on the look on his face, that possibility seemed unlikely.

"Why?" he ground out.

She laid herself bare. "Because I think you feel this…draw between us as much as I do."

"Maybe."

She started to unlace their fingers, but he squeezed her hand tightly. "Okay. Yes."

They stood by the fire, encircled in their own little world as lust and tension swirled between them.

"What are we going to do about it?"

"I know what I'd like to do," she said breathlessly. All the fantasies she'd imagined in the dark of the night rushed into her brain. When she knew what she wanted, she went after it. And right now, she wanted Jake Brown.

"Come home with me."

8

———

This was probably a mistake.

Definitely a mistake.

"Ride share?" She didn't have a car. There was no need in the city. She took cabs or ride shares whenever she needed to get anywhere.

"I've got my truck."

"A truck in this city?"

"You can take the boy out of the country, but you can't take the country out of the boy." He'd thickened his accent and deepened his drawl, revealing a hint of the South. His rumbling voice sent a shiver down her spine.

Zara had time to change her mind. But she didn't want to.

"What made you come *here* tonight?"

"Didn't want to be alone." He held her hand as he led her toward his ride.

Did that mean he'd been planning to pick up any random woman? "I've come back here several times since I moved in, but I haven't seen you since…"

"This was my first time back." He unlocked the truck and helped her up. The skirt of her suit slid up, exposing her pantyhose-clad thigh. His fingers trailed up the nylon until he reached the hem of her skirt.

He traced the line of fabric, and shivers tingled up her leg, zapping straight to her clit. She gasped. "What was your plan?"

"Didn't really have one. I didn't want to be alone."

The shivers disappeared, replaced by disappointment. "Anyone would do?"

"No." He squeezed her knee and leaned in to nuzzle the sensitive spot below her ear. Her nipples hardened into aching peaks, and desire flooded her. "Truth? I was hoping to see you."

The memory of all the things he could do with those talented fingers cascaded through her brain. Jake leaned against the door frame, his body crowding hers, and he took her mouth with a commanding kiss.

He plundered, his tongue dueling with hers, his kisses voracious, consuming her mouth as if he couldn't get enough.

Zara moaned, and he pulled away.

"I hope you live close by, because I don't." His erection strained against the zipper of his khakis. Zara couldn't resist the impulse to caress him. She smoothed her palm over the front of his pants and squeezed.

"Ten minutes. Depending on traffic."

"Shit, Zara." He removed her hand and tucked it in her lap. After slamming the door shut, he hopped into the truck and started the engine.

She reached across the middle console but before she could touch him, he barked, "Hands to yourself."

She loved that he responded to her so passionately. She loved that he was as turned on as she was.

Her fingers brushed over a stack of well-worn comic books in haphazardly stacked in the console tray. "Luke Cage?"

"Uh, yeah. He's a Marvel Super Hero with superhuman strength who fights for justice."

The hint of uncertainty in his voice charmed her. "Kind of like you?"

"I'm not a hero." He brushed aside the comment.

But he'd fought for his sister.

"My sister used to give them to me." He laughed softly. "They were bribes to keep me busy during her dance lessons. My mom was a single mother, so I had to tag along to Cia's ballet classes."

Her heart melted at the affection in his voice.

"That's sweet."

"I'll show you sweet," he growled, clearly attempting to reestablish the lust-filled race to the car. "Where to?"

She gave him her address. He drove quickly and competently to her rowhouse. Incredibly, he found a parking space right in front. This was meant to be.

He helped her out of the truck, pinning her to the side for a kiss that sizzled down to her toes. Then they ran for her home.

She adored the historic building with its large doors and heavy brass knockers, but as she struggled with the old-fashioned key, she was regretting her choice. Jake locked his truck with a beep and took the keys from her.

Her voice was breathless. "It sticks sometimes. I've been meaning to get it fixed." She hadn't had the time.

He jiggled the lock and expertly opened the door. A dark car drove slowly down her street, taking so long that she glanced back as the front door swung shut.

She dropped her computer case and purse by the door as Jake set her keys on the small cherry console table she'd placed in the large foyer.

She forgot all about the car as he stalked toward her, desire stamped in the harsh lines of his cheekbones. His intensity weakened her knees, and she dipped back against the door. Her hips canted forward, and her heart thundered in her ears.

"You want this?" he asked.

She reached for him, pulling him into her personal space, his erection bumping up against the concave of her belly.

"Absolutely."

"Thank fuck." He cupped her jaw in his large, competent hands. He tilted his head and devoured her.

She pulled the tails of his shirt from his pants and smoothed her palms over his warm skin. Jake's fingers dove inside her silk shirt and scooped her breasts from the lace cups. He rubbed his thumbs over her distended nipples. "Can't wait to taste you again."

The air around them heated, thickened. The scent of pine rose from his warm skin, triggering more memories.

The last time they'd come together, they had been strangers in the dark. But now Zara knew more about him. He had a wounded heart he guarded tightly.

She yearned to discover all the vulnerable places he kept hidden from the world.

She wanted to give him the same pleasure he'd given her. Zara unbuckled his belt and opened his pants, needing to touch him. His silky length was hot and hard in her hand, her fingers pale against his long brown length. She squeezed him, the tip leaking and lubricating her palm.

Her body softened as his hardened.

Jake peeled her fingers from his erection. "Slow down, or I'm going to embarrass myself."

She grabbed his hand and tugged him up the stairs toward her bedroom. They tumbled inside and she cringed when she remembered she'd left a mess.

"It's messy." She kissed him desperately as she shoved his

pants and underwear to his ankles. His erection parted his shirt tails, arrowing toward her.

He broke the kiss to scoop her breasts together and kiss down to the tips. "Don't care." He sucked her nipples into his mouth. Lust cascaded through her as he feasted on her body.

Zara stripped quickly then gripped his head, holding him to her breasts, and arched into him.

He continued to kiss her as he stripped off his shirt. Her hands roved over his chest and arms, her fingers tingling as she reveled in his smooth skin and powerful body.

The bed, at least, had been made. Jake ripped the covers back, lifted her, and tossed her on the mattress in a feat of physical prowess. Her heart trilled at the casual show of strength. He crawled between her legs, running his hands up her calves and thighs. Her legs moved restlessly as he kissed the crease of her hip and licked her sharp hipbones. Her sex throbbed as she waited desperately for him to touch her clit.

She couldn't reach much of him, but touched the side of his face, then ran her fingers through his short curls.

He played with her nipples, plucking and pinching, the sensations zooming down to her clit. He scooped his palms under her ass and lifted her to his mouth.

"Finally." She sighed.

He dove into pleasuring her. Licking, sucking, swirling his tongue over her. Tingles spread through her entire body, rushing her toward the cliff.

She was on the edge. She tried to tug at him. "I'm going to come."

"Can't wait." He blew against her aroused flesh and pinched her nipples.

Zara exploded in a burst of pleasure so intense her vision blurred. He ate and ate and ate, stimulating her until she couldn't take it anymore.

She collapsed beneath his hands, overcome, her heart full, her chest expanding with gratitude, tears filling her eyes. All the loneliness and doubts that plagued her over the past few months dissolved, evaporating into the ether, drifting away on a cloud of pleasure and something deeper that she refused to name.

Her limbs trembled, and her heart beat a syncopated rhythm emphasizing the feeling as if she'd come home.

Jake sat up and grinned, his face slick with her come.

This man had given so much to her. His kindness, his trust, his affection, his desire. She wanted to give him the same in return.

9

Triumph gripped his heart.

Jake's head spun. Dizzy from lust, he burned with the need to get inside her. His erection pointed toward her, begging for her touch.

As a lover, Zara didn't hold back. Her innate reserve evaporated, and she threw herself into the physical, reveling in every sensation, reveling in his attention.

Her ability to receive pleasure with an open heart was astonishing, because the façade she presented to the world was far more measured, proper.

Once her clothes came off, like a key sliding the pins in place, her inhibitions shifted and unlocked her reserve.

Her wild abandonment set off a chain reaction within him. Giving her pleasure filled his chest with an answering swell of pleasure, choking him up.

"My turn." She pushed so he rolled over onto his back. She straddled him, her sex wet and glistening.

"I can taste you."

He couldn't stop touching her, trailing his fingers along her side then over her hip bones, rubbing her slick lips. Her soft skin pebbled beneath glide of his fingers. The scent of her desire and the hint of floral perfume filled his senses.

He tended to have lovers who assumed he would do most of the work. But she didn't have the same expectation.

She threaded their fingers together, inhibiting his ability to touch her, then she bent to his cock. At first her licks were soft; the light touch almost tickled. She explored him using her mouth with a hesitancy that was surprising.

The last time they'd been together had been less intimate and more physical. But now she took her time, alternating between sucking the head of his cock and then nipping at his hip bones.

"I like this muscle right here." She licked his inguinal muscle with one long stroke of her pink tongue, then released his hands so she could cup his balls.

His heart banged in his chest.

Her fingers were doing things to him.

"That feels amazing."

Her body was all angles and sharp lines, her muscles trim and sleek.

Maybe she didn't let down her guard with everyone. Maybe no one else saw the passionate woman beneath the façade. And maybe she only revealed that special place only to him. That thought expanded his chest, more vital than the lust that swelled the rest of him.

They fit. She fit.

That lost feeling that struck him at odd times disappeared when he was with her. As if she filled up those lonely parts of him and made him whole.

Which was weird. This was about sex. About physical pleasure and stress release. Not about anything more. Right?

Her hands were soft, her fingers delicately finessing more

from his body. His erection throbbed as desire pooled heavy in his balls.

"I'm going to come all over you if I can't get inside you soon." He wanted to join them together. Wanted to dominate her body the way she was dominating his mind.

Imprint on her so she wouldn't ever forget him.

This was probably a mistake, but he wanted it to be the best mistake he ever made.

"I want to come inside you."

"Yes." She lifted up so her slick sex rubbed back and forth over his cock.

He groaned. "We need a condom."

It wasn't sexy, but she didn't even blink. "Yep." She reached into her nightstand and pulled out a packet of three.

Thank goodness she had some right there.

He'd worry later about the fact that he was jealous as hell of whomever she'd been thinking of when she put them there.

Jake ab-curled up and tore open the package.

She was sitting on his thighs, her legs spread wide. The scent of sex and her subtle perfume swirled around them. His fingers trembled as he rolled the condom over his painfully erect cock.

Her gaze was laser focused on him as she licked her lips.

He took a moment to absorb the wanton picture she made. Her nipples glistened a deep pink, wet from his mouth, the hardened tips pointed at him, and a rosy flush covered her pale chest. His beard scruff had marked her skin. She wouldn't be able to forget him tomorrow.

She lifted up on her knees, her strong thighs bracketing his hips, and he slid inside her.

Their gazes caught, held, the moment unbearably intimate as he stared into her blue eyes and dropped the shields he kept in place, keeping him alone and safe. He opened his heart, letting a swell of gratitude overwhelm him. Wonder choked his throat, and his breath caught.

In this moment, he basked in awe at the gift of her trust, and he let her see inside him as he pushed up into her. She didn't look away, as if she could see inside his soul, and accepted him for who he was, flaws and all.

He seated to the hilt, the ridge of his cock pressing against her clit as she began a slow ride. Jake curled his palms under her ass and rocked into her firm curves.

Urgency was replaced by this languid desire, slowly, leisurely building as they connected on a deeper plane.

Their pace increased, her walls squeezing around him, his cock swelling harder. Desire coiled in his gut and gathered in his balls. Still he didn't look away from her gaze.

Jake curled up and sucked her nipple into his mouth. She clutched his head to her breasts. Her heart thundered against his forehead as her channel squeezed him tight.

The leisurely pace disappeared. They banged against each other, the thrust and withdraw frantic. He couldn't wait for his orgasm but didn't want this connection to end.

Zara's breath huffed out as she bounced on him, her small breasts bobbing. Fierce concentration claimed her face until she came with a keening cry, their connection broken as she threw back her head, and her channel pulsed around him. The contractions squeezed his cock, catapulting him into an explosive orgasm, his come jetting out in hard, concentrated pulses.

Sweat coated his skin as she clutched him to her. He rested his ear against her chest and listened as her heartbeat slowed. No words were needed.

Confusion and sadness had been his companions over the past few months as the world around him irrevocably changed, and everyone he knew seemed to pair off under the guise of that nebulous filament called love.

All that washed away as he came down from his orgasm. That sense of coming home, of peace, washed over him in a wave of pure joy.

Zara draped her arms over his shoulders and rested her head in the crook of his neck. Short puffs of breath tickled his sensitized skin as she lazily licked him.

"That was…."

She didn't continue. His anticipation morphed into curiosity as he waited. She traced the hard line of his neck and then pulled his earlobe into her mouth. Her perfect white teeth nipped at the sensitive skin.

"You going to finish that sentence?" His voice was rough, gravelly.

"I'm trying to find the perfect word." She kissed her way along his jaw. Miraculously, his cock was growing again. It should be impossible. He'd just come like a rock star and yet his body didn't seem to understand that he should be completely spent.

He decided to finish for her. "A good warm up?"

Her laugh shook her chest, and she leaned away from him. Her lips, rosy and plump from their kisses, widened into a mischievous smile.

"Works for me."

Now this she could get used to.

Zara woke leisurely, a warm muscled arm around her waist, and Jake's hairy leg thrown over her hip.

She ached in wonderful places.

Jake was an amazing lover. Was having sex with a coworker a mistake? Maybe. But they worked out of different offices. She'd only seen Jake at work once. It should be fine.

Just because they'd had sex last night didn't mean he'd want a repeat. But…he hadn't left, so that was a good sign. Right?

She was totally overthinking this.

God, would she ever completely regain her confidence?

He'd taken care of her well last night. He'd been attentive and generous, the same as the last time. But now that it was morning, doubts crowded in, making her begin to question things. What would this be like? The last time he'd snuck out in the early morning. Would he do the same today?

How would she feel about that?

She wasn't in the right headspace to start a relationship.

Hopefully, he'd understand that. Maybe she was getting slightly ahead of herself… and him. No one mentioned relationships.

He stretched behind her, arching his back and lifting his hands over his head. His morning erection nudged her butt.

He nuzzled the back of her neck and muttered, "Good morning," in that gruff way of his that set her nerve endings tingling. She needed to turn off her brain and be present in the moment. At least for now.

"Morning." Her breath caught as he played with her body, strumming his fingers along her spare angles. She didn't have a traditional female body by today's standards, with curves and big boobs.

Jake didn't seem bothered by that lack while he worshipped her body with reverence. Her insecurities came out as he swept his hand over her flat belly toward her chest.

"You don't mind my lack of curves."

He rolled her over so fast her head spun. "You're all sleek lines and fascinating angles. I like discovering all those hidden spots that turn you on."

She was quiet, a simple pleasure stealing through her.

"Who criticized your body?" They lay side by side, his face close to hers.

David had subtly disparaged her shape after they'd been dating for a few months, even mentioning a boob job. That had been *before* he'd hit her.

Shame curdled her stomach. She resisted the urge to hunch in on herself as she remembered the hurtful words David had hurled at her. He'd been particularly vicious when she'd finally left. Zara wanted to duck her head, but she lifted her chin and shrugged.

"Never mind." It didn't matter. It *shouldn't* matter.

His eyebrows arched down. "You're smart, competent, a

team leader, and gorgeous. You're running a PR office in one of the most politically charged, image-conscious cities in the world, and according to Jill, you're killing it."

A peculiar burn settled low in her belly. She was more touched by his acknowledgement of her accomplishments than her looks. After all, her face and body were genetics, nothing that she'd had any hand in creating. But her work… that was all her doing.

"So if I mentioned I was getting a boob job…"

"For what it's worth, I think you're beautiful the way you are." He frowned. "But it's your body, and you're allowed to do whatever you want with it."

"Good answer." Her mouth curled up at the edges. "I have a few ideas about what I'd like to do with it."

He raised his brows, even as his erection poked her in the stomach. "Anything I can help with?"

He wasn't leaving yet. Her heart fluttered in her chest like fireflies in a jar.

She slung her leg over his hip. "We only have one condom left."

He straightened a little. "Did you…buy them for anyone specific?"

Was he jealous? There was a hint of something in his voice that she couldn't place. "They were an 'in case I ran into this super-hot guy I met a few months ago' purchase."

She wanted to say more, like he'd made her feel things, nascent emotions, that excited her but also kind of scared her. The last time she'd felt this anticipation, this mix of possibilities it had turned horribly wrong.

Jake ceded to her power without any kind of struggle. He'd given her something, even if he hadn't realized it. But they weren't intimate. They were lovers who'd shared their bodies, not their souls. And just because she thought she'd felt something didn't mean she was ready to bare that part of herself.

"Ah." It was a noncommittal response, but pleasure shone from his topaz eyes. "Lucky for you, you did."

Time to get this on lighter footing. "Oh, did you think I was talking about you?"

He grasped her around the waist and used his super strength to lift her up, and she shrieked. Jeez, he was strong as he held her over his body. She grasped his shoulders.

"You want to change that answer?" he growled.

"You're so big and strong." Her voice came out breathless. Her heart beat in an erratic rhythm. If he ever wanted to, his fists would be devastating. Unlike David, who wasn't that big of a guy, Jake Brown was muscled and clearly took very good care of his body. Momentary insecurity trickled through her. Should she be worried?

"I would never hurt you." He lowered her carefully on top of his body, his touch gentle.

"I know that."

"I'm not sure you do." He tucked her hair behind her ear and pressed a gentle kiss to her lips.

She wanted to apologize, but her throat was suddenly clogged. She tucked her head into his neck, his heartbeat thundering in her ear. She lay on top of him, his muscled body cradling hers. "I've got some issues to work through," she confessed.

He snorted. "Don't we all?"

She wanted to get back to that playful atmosphere from a few minutes ago. But how?

"Can we take a moment?"

"Take as long as you'd like." His voice rumbled in her ear. "I don't have anywhere to be today."

She lay and listened to his heart rate slow and steady. The

silence turned companionable, and he gently stroked his hand down her back and over her butt, his touch comforting and not sexual. Their connection more intimate than the sex.

Intimacy was a lot harder than sex. She'd given him a glimpse of her emotional vulnerability. Enough for him to use that information against her if he ever wanted to. Panic began to flutter in her chest.

What had she been thinking? She wasn't ready. Having impersonal sex with a stranger was a step in the right direction but clearly, she had more work to do based on her panic right now.

Jake had been a nice distraction. But she needed to focus on the job, focus on making Xavier a household name and eventually bringing ALI with him. Her career was the goal here. This, whatever it was, had been a bright moment, not a commitment.

His stomach rumbled.

"You want coffee?" She pushed off his body and jumped out of the bed, scrambling to the door to grab her robe. Her nudity only exacerbated her vulnerability. The short silky floral wasn't much protection, but she needed to cover up. She scoured her brain, trying to think about what food she had in her refrigerator.

She rushed out the words like she wanted to rush out of this room. "Stay there. Make yourself comfortable. I know I have coffee." But food might be another matter. She was never home. "Oh, and protein bars."

He chuckled. "That works."

"Cool." And she ran.

11

———

Zara scurried away.

Jake wasn't sure what just happened, but Zara had left the room as if being chased by a bad guy. Someone had hurt her.

That was Jake's kryptonite. Women who'd been hurt. Last night, he'd been in a mental headspace that was not good. She'd given him her trust and her body. For that, he would be forever grateful.

He tugged on his khakis, a wrinkled mess from the floor, and smiled.

He hadn't had much time to look around last night; he'd been too busy ripping her clothes off. But as he shrugged into his button-down shirt, he checked out her bedroom. He studied the high ceilings and fancy molding, the gleaming wood floors, and the antique furniture.

He remembered the drive here. They were in an expensive part of town.

A peculiar discomfort began to simmer in his chest. He wandered down the curved staircase and took in the very fancy crystal chandelier hanging in the entry.

As he made his way into the kitchen, he noted the details: the six-burner plus a grill cooktop and the set of double ovens, the gleaming quartz countertops and the wine fridge. Her refrigerator cost as much as his truck. He knew because they'd had a client once who'd cried about leaving the behemoth behind. Her home screamed money.

How could he have missed that?

"Coffee is almost done," she said brightly, her gaze darting from him to the window over the sink. "Have a seat."

He sank onto one of the stools at the breakfast bar/island.

The silence in the room lengthened as he observed her. She fluttered around, never settling. And her awkwardness fed his.

"This doesn't have to be weird," he finally said.

"You're right." Her shoulders relaxed. "I'm a little out of practice."

"Me, too."

She scoffed. "Really?"

He didn't take offense. "Despite how we initially met, I don't usually hook up with strangers."

She studied him as she handed him a white porcelain mug with an illuminated-script, forest-green C adorned with vines and pale green grapes. "Me, either."

She set out a small porcelain pitcher with half and half and a rectangular glass container with packets of sugar and sweetener.

Jake sipped his dark, rich coffee. It was excellent.

She poured herself a cup of coffee. "Let's sit on the sun porch."

"You realize it's winter."

She rolled her eyes. "It's a beautiful spot, and it reminds me of home by bringing a little bit of the outdoors inside."

He was realizing now that they'd skipped quite a bit when they'd met, and he was filled with curiosity.

"Where is home?"

"California. Northern California."

He could see that. She had that cool elegance and confidence in the way she moved.

Jake commented casually, "That's a big move." Of course, he'd moved from the south to D.C. which wasn't as far geographically, but culturally, the urban center was on another planet compared to his rural southern roots.

Discomfort flashed in her eyes.

"Your move was big." She deflected, and Jake wondered why she didn't want to talk about it.

"Sure, I came from rural Mississippi." But he didn't call it home. Not anymore.

She blinked. "I thought I heard a bit of twang once, but you don't have an accent."

He'd worked hard to get rid of it.

"Is your family still there?"

"No. After my sister…" He trailed off. His mother barely spoke to him these days. They endured awkward visits once a month or so. When he'd attacked his sister's killer, he'd almost gotten thrown in jail himself. A judge who understood the outsized impact that the Drayton family had on town affairs had saved him by giving him the option of going into the military instead of jail. That, and he'd been seventeen.

She put her hand on his wrist, her long elegant fingers squeezed him. "I'm so sorry about your sister. Any news on that?"

"I have to go in front of the parole board next week."

"Good luck."

He couldn't even bear the thought that Edward Drayton the Fourth might get released. Jake's fists clenched.

"I can't let him get out."

"Have you talked to anyone about it?"

He looked at her blankly. "Uh, no."

"Well, I'm here if you need to talk."

Not in a million years. "Sure."

Instead of getting annoyed, she laughed and let it drop. The earlier tension broke, and they settled into an easy rhythm chatting about favorite activities.

"You look like a runner," he said.

"I do like to run, but between the weather and finding a safe space, I haven't done much since I moved to D.C."

"Then what do you do?" Because she definitely worked out.

"Tennis."

A country club sport.

He couldn't help the instinctive shudder. He knew his aversion to rich folk wasn't rational. But it stuck in his craw.

"You're rich?"

She tilted her head, the soft morning light hitting the line of her jaw. Her clear blue eyes narrowed. "No."

He called bullshit.

"But my parents are."

Another trust fund baby. He couldn't seem to get away from them.

"That seems to be a problem for you." She set her empty mug on the counter, their earlier ease disappearing. The awkward gap in the conversation lengthened.

He let out his breath he didn't even realize he'd been holding. He didn't date rich women. He knew it was his issue, but there were plenty of women to have sex with.

What was he saying? He didn't date, period. But for a little while, he'd had a glimmering hope that maybe they could be more than just a hookup.

"Alrighty then." Zara smiled tightly. "One quick thing, I meant to call the other office yesterday, but I got sidetracked by Xavier's request to meet last night. I had a couple call in with a really weird request. I said I'd pass it on to your office."

"What did they want?"

"So strange. They were looking for their son, Ben. And wanted to know if Adams- Larsen might know where he is."

Jake didn't move a muscle. Shit.

"Isn't that weird?"

"Yeah. Weird." He sipped his coffee hoping she would drop it. This was a problem.

"You don't know anything about him? He wasn't a client of your office?"

And…this was what Viktor had meant. How do you have a relationship when one of you is lying to the other basically all the time? Jake knew better. But for a few hours, he'd thought maybe they could be more than quick hook-ups in the dark. Although since she'd bolted from bed, she'd probably also been having second thoughts.

"Nope."

"Not surprising. He's young." She tilted her head and studied him. Then her mouth tightened. "You ever going to tell me what you do?"

Jake gulped the rest of his coffee. "Thanks for the coffee."

"You're leaving?" She didn't look upset. She looked suspicious.

"You said you had a lot of work today. I don't want to keep you." He didn't want to go, but it was the best course of action.

"Do you want the couple's phone number?"

"Sure. I'll have someone call them."

"Right." Now her voice was flat.

He didn't think anything he said would make this cluster better, so he kept his mouth shut.

"Thanks for the ride." She flushed. "Home from my meeting."

The blush was cute. But he needed to stay away from cute. There couldn't be a repeat of last night.

"There's something off about Xavier." He threw it out mostly because he wanted to distract her from his reaction about Ben. But it was true.

Now she rolled her eyes. "His net worth? Since you take issue with having money."

"Be careful around him." Jake set his coffee cup in the sink.

Zara sighed heavily. "He isn't a threat. He's a sitting congressman."

Jake would keep an eye on the doings of Rodriguez. Just because he and Zara were a bad idea didn't mean he couldn't be protective of her. And they so totally were a bad idea.

Coming home with her was a mistake.

He'd known it.

He wasn't sorry. It had been the best night he'd had since… the last time they were together. But that didn't mean they could have a three-peat.

Staying away from her was the best thing he could do for both of them.

Even if it was going to hurt.

12

A FEW MONTHS LATER

"I'm going to need you to pick up Zara Cooper," Jill said.

Jake's heart stopped. He'd actively avoided thinking about her since their last unfortunate encounter. Which, of course, meant he thought about her a lot.

She deserved a man who would share her life and hopes and dreams. That couldn't be him, no matter how much he longed to see her again and no matter how much he wished things were different.

It hadn't been easy to stay away from her, but he'd been consumed with taking care of Viktor.

Viktor's entire world had imploded when the love of his life had blown up. He was wrecked, beyond devastated.

Grief pulsed in the air around his friend, his sorrow so immense that it was painful to be in the same space. But Jake kept him company whenever Vik would let him.

As a matter of fact, Jill and Marsh had kept him in the office. He was between assignments right now, kind of floating around filling in where needed.

He would prefer to be busy rather than have too much time on his hands, but watching out for Viktor was important.

His friend was hurting.

Over the past few months, his co-workers had all paired off with new loves. Ever since Jake had relocated young Layla and her boyfriend, Ben, who had insisted they couldn't live without each other, the world had been shoving examples of 'true love' in his face.

He didn't understand why that was happening.

Viktor falling in love had been a complete surprise. Viktor's lover had been even more unexpected. The Russian assassin was one scary dude, and yet he'd been tender with Viktor while fierce with anyone who threatened Viktor and ready to defend his love at any cost.

"You okay?" Jill spoke again and Jake realized his attention had drifted. He guessed that was an improvement over the anger that had dogged him lately.

"Yeah. Fine." Worry nagged at him. "Everything okay with her?"

Jillian shrugged into a black wool suit jacket, dressed in her customary long tight skirt and silk blouse. "We're doing a press conference."

"Wait. What?"

"Marsh and I decided it was time. We need to head off the rumors."

Shouldn't everyone in the office have been consulted? Of course, Jillian and Marsh owned the business. They could decide to do whatever they wanted. But…

"What does Zara have to do with it?" Jake pulled back on the aggression coursing through him.

Jill frowned at his tone. Had he seemed too familiar? He didn't think Zara would be judged for having sex with him. Especially since everyone in the office had hooked up on recent ops. But the need to protect her burned beneath his breastbone. It was no one's business but theirs.

"She's going to do the press conference and field the questions."

"Did you tell her what we really do?" Jake's heart sped up. If she knew what they did, perhaps he could spend time with her. He shouldn't be thinking about him and Zara right now, but…

"No."

At first, he thought she meant, no, you can't date Zara. But then her meaning sunk in.

"You're throwing her to the press?" His voice rose.

"She's a seasoned professional." Jill smoothed her palm over her perfectly neat hair. "And she's doing a fantastic job. She's grown the revenues of our PR office exponentially since she took over."

"I'm against this."

Marsh walked into Jill's office. "What's up?"

"You're doing a press conference?" Jake practically snarled.

Marsh sighed. "It's time."

What?

"We knew our original business model had an expiration date. With everything that's happened over the past few months, the change was inevitable."

"We aren't going to help people anymore?" The bottom dropped out of his stomach.

The world was shifting on its axis. Everyone hooking up. Their business model changing.

He wanted to stay in that sameness that kept him safe and worked for him. He didn't want to change. He didn't want upheaval. He wanted to keep doing what he'd been doing.

"Of course we are." Jill studied him patiently. Like he was the one overreacting, instead of them being calm and nonchalant as they imploded the best job he'd ever had. Not just a job, his life.

"Then why are we putting Zara through this?" Without giving her any background information. Letting her go in blind and be blindsided. This was fucked. Jake clenched his fists, trying to hold in his anger.

"Zara?" Marsh raised his eyebrows. "Something you need to tell us?"

"I'm just saying that seems like a bad idea, and I am against it."

"Jake," Jill said gently. "Your objection is duly noted."

"But you're going to do it anyway."

"We have to. There's too much pressure on everyone. If we control the narrative, then we can manage what information the public sees and consumes, and we can continue to keep our real and critical client list confidential. We're trying to head off a congressional investigation."

"Why use Zara?"

"We want her to be the face of the company." Keep everyone else hidden was left unsaid.

"She could become a target." Fear rumbled in his chest. He hated this.

Marsh shook his head. "We don't anticipate that happening."

"What if you're wrong?"

"Then we have a company full of trained bodyguards." Jill threw up her hands in exasperation. "She's a grown woman and she can handle herself. That's why we hired her."

"For public relations. She isn't an operator."

"Fine. You're in charge of her security." Marsh shot back.

Jill nodded. "Good idea."

Jake opened his mouth to argue and then shut it. She

wouldn't be happy about that. He hadn't reached out since he'd left her rowhouse like his head was on fire.

"Jake. We will be there. We're going to let Zara handle the press. She's a professional. But if something comes up, we can field specific questions. If we don't read her in, then she isn't lying to anyone."

"I want to be there." Hopefully, that wouldn't make her uncomfortable. Of course, she hadn't reached out to him either. So maybe they were fine. Nothing to see here.

"Absolutely. You can monitor the crowd."

All the yearning he'd suppressed came roaring back. Anticipation fizzed in his bloodstream, vibrations surging through him.

"I need one of you to pick her up. I want to check on Viktor before the press conference."

Marsh nodded. "I'll get her."

"I'll see you there."

He'd protect her from everyone—even if he couldn't protect her from himself. He'd make damn sure no one else was a threat.

A few hours later, clicks and snaps echoed in the ballroom of one of the generic chain hotels downtown. He was pleased with their decision to keep the location neutral. Subtle snicks and hisses provided background noise as the room's inhabitants waited for the presser to start. Jake leaned against the side wall of the room, trying to make himself unobtrusive.

Unease skittered along his spine.

This was going to put Zara in the crosshairs of anyone who thought they had a beef with ALIAS. Fortunately, most people had no idea that ALIAS was responsible for the disappearance of their target. But their clients disappeared for a reason, and he refused to let Zara to become a victim of violence.

Zara walked up to the podium and smiled at the crowded press of journalists. "Good afternoon, everyone."

She looked amazing.

Even more impressive, she exuded a serene confidence that told the world she knew who she was and what she was doing. It was extremely attractive.

She had on a pink wool suit with a short skirt and an almost cropped jacket with fancy round shiny gold buttons. It looked expensive. Her hair was more styled than she regularly wore it, and her lipstick perfectly matched the pink nubs in the suit. Her heels had a low profile that accented her gorgeous, sleek, muscled legs.

Legs he'd had wrapped around his hips while he powered into her.

Shit. Not the right image to think about right now. Jake willed those thoughts away and hoped no one noticed that he'd lost his focus for a hot minute.

He'd been having random flashes of their last encounter for weeks.

He'd purposely pushed Zara away. He had no right to be sad or long for another shot with her.

Zara appeared to be in her element as she delivered the statement prepared by Jill and Marsh. They sat to the side of the dais, relaxed and confident, ready to jump in if need be. But they'd be out of the view of the photographers' shot. He was hoping this would be a short clip at the end of a busy news day or even lost to a new scandal.

"We've prepared a short statement, and everyone should have received a press release when they showed their credentials. Then we'll take a few questions."

While everyone else saw a composed confident woman, Jake noted the strain around her eyes. The little crinkle that meant she wasn't completely comfortable with the circumstances. He didn't like the fact that he could read her so easily.

He darted his gaze, taking in the expressions of the journalists watching Zara.

No one else seemed aware of her consternation.

To Jake, it was plain as day.

Her gaze moved around the room, skimming right over him. But she knew he was here. He hoped she would view his presence as support.

Zara laid out the facts.

ALIAS had been in the news recently with rumors about their business. Normally, they wouldn't respond but the rumors were out of control.

They were helpful in catching an international criminal. They did reputation management with a very selective client list and occasionally client protection. They also handled media relations.

Basically, she hadn't given them anything new.

Before she'd even finished speaking, the hands went up. Zara pointed to a slick guy in a grey pinstripe suit and the standard plain red tie.

"What can you tell us about your clients?"

"Nothing. Our client list in confidential." Zara's smile widened. "Same as always."

"Is it true you shielded Bitsy Vandenbeek?"

"I already told you, I can't reveal our clients." Zara paused. "Feel free to ask her."

Jill and Marsh must have cleared that with Bitsy before this news conference. The spoiled, but smart, heiress who'd been in danger after hearing that that her stepfather had his mistress murdered had been the beginning of clients who they didn't relocate.

More questions from the reporters. "Who are your clients?"

"The whole point of our business is that we don't advertise who we've helped," she said patiently.

They asked the same questions with slightly different spins for the next ten minutes. They named off a few more people who perhaps had been clients. Jake could tell the strain was starting to get to her.

"Do you fake people's deaths?"

Jake didn't move, didn't even blink. Where the fuck had that come from?

Of course, they didn't fake people's deaths, but they did make people disappear.

"What?" Zara laughed. She had this waterfall of laughter that sounded like a gurgling stream near the woods that he'd played in as a kid. It was the second thing he'd noticed about her when they'd hooked up. "Of course not. What…are we living in a spy novel?"

Jake made note of Jill and Marsh. Their expressions hadn't changed. Not even surprise. Had they known that question was coming? And what the fuck were they going to do if the reporter kept digging?

She paused, clearly taken aback by what she thought was a silly question but then answered very succinctly. "Of course not. We do not kill off people, literally or figuratively. That would be illegal. We just protect them while handling their very delicate public relations. Which is in high demand in this town."

The press laughed.

Pride for her composure and confidence swelled through him.

Because they had hooked up, their intimacy had also given him a window into her insecurities. He admired her competence and appreciated her ability to handle this impromptu sham of a press conference.

Too bad she was lying. Even if she didn't know it.

13

———

Zara fielded questions from the reporters.

She concealed her frustration with Jillian and Marsh. If they'd given her more information, she could have crafted a more precise statement that would have curtailed the crazier questions. She could have shaped the discussion. But they'd given her the statement and an extremely generalized list of things they handled.

She'd always known that the other branch of Adams-Larsen was where the real VIP clients landed. But until recently, she hadn't realized that the agency protected people. She wondered if that's what Jake did.

This and that was…bodyguarding of sorts?

That made more sense as to why a guy like Jake worked for them. He was here. She'd actively avoided looking at him. As her mind wandered, she wondered, *why* was he here? She didn't want to see him. The last time they'd been together, he'd run away. Since then, he hadn't reached out once.

Her emotions were all over the map. She liked him—when he was having sex with her and talking. But she didn't like the awkward silences and pauses when she'd asked questions he wouldn't answer. Of course, those evasions made a lot more sense now.

Without volition, her gaze slid to him. He looked good, dammit.

While she, on the other hand, had struggled since he'd walked out the door.

She hoped this would be over soon. She preferred to be behind a desk, not a podium. She wanted to influence the news, not be a part of it.

As she'd read through the statement and a list of FAQs regarding the presser, something niggled at the back of her brain.

What was she missing?

She wasn't stupid. She'd known that her bosses were keeping things from her.

Jake leaned against the wall on the far side of the room, his gaze never stopped moving as he scanned the inhabitants.

If anything was guaranteed to throw off her poise, it was coming face to face with her one-night stand. Twice night stand?

Figured that the first time she had thrown away all caution and picked up a guy in a bar, she would manage to sleep with a guy and then find out he worked for the same company. And now, he was here watching her.

After basically running out of her house and never calling again.

Of course, she'd shared confidences that she never would have if she'd known she would see him again.

And she'd made a vow after that night to swear off forbidden relationships.

When she wasn't re-living the best sex of her life, dammit, she was remembering his confession. He hadn't given specific details, just admitted that he'd had a client, and he'd had to do something hard, something that made him sick.

It was hard to reconcile the tortured guy who'd called to her soul in that bar, with the confident, physically impressive, taciturn man leaning up against the side wall of the ballroom, his gaze never resting as he watched the crowd—and not her, thank goodness.

Not to mention she had shared intimate details of her life with him. About her idiot ex- who'd damaged her self-esteem and made her doubt herself. She didn't need him sharing her insecurities with her bosses.

She was a smart, confident, capable woman. Dammit.

She told her mirror so every morning. She didn't think the affirmations were working. She knew she was smart. She knew she was capable. But confident? Only when she was in front of the press or working for a client.

Her personal life was another story. She was a mess. David had damaged her belief in herself. And she needed to keep her damn focus on this room full of reporters.

"Why now?" The persistent reporter from the *Washington Post* shouted out.

Zara glanced at Jillian. She gave a chin lift.

"There have been enough speculation pieces lately that the principals decided it was time to defend their business."

Jillian nodded again.

"While we would normally don't reveal any personal details, they decided to clarify their actions," Zara continued. "We helped our founder's boyfriend track down an international criminal."

And that was the bombshell that would throw all the attention away from the company. Jillian had been helping her boyfriend.

She fielded a few questions about Jillian and Hamish.

They'd met through mutual friends while he'd been here searching for an Irish mobster wanted in the UK. They'd been attacked and defended themselves. They'd fallen in love, and he planned to relocate to the US permanently.

More questions were thrown at her about the criminal, but in this, she was covered.

"We can't comment on an ongoing case. But rest assured, Adams-Larsen helped apprehend a dangerous criminal and have the person extradited."

Zara and Jillian had gamed this out. The plan had been to keep it private unless the need to pull a partial hangout became necessary. She'd never personally used this technique, but giving the press a sensational statement that trumped the initial questions would take the focus off the things Jillian and Marsh didn't want more light on and should keep other questions at bay.

She wished she had more information.

The reporters had gobbled up the more sensational story and run with it.

"Are you going to release your client list?" The slick guy in the suit shouted.

"No." Zara hesitated. "But we changed our policy, and if a client wants to let their friends or associates know they used our services, we won't object."

She glanced around the room, noticed Jake's scowl. Lovely. She wondered what he was upset about now. Didn't matter; she'd followed the wishes of their bosses.

"Thank you all for coming!"

The reporters continued to shout questions at her as she closed her portfolio. She thought overall it had gone well. Except for asking about faking people's deaths. That was weird.

But suddenly, she recalled the couple who'd called her office right before she'd hooked up with Jake. They had been searching for their son, Ben. Jake had seemed a little squirrely when she'd mentioned them.

Could he have been a client?

14

———

Jake hated the past thirty minutes.

He stalked to the small prep room off the ballroom, scouting to make sure none of the hovering reporters got too close. Zara was done answering questions.

Once he made sure the room was clear, he gestured to her that it was okay to go in. Jill and Marsh followed.

Zara rolled her eyes at him. "I'm not a client."

"Jill and Marsh want you protected."

She jerked to a halt, her eyes wide. "Is that necessary?"

"Actually, Jake was concerned for your safety," Jill said smoothly, ratting him out.

Zara's startled gaze shifted to him.

"Precautionary," he said gruffly.

Her shoulders dropped.

"Nice job out there." Marsh smiled at her.

Jake wished he could be more like Marsh and project that casual vibe. Women loved Marsh. And he loved them right back. But these days he was entwined with his artist, Ayesha, and seemed to be enamored.

"Jake will get you back to the office."

"That's not necessary." She brushed aside the offer. The frown of dismay on her face was hard to miss.

"Precautionary." Jake felt compelled to say again.

"I don't want to take you out of your way."

"It's not an inconvenience at all." Total lie. He was feeling equal parts anticipation and dread. Unfortunately, Zara looked like all she was feeling was dread.

He had been kind of a dick when he left her place the last time.

Lately, Jake had been preoccupied with watching out for Viktor, but he'd dreamed of her. And in the middle of the day, he'd drift off, thinking about their nights together. She'd been an uninhibited lover, and vocal, quite unexpected since she oozed old money vibes. He wasn't sure how he'd missed that when he'd first met her.

In his defense, his headspace hadn't been great at the time.

In his mind, he'd jumbled the job with Layla and Ben and his one-night stand with Zara into a mix of regret and longing.

He'd had difficulty focusing on work, the one constant in his life, his reason for everything. He'd yearned to see her again but knew that nothing had changed. That see-saw of emotions battered him.

Now he got to drive her back to the office. His body jazzed at the thrill of spending time with her.

And shit, he'd lost the thread of the conversation. Jake flipped the keys of the office Honda Accord around his fingers.

"Let me know when you're ready."

She looked like she wanted to object again.

"Everything okay?" Jill frowned at Jake.

He hadn't breathed a word about their hookup to anyone at the office.

Zara shot him a sharp look, then smiled tightly. "Absolutely fine."

"Nice job, Zara. We'll probably get calls for the next week or so, but then I expect things will die down." Jill shrugged into a long wool coat. "And go back to normal."

"I'll keep a log of any unusual calls and send it to Hannah daily." Zara was all business now.

"Sounds good."

Jake had a pit in his gut that he'd learned never to ignore. "What about blowback?" His shoulders inched up to his ears as his tension ratcheted up. And yeah, maybe he needed to regulate his tone.

He worried that the press conference had given a face to Adams-Larsen, and now she could be targeted by someone looking for answers. They were being very lackadaisical about Zara's safety.

Marsh crossed his arms over his chest. "Why don't you hang out at the ALI office for the next few days to ease your concerns? We'd discussed protection for today, but it isn't a bad idea to continue until the speculation dies out."

What? No!

"Oh, that's *totally* not necessary." No one could miss the panic in Zara's voice.

"Actually, not a bad idea." Jill studied them. "You're in between assignments anyway, and Viktor is about to take a vacation."

That was news to Jake.

"He needs time to get his head straight."

Jake raised his eyebrows. Viktor's lover had blown up practically in front of him. He would have used different language. Maybe say 'recover from his total devastation or ease his heartbreak.'

"Okay." He was going to see Zara every day. His body buzzed with awareness, but his brain told him to hold back. The same reasons for staying away from her still existed. So now he'd be tortured with being near to her and unable to do anything about it.

"Consider yourself on the job."

ZARA LOOKED around the garage for Jake's truck. Instead, he led her to a nondescript Honda Accord.

"This is yours?" Zara blinked.

"Office pool car."

"It's…"

"Blends in, completely ubiquitous. It's a great car for being inconspicuous."

"Ah."

He slid into the driver's seat and waited for her to buckle up. He was a giant in the driver's seat of this little car, and the interior seemed to shrink even more with her presence.

The silence in the car became oppressive as they studiously avoided each other. Zara had picked up one of the more recent Cage comics, City of Fire series, that he'd tossed in the car and was flipping through the pages.

"So, how have you been?" he asked awkwardly.

"Do you really care?"

Shit. He hadn't expected that. She was usually polite.

"Never mind. I'm fine." She slammed the comic book closed. "So you provide protection for clients?"

He stiffened.

"That's the little bit of this, little bit of that?"

It was one of his jobs…along with witness relocation and misdirection.

"Part of it."

He couldn't share what he really did. He didn't like keeping her in the dark, but it wasn't his decision to withhold information, and Jill and Marsh had expressly prohibited telling her the truth.

Guilt flooded him. "I'm sorry."

"No. I'm sorry. I can see that you aren't allowed to share." He inclined his head.

"That's why you didn't call?" The forlorn plaintive note in her voice surprised him.

He was silent.

He hadn't called because he liked her too much. Their connection transcended the physical, but he couldn't stomach continually lying to her. He was silent too long.

"Right." Her short laugh was irritated. "Not my business. We didn't make any kind of commitment to each other. Our night was…stress release."

Stress release?

That pissed him off. His temper rose, and the urge to lash out was strong. But he'd grown out of that kind of response. He controlled his temper rather than letting his temper control him. She had handed him the perfect out. But he couldn't take it.

"It was more than that, and you know it," he shot back.

"Then why haven't you called me?"

"It's complicated." Jake sighed.

"Are you seeing someone else?"

"No! Of course not." Jake held in the words he wanted to say. *I dream of you all the time. I wish things were different, and we could spend time together. But you deserve a guy who will put you first, not put strangers who need justice within a flawed system before you.*

His job was his redemption. And that redemption didn't include love.

"There are things I can't share with you, and that makes it hard."

"So those signals you were sending about wanting more really did exist?"

"Yes."

"I wasn't imagining it." The relief in her voice that surprised him.

He had a chance here to be honest where he could. "Not at all." He'd wanted to continue what they'd started. But it wasn't to be.

"Have you ever lied to me?"

Lied? No. Obscured the truth? Probably. "No."

"Does it have to do with what the reputation management branch really does?"

He should have known she'd figure out there was more going on than that sham press conference. She was smart and extremely competent.

"How's the job with Rodriguez going?" His deflection was answer enough.

He was hoping she'd say he had decided not to work with her.

"Great." Her whole face lit up. "We've got a preliminary plan in place, and he's already implemented some of my suggestions."

Suspicion lingered about the guy. Under the surface, it tickled at his consciousness with an intense knowing. "There's something about him. I wish you'd get rid of him."

"You aren't in a position to tell me what I can and can't do." And you never will be was unspoken.

"I like to think we're friends."

She snorted.

"Okay, well, if we were friends, I would tell you that there's something about him I don't like." It was more than that, but he had his own freaking problems, and she didn't want to listen.

"What's the Viktor issue?" she asked abruptly.

Jake tightened his hands on the wheel. "He's been having a rough time."

She dropped that line of questioning, and Jake relaxed his hands.

"Okay. Why in the world would a reporter ask if we fake people's death?"

Ugh. His hands tightened on the wheel again. He guessed it had been someone with either Russian media connections or someone who owed the Russian ambassador a favor who wanted to confirm again that Sasha Loblaw was gone.

You'd think with as many people as Russia assassinated that they would know when their target was dead.

"Viktor is having a hard time because his boyfriend died." Of the last two questions she'd asked, that was the less dramatic and revealing answer.

"That's terrible."

"Yeah." He blew out a breath. "He's devastated." He left out that Sasha was a Russian assassin, security for the Russian ambassador to the US, and supposedly the highest-ranking FSB—Russian intelligence agency—agent in the country.

And that he'd blown up in a car bombing.

No need to freak her out.

"Do you really think we need protection at the office?"

"I think there are a lot of volatile people out there," he said evenly. They really hadn't given any detailed information about their true activities. Jake had a feeling he'd be doing more straight up protection now – at least until this all died down. "We've had a couple of dust-ups with the authorities lately."

ALIAS had been in the news several times recently.

Their notoriety started when a Russian was accidently killed in the ALIAS office a few months ago. They had been temporarily hiding two people as a favor to a friend of Jill's at the CIA. Then a stalking case with Judge Adams, although the government had kept most of that out of the papers. The biggie was the client who had been guilty and severely misled ALIAS. That was the op where Jill and Hamish had gotten together and provided the shocking reveal for today. After she'd brought up that, the press had quieted down.

She shivered. "Am I at risk?"

"Probably not." But he didn't want to take any chances. "That's why I'll be there."

Was it wrong that he was thrilled to spend time with her while she was worried about her safety?

Zara blew out a breath.

He hoped he was over-reacting and everything would be quiet.

"I won't put you in danger."

"Thank you." She shifted in the seat, her voice trembling.

"They'll have to go through me first." It was a vow.

15

Zara couldn't sit still.

Her fingers shook, her stomach jittered, her blood fizzed. She fidgeted in the seat of the small car again and crossed her legs. Then she uncrossed them. Finally, she grabbed the comic book again and stared blindly at the cover with the buff Black superhero surrounded by fire.

He'd just told her that he would protect her like the super-hero on the cover. But she didn't like the idea of Jake in danger, either. He wasn't impervious to bullets or fire.

Jake studied the rearview mirror and made a turn. "You okay?"

"Fine." Her voice caught. She wasn't fine.

The press conference was over. She'd handled it, but she couldn't seem to stop shaking. She didn't know what was wrong with her. "I don't know."

"Adrenaline let down." Jake glanced over at her, his topaz gaze assessing. "You did a great job."

Zara waved away his compliment. "I prefer to be maneuvering from behind the curtain, not at the podium."

Her clients were supposed to be the story. Not her. She'd felt incredibly exposed during that press conference.

She thought about some of the questions thrown at her.

"Why did you protect Bitsy VanDenBeek?"

"I can neither confirm nor deny." He shot her a quick smile, then his gaze went to the rearview mirror. "You said it perfectly. If you guessed who our clients are, we didn't do a very good job."

A non-answer.

"But out of curiosity, what makes you think we did?" He tightened his fingers slightly.

That non-answer was answer enough. "Your body language when the reporter asked."

"No way." He shook his head. "Nice try."

If he didn't want to believe her, that was up to him. But now she knew something new about him.

He took a quick right turn down the wrong street.

"You went the wrong way." She leaned forward in her seat. The turn-off for the office was a few streets down and in the opposite direction.

He glanced in the mirror again.

He turned right again.

"Um, Jake?"

"Doing an SDR."

"SDR?"

"Surveillance detection route." He took another right turn. "Checking for tails."

"Is that necessary?" Guess this was part of the protection package.

"Yes."

"Are we being followed?" Her voice rose. He'd said this was precautionary. Was there something else her bosses weren't telling her? Of course, there was more. Their whole agency was one big secret. She didn't know of any PR firms that provided protection. What the hell had she gotten herself into?

Jake checked the mirror again. "Apparently not."

"The office address is in the public domain." Which set her jittering again. "Why would anyone care if we offered protection for people?"

"Curiosity. Research."

She thought back to what she knew about Bitsy VanDenBeek. She'd been sequestered away in Lake Tahoe because her life had been in danger. "Why would anyone want details about past clients?"

"In this town, information is currency. Everything can be bought and everything can be leveraged." His cynical words struck her. She knew that of course. Half of what she did was leverage the *right* information.

She needed to think this through.

"I hope your computer files are protected." So much was on servers these days. Her office had excellent firewalls and cyber security in place. Some clients were more sensitive than others.

Especially Xavier.

Her cell phone rang. Xavier.

"Hello?"

His voice was clipped. "I just saw the press conference."

Her stomach dropped. He did not sound happy. "That pertained to a separate branch of the business."

"No more meeting in public."

At least he hadn't said no more meetings. Her heart thudded hard in her chest, the jittery feeling back in her fingers and toes.

"Whatever you prefer." He was her biggest client. If he

referred friends, she could continue to grow the office exponentially.

"From now, on we will meet at my home." Xavier didn't let her answer. "Tomorrow. Eight AM."

He hung up.

Zara blew out a breath.

"Everything okay?"

"A client who wasn't happy with the presser."

Jake turned again then relaxed. She guessed no one was following them. Zara loosened her hold on her phone.

"Huh." Jake headed toward the office. Finally. "Did he terminate the contract?"

"Nope."

"Too bad."

"What?" She didn't mention it was Xavier.

"I've read up on your golden boy."

"You really have a hard-on for this guy."

He shrugged. "I have good instincts."

"Well, he's a philanthropist, and he's done great things for many fabulous organizations, and now he's working for the government to effect systemic change."

"Doesn't mean I'm wrong."

Damn, he was stubborn.

He pulled into the back parking lot of the office, effectively ending the conversation.

A few hours later, Zara arched her back and stretched her arms over her head. Concentrating had been a bitch today.

She'd poured over the next set of plans she'd drafted for Xavier. She was really pleased with what she'd come up with. Hopefully, she could placate his concerns when they met tomorrow.

He had sounded pissed on the phone but he hadn't fired her. Thank goodness.

No matter what Jake thought, Xavier was an excellent client, and she couldn't believe that she could have a hand in helping him get elected. Sure, she wished that people would know she was behind his current appearances and schedule. She was vain enough to want the recognition, to want the win, to be acknowledged for her contribution. But she understood that he was extremely protective of his brand.

She still held out hope that he would give her credit when the time was right.

She had some new events for him to add to his calendar.

Two of her favorites involved environmental causes. She'd suggested an appearance at a local fair focused on the environment by reducing plastic use and another to visit a new composting facility that was creating jobs and reducing landfill. She didn't have any experience with politicians, but she liked to think she understood what made him tick.

A few years ago, her family had begun a program to grow their grapes organically to reduce the amount of chemicals leaching into groundwater and contaminating lakes and streams. Shifting to the use of natural pests and cover crops to control infestations and weeds and organic fertilization of the crops took time and patience.

She liked to think she was working toward a better future for everyone by elevating Xavier's profile with time and patience.

Xavier and his wife were second generation Americans and understood the need to be good stewards for the future. He had created scholarships for first kids in the family to attend college.

So much to admire.

Their success story needed amplifying, especially building a literal fortune from very humble beginnings and then paying that success forward.

She found herself getting heated just thinking about Jake's reaction to money. What was that about? He definitely had a chip on his shoulder.

She tried to stay hyper-focused on work, but little things kept pulling her back to Jake.

She dreamed of him regularly. His generosity in bed and the feeling of connection. She re-lived those moments, staring into his eyes as they came together. That sense of bonding, leaving their own selves to become something more together.

She needed to forget about him, them. Move on.

Easier said than done, since he had taken over the conference room with his laptop and cell phone. The door was open so he could see and hear the front entrance. He'd locked the door after six. The rest of the staff was gone for the day, but Zara had work to catch up on because of the time spent on the press conference.

"You can go if you want."

He glanced up, his topaz gaze piercing. "Are you leaving?"

"Not yet."

He continued to study her, his expression intense. A tingling started in her toes and spread throughout her, responding to the memory of staring into his gaze. Desire flit through her body like butterflies, her heart tripping. Because she could see that he felt it, too.

He shook his head, as if trying to shake off the energy that buzzed between them. "I'll stay as well." He went back to pounding away on his laptop. He made quite the contradictory picture, the large athletic hulk beating up the keys of the delicate machine. Her lips twitched.

The doorbell rang.

Jake stood. "You expecting anyone?"

"No." She shook her head.

"I'll get it."

Jake opened the door. "Can I help you?"

His deep voice rumbled, and desire fluttered deep in her belly as the sound triggered memories of their nights together.

"Hello. We're looking for Jake."

That was weird. Why would they be looking for him?

He didn't work in this office.

She couldn't see beyond him. But the leather holster at his waist with a gun in it jolted her. Logically, she knew that he might be armed, but seeing the evidence threw her. That frisson of desire curdled replaced by the cold shock of fear.

"You found him." There was a cautious curiosity in his voice, but Zara studied his body language. He was tense. She wasn't even sure what gave it away because he really hadn't moved or reacted to them in any way.

"We're looking for our son."

Jake continued to block the doorway.

"This is a public relations office," Jake said mildly.

"We saw the press conference on the news, and we knew we had to come." The woman's voice trembled. "Our son, Ben, is missing."

16

____

 uck.

Ben Hansen's parents stood on the doorstep.

Karen Hansen had perfectly styled hair, and her blue eyes, the same shade as Ben's, glittered with unshed tears. Her clothes hung loose on her frame, and the large, but not too ostentatious, diamond band on her ring finger tilted sideways as if she'd lost weight. Charlie, Charles Benjamin Jr., wore the quintessential country club outfit, light blue button down, neatly pressed khaki pants, and a navy blazer with penny loafers, telegraphing money and status.

Jake had done research on them before he moved Ben.

He'd known they were going to be an issue. He'd told Ben that his parents wouldn't accept that he wanted to have an adventure. But Ben and Layla had been adamant that they were going to be together, whether Jake facilitated or not.

With ALIAS, they were safe, as long as Ben didn't contact his parents, and Ben and Layla stayed far away from D.C.

Jake kept his body loose, and his expression one of mildly interested concern.

"I'm sorry your son is missing, ma'am." Jake gentled his

voice. He was sorry, but that didn't mean he could help them. "But we don't find missing people."

"You know him." The father was more aggressive. "You were in his records."

Jake didn't move. "I don't know what you are talking about."

"Did you make him disappear?" The father's fists were clenched, and his face was turning a worrying shade of red, similar to the tomatoes his momma used to grow in her garden.

Make him? Nope. Ben had insisted on going to Layla—against Jake's better judgement.

Unfortunately, Jake couldn't let these people know that Ben had chosen to disappear.

He frowned with a manufactured confusion. "I don't understand why you would think that." He chose his words carefully, intent on not lying.

The mother clutched a piece of paper desperate and tight in her white fingers. "He had a handwritten note in one of his study guides with your name and this address."

Double fuck. They'd erased all the digital footprints that connected Ben, Layla, and ALIAS. They'd deleted all texts and communication between Ben and Layla. But Layla must have shared Jake's name with Ben, and he'd written it down. He needed to shut this down fast.

Hopefully, Zara was engrossed in her work and wasn't listening.

"I'm sorry, but I don't work here. I'm only visiting my friend."

"Please. You have to help us." Her voice shook. "We've poured through everything. Every note, every book, every paper. He's...gone."

"We have money," the father ground out, hoarse and raw. "We can pay you."

"It's not a question of payment." Jake forced his heart to slow. "I can't help you."

Not won't. Can't. He was careful in his wording.

"You don't understand."

But he did. "I do. I lost my sister many years ago." He was brutally honest. "I know how you feel."

Ben's mother reached out and grabbed his hand, her fingers bony and stick-like against his much larger ones. "Then help us."

Their grief pulsed in the air between them.

This was why he'd been against Ben following Layla. Dammit. "I'm very sorry, but I don't know anything about looking for a missing person."

"You lost your sister!"

"She was murdered."

Ben's mom paled and swayed. "Dead?"

Shit. He was seriously thrown off by their appearance. "I did not mean to imply that Ben is dead." Jake's voice deepened. "My apologies."

"It's the not knowing." The father's rage morphed, and his shoulders slumped. "Where he is."

Jake's chest tightened. His heart ached for these people, but telling them where Ben was would only put them all in danger.

As far as he knew, there hadn't been any recent chatter about Layla Habib. But the assumption was that the Iranians still had a FATWA on her head. To reveal her would put both Layla and Ben in mortal danger. At the moment, no one knew that they were a couple.

She and Ben were happily living together far from here.

Ben bought a laundromat and was running the small business. Layla had started writing a PI mystery series.

Most of that information he shouldn't have, and he would admit to no one that he'd followed up on them. That wasn't how ALIAS worked. They placed their clients and then cut all contact. It was better—safer—for everyone.

They split the details of each relocation into sections, and the clients had case numbers assigned with no reference to their legal names. By separating the information among the different employees, they could keep their clients safe. No one person had all the details. Layla had been a special case. At Jill and Marsh's insistence, Jake had approached her, and the timing had been condensed.

The system wasn't perfect, and there were ways around the safeguards —which was how Jake knew more about Layla and Ben than he should.

Zara leaned around Jake. "I'm so sorry. I couldn't help but overhear. Did you speak to the police?"

Shit. That was the last thing he needed.

"They won't help us," Karen said. "Because he withdrew money and left a note. He left voluntarily, so they don't believe us. But we *know* something is wrong."

Zara blinked. "Oh. Umm. Maybe he wanted to be on his own for a while." Her voice was soothing.

"He wouldn't do that to us." His father clenched his fists as if trying to keep his emotions from spilling out. "He was in school to learn management so he could take over the family business. We had plans."

"He wouldn't just leave," Karen whispered. "He loved us. We were close."

Zara clasped Karen Hansen's hand. "I'm sorry. Maybe he'll come back home soon."

"He wouldn't do this to us." Charlie's shoulders slumped further, his eyes tired and sad. "He wouldn't."

"I'm sorry I couldn't help." And he was.

"We aren't going to give up looking for him." Ben's father handed him a business card with a hand-written cell number on it. "That's my private line. Please call us if you find out anything about our son."

Jake shut the door quietly. He wanted to punch the wall, but he forced his muscles to relax and turned to go back to the conference room.

Fuck, fuck, fuck. His frustration boiled to the surface. Tension tightened his neck until he thought it might snap off.

Zara grabbed his bicep. "Not so fast."

Jake stilled. She hadn't touched him since he'd left her rowhouse months ago. The same as every prior time, his body responded with devastating enthusiasm. He wanted to turn and wrap her in his arms. Take solace, obscure the frustration coursing through him. He'd known that when Ben disappeared, his family would be an issue. But he'd given in because the kid was going to do it whether Jake helped or not. And if he hadn't helped them, Layla and Ben would likely be dead.

"I thought you were working?" He made it a question.

"We need to talk about what happened."

He cleared his face before turning around.

"Did ALIAS ... fake his death?"

"What?" Now Jake laughed. The question threw him because it was not at all what he expected. He should be used to her surprising him by now. "Of course not."

She studied him suspiciously.

She didn't believe him. His throat tightened. "I feel badly for them, but it sounds like the kid wanted to get away."

One of the first protocols of relocating a client was they had to cut all ties to their former life. That was how plenty of people in the official US Marshal witness protection program were found. They called or wrote letters to their loved ones missing that contact.

But the bad guys watched their loved ones, waiting for them to mess up.

The bad guys shouldn't be watching Ben's family. They shouldn't know about Ben at all.

He needed to have a contact send the parents a postcard, pretending to be Ben and asking for time, to get them to back off.

Zara wrapped her arms around her middle. "Sometimes adult children don't know how to tell their parents how they really feel."

"Speaking from experience?"

She shrugged. "I love my parents, but they had a hard time accepting that I wasn't interested in our family business."

Jake's brain was working, making connections, putting things together. "Is that why you moved across the country?"

Her face went blank, and she uncrossed her arms to hang loose at her sides. "There were multiple reasons."

He wanted to dig in and find her secrets. He wanted to know her. Her vulnerabilities and her strengths. Because there was a whole lot unsaid in that sentence. He remembered their first meeting. "Finding yourself?"

Her startled gaze shot to him. "Something like that." Her body wilted, as if suddenly holding up was too much effort.

He nudged her subtly. "It's been a long day."

"Yes."

Jake wanted to wrap her in his arms. They could find comfort in each other. But he would continue to have to lie to her and that was getting harder and harder to do.

"I'll follow you home."

"Is that really necessary?"

"Being cautious."

"I took a ride service," she finally admitted. She pulled out her phone and tapped the screen. "I don't have a car."

"Then I'll give you a ride."

The look on her face stopped him. Her reluctance to spend more time with him quelled that urge to give her a hug. His heart thudded hard. She didn't want to be with him. That was his fault. He'd hurt her. That had been apparent earlier. He hated that.

She sighed and nodded. "If you insist."

Well then, he needed to get over his butt hurt feelings and keep her safe. "I do."

She made a panicked face as if a distasteful thought had occurred to her. "How long do we have to do this?"

Could she make her reluctance any more obvious?

He didn't want to scare her. But Ben's parents had tracked down the office after the press conference, and the possibility of others doing the same existed. Charlie and Karen Hansen had been harmless, but others might not be. He wasn't about to let her get hurt on his watch.

"As long as it takes."

17

———————

*S**he needed caffeine bad.*

The next morning, Zara slid into the front seat of another Honda.

"Morning." She couldn't say it was good. She'd spent the night tossing and turning with strange dreams of parents coming to her doors and Jake turning them away. Her subconscious was clearly fixated on the confrontation with Ben Hansen's parents, but when she had dreams like this, it usually meant she was missing something.

As a result, she was bleary-eyed and short on caffeine. And she'd discovered she was out of her favorite coffee.

"Good morning." His deep voice rumbled through her.

She shifted in her seat. She seemed to be spending a lot of time in cars with Jake, and he continued to be a mystery on so many levels.

One thing was sure. Her instincts were back.

When she'd seen him in the bar the night they met, she'd been sure she'd be safe with him. She'd been absolutely on target —even if she did want to snap his head off right now. She shot him a disgruntled look.

"Coffee in the cup holder." He grinned at her.

"What?" She snatched up the cup. She didn't even care if it was good coffee. She needed a serious hit of caffeine. She took a giant gulp, the drink hot, but not scalding. "Oh my God, I could kiss you." She tossed out the words without thinking. Her breath caught.

He laughed, completely unfazed by her declaration. "Wow. I wish I'd know that was all it would take sooner."

A flush of embarrassment rolled through her. "Sorry," she muttered.

"Zara. I knew you were kidding."

She took another sip and moaned. It was really good coffee.

Her brain started to kick into gear. "How did you know I would need coffee?"

"I remembered."

From the morning after the night at her place. Her body flushed, this time with desire. "Where did you find this?" She took her beans seriously, and so far, she hadn't been able to find a coffee shop that compared to her old neighborhood shop in San Francisco.

He cleared his throat. "You clearly aren't a morning person."

Trying to distract from the fact that he knew intimately why she wasn't a morning person she said, "You didn't tell me where you got it. I need to live there." Her words were fervent as she clutched the cup to her chest.

He snorted.

"C'mon. Spill."

"Ah." Jake avoided her gaze. "I made it."

Wait. What? "Get out."

He signaled a lane change and shrugged.

"How?"

"The usual way. I ground the beans and used filtered water."

Smart ass.

"You like good coffee." A statement, not a question.

Her, too. It was a small thing but felt significant.

"Don't most people?" he deflected.

"Most people don't have the palate to differentiate between good and great coffee." Her ex, the asshole, used to give her a hard time about her predilection for superior coffee.

"Never really thought about it."

"In my family, we learned to activate our palate before we could drive."

She'd developed a refined palate at an early age. Her whole family was well-versed in how to distinguish different flavors: sweet, salty, sour, bitter, umami; deconstruct the tastes through smell, color, and clarity.

"Why?"

"My family makes wine. We've all taken sommelier classes."

Jake rolled his eyes. "Sommelier."

"A wine steward who has trained in all aspects of wine knowledge and been certified—"

He showed her his hand. "I know what a sommelier is, I just don't have use for one."

Ever. Was implied.

She tried not to be offended.

"Well, I would try to do a comparison about why it matters based on your profession, but since I have no idea what you do, beyond *this and that* I can't."

"Fair point."

He didn't elaborate.

"I'm not a Master Sommelier, obviously. But having an advanced palate is a skill."

"I've always been able to taste nuance." Jake shrugged. "It's not that big of a deal."

Wrong. It was unusual. Even if he wasn't a super taster—since he drank strong coffee, it indicated he likely didn't have the super taster receptor—he clearly was able to distinguish flavors. He made incredible coffee.

God, he really was perfect. If only he weren't keeping things from her.

That's when it hit her.

Her dreams narrowed into pinpoint focus. "You were involved with Ben's disappearance.

"Where the hell did that come from?" Jake took a sip of his coffee.

"My dreams." She squeezed the cup tighter. "Something about yesterday kept bugging me. I had dreams all night about yesterday's encounter with that couple."

His language was nuanced, too. When he'd answered Ben's parents, he'd very deliberately replied, *I didn't make him disappear.*

"You didn't *make* him disappear."

Jake's hands were loose on the wheel. But his trap muscles were rock hard. "I didn't."

"But did you *help* him disappear?"

His mouth tightened. "What's the difference?"

He was smarter than that. He knew what she meant. He was evading the question. "Are you going to answer me?"

"Ben is not a client of ALIAS." Jake clipped out.

They were almost at Xavier's mansion. She wasn't convinced. "You're sure?"

"I'm absolutely positive."

She didn't believe him. "So you had nothing to do with his disappearance."

He pulled up to the iron gate with a security guard gatehouse and rolled down the window to speak with the uniformed guard at the gate, effectively cutting off their conversation.

He never answered.

"Name." The guard frowned tersely. He wore khaki pants and a navy-blue polo with the XR Global Innovations logo over the left pec. His arm muscles bulged, and the holster at his waist surprised her.

"Zara Cooper to see Mr. Rodriguez," Jake replied equally tersely.

"I only have Ms. Cooper on the list." He consulted an iPad which showed a picture of Zara and with her credentials and listed her business address. "Who are you?"

"She's my principal." Jake reached into his pocket, and the guard tensed visibly.

"Easy. Just getting my ID." Jake pulled out his wallet.

The guard studied the card for a moment. Then he lifted the iPad and tried to snap a photo of the ID, but Jake flipped it closed as the guard pressed the button.

The guard looked like he was going to argue but then sighed. He snapped a picture of Jake's face instead.

Zara blinked at the intense security. Jake clearly didn't like that the guy had his picture. The guard handed Jake a clip-on visitor tag clearly fitted with RFID technology.

"Attach this to your person, ma'am."

He addressed Jake again. "You can drop her off and then pull over there to the side. Do not exit the vehicle."

Jake rolled up the window and proceeded around the large circular driveway with an excessive five-tiered fountain. He stopped at the expansive half-round steps leading to the massive wooden front doors.

"That seemed a little over the top." A quiet discontent rippled through her. Xavier had seemed so down to earth when they'd met previously. Sure, he always had bodyguards, but they stayed in the background.

However, the armed, very serious guard certainly dispelled that 'every man' vibe that he emitted in person.

"He's a very wealthy man and a US congressman. He probably needs it."

But a note in Jake's voice made her think that he agreed with her assessment.

Zara gathered her briefcase and folio. She'd dressed more formally for this meeting, making sure to present as professional appearance as possible. She wanted to put Xavier's mind at ease. He'd been pissed on the phone yesterday.

As she got out of the car, Jake cautioned, "Be careful."

It was the residence of a very wealthy man, and the security was insane. What could possibly go wrong?

18

A uniformed maid in a black dress with three quarter-length sleeves and a white peter pan collar led Zara into a traditionally appointed study with dark mahogany bookshelves, studded leather chairs, a large mahogany desk, and a globe stand. French doors led to a concrete pool deck with another large fountain, pergola, and chaise lounges set at an angle along the edge of the pool. A light steam rose off the turquoise water, and rolled bold navy-blue-striped towels perched at the end of each chaise.

"May I offer you a drink?"

"Water would be great."

"Still, sparkling, or tap?"

Zara blinked. It was like a restaurant. "Tap is fine."

The maid nodded.

"I'll get that for you. Mr. and Mrs. Rodriguez will be along in a moment." She shut the door quietly.

Zara didn't want to sit until Xavier and Carolina entered the room, so she studied the books on the shelves. Subjects were a wide range of non-fiction, from history to cold war policy to sustainable agriculture and organic farming techniques to biographies of successful entrepreneurs. *Losing My Virginity* by Richard Branson, *Business @ the Speed of Thought* by Bill Gates, essays from Warren Buffet, *Made in America* by Sam Walton, *Shoe Dog* by Phil Night, *Onward* by Howard Shultz, *How to Win at the Sport of Business* by Mark Cuban. *ReWork* by Jason Fried and David Heinemeier Hansson.

Biographies about Churchill, Alexander Hamilton, Nelson Mandela, George Washington, Abraham Lincoln and other historical world leaders.

Death in a Lonely Land: More Hunting, Fishing, and Shooting on Five Continents by Peter Hathaway Capstick. More books on hunting big game.

Valley of the Moon by Jack London.

It took her a few minutes to realize there weren't any books about or by women. Strange.

The doors opened, and Xavier strode in with the swagger of a man who could buy and sell small countries. Carolina followed at a slower pace, dressed again in that wealthy woman chic that seemed out of step with her personality.

"Welcome to our home." Carolina's lips quirked tentatively as her gaze skittered away from Zara's.

"Thank you." The house was too stuffy and dark for Zara's taste, but she could see the appeal if you were trying to convince people of your net worth. Or your worthiness. But she felt like the whole setup was trying too hard to look perfect.

"Have a seat." Xavier gestured to the seating area of two burgundy leather sofas and flanked by one wing chair with a large square coffee table between them. Xavier took the one overlarge wing chair.

Zara couldn't help but stare. Mounted behind the imposing

desk, in perfect view of the seating area, the head of the animal with circular horns sent the message, "I can dominate you like I dominated this animal."

"You like it?"

She tried to keep her distaste to herself. "It's unusual. What kind of animal is—" *she?*"—it?"

"That's a Persian Gazelle. Fallow deer." He smiled proudly. "They are extremely rare."

Her stomach rolled. She was a believer in preserving nature, not running around shooting it. Logically, she understood that it was necessary to balance out herds when natural predators had been eliminated. But she wasn't a fan.

Xavier was her client, not her friend, so she held back her disapproval. "She was beautiful."

He continued to beam at the dead animal on the wall. "Very rewarding hunting trip. They are only available by special permit in Iran."

Iran. That was unusual.

"Mountain hunting is an extreme sport. They don't drug the animals to slow them down. There are no feeding troughs. You need technical skills, navigation, route planning." He ticked off the requirements on his fingers. "Physical skills, carrying heavy gear, extended strenuous hiking, stealth. You have to be an excellent shot to bag an animal like that. It's the ultimate game."

He turned away from the taxidermied head.

Game. As if taking a life were of no consequence.

Zara wondered if she could position her body so she didn't have to gaze at the poor dead animal.

As if she sensed Zara's uneasiness, Carolina sat on the end of the sofa furthest from the deer, allowing Zara to turn her head so that the deer wouldn't be completely visible.

Zara's tension loosened.

Xavier frowned at his wife.

Was that a tactic he used to make his guests uncomfortable?

Look at this wild animal that I killed with my gun. No one is safe.

Now she was starting to sound like Jake.

19

"Let's get down to business." Xavier said, "In all honesty, I thought about cancelling our agreement." Zara's stomach churned again. "The other branch's activities are not indicative of ALI. I believe we can continue to give you good value. I am ready and willing to make sure everything is handled appropriately."

"I like you, Zara." Xavier steepled his fingers together in a move that seemed calculated. "Which is why we are continuing. But I do expect that Adams-Larsen's public relations issues will not affect me."

"Absolutely, sir."

"I'd hate for our relationship to end up like my beautiful Persian Gazelle."

Dead? Hung up on a wall as a warning? The threat was implied. But she wasn't sure exactly what he was threatening.

She'd hired more people to take over the new accounts they'd brought in, and she was handling his account personally. So far Jillian had been pleased with her performance. But if she lost his business, that would severely impact the bottom line of ALI.

"You have my personal guarantee." She met his gaze directly and shivered at his frosty expression.

"Glad to hear it."

Zara opened her portfolio and removed the schedule of events that she had laid out for him to attend. She set the black leather portfolio on the end table next to her.

"This is a tentative schedule for the next month. You'll need to check your calendar and make sure that there are no conflicts before we go ahead and book you." She handed one copy to Xavier. "Do you want to go over these?"

Xavier shook his head. "Carolina, please make sure that I am good to go."

Zara handed another sheet to his wife. A slight discoloration on her hand caught Zara's eye. Carolina tucked her hand beneath the paper not meeting Zara's gaze. "Of course, *mi amor.*"

"I have ideas about other things we can include."

Zara smiled. "That's great." Having Xavier as an active contributor would make her work easier.

"What's this 'A New Home' fundraiser?"

"A national organization that helps women and children escape domestic violence. They build townhouses and offer safe space for families escaping violence. There are work and school requirements for both mother and children." Zara probably went on too long, but this organization had a mission that had become near to her heart.

He used a Montblanc fountain pen encrusted with precious stones to cross out that line. "That is a domestic issue with no winners. I am not going to piss off fifty percent of the voters."

Zara's heart fell. As a champion of the underdog and disadvantaged, she'd been sure he would be drawn to the issue of helping people survive a situation with difficult odds.

Instead, he brushed aside her suggestion with a callousness that surprised Zara.

Carolina didn't even flinch. Which also surprised Zara. In the past she had been a supporter for survivors of domestic abuse, citing a family member, she'd refused to say which one, who had been a victim of abuse.

"Find an event or organization that champions renewable energy, electric vehicles. I recently closed a deal that will make it very lucrative for me in that space."

He'd been a major supporter of renewable energy in California. The way he pushed that as an option held a certain calculation. Apprehension skittered down her spine. In his home, he acted less smooth and with more than a hint of arrogance, and his wealth was on obvious display.

"This is a good start." Xavier tossed the paper back at her.

Start. She mentally sighed. She'd spent days on this plan. "Let me revisit and get back to you."

"I believe there is a conflict with this one." Carolina had taken a simple red marker and circled one event celebrating an urban farming project that utilized rooftops as green space for community gardens in the city and which produced fresh produce for food banks.

The super cool project was developed by Penny Hastings, a woman farmer from Massachusetts. Zara had loved that one because the event served a double purpose, the same as the projects themselves did. It was a perfect fit for his agenda.

"What conflict?" he barked out.

"The girls have their Spring school talent show."

He smiled tightly. "We discussed that moving forward with this plan that we would all have to make sacrifices. That stays."

Carolina nodded meekly.

An uncomfortable tension permeated the room. Zara slid the papers back into her briefcase. "I'll be in touch."

"One more thing." Xavier's voice could cut granite.

Zara blinked.

"I didn't appreciate the surprise guest this morning."

Surprise guest? He was talking about Jake. She grimaced. "My apologies. Due to…company concerns, he is providing protection for me." He of all people should understand the need for a bodyguard. Even if she didn't want one.

"Don't come with extra people again. Inform my staff."

"Of course." Zara nodded, a fine trembling in her hands betraying her unease. Hopefully, he hadn't noticed.

"I'll see Zara out," Carolina said.

"Brigitte will see her out," Xavier said smoothly as he ran a hand down his funky tie. Zara recognized the design from an up-and-coming Latina fashion designer from California. "We've got some things to discuss."

Carolina blanched.

The maid was back. Zara said her goodbyes and followed the maid to the front door.

Her stomach twisted with an unnamed disquiet. She was almost at the over-sized front doors when she realized her tote bag was too light.

"Shoot. I left my portfolio."

"I'll get it, ma'am."

Ma'am? What was she, an octogenarian?

"That's not necessary." She'd already put her foot in it. "I'll run back and grab it."

Zara knocked briskly and then pulled open the door. Brigitte had her hand on her arm to try and stop her.

"Sorry to interrupt, but I accidently left my portfolio." She was speaking rapidly trying to apologize which was why it took her more than a few seconds to process the scene before her.

Xavier gripped his wife's biceps so tightly his knuckles were white, his usually handsome face crunched in wrinkles of rage. Carolina's hair was askew and a red palm print marked her cheek. Her hands hung limply at her sides. She averted her wounded gaze from Zara's.

A shocked silence held everyone still.

"I'm sorry to interrupt, sir. I know you don't like to be disturbed." The maid's conciliatory tone set Zara's teeth on edge. This was clearly not an unusual sight.

Xavier let go of his wife and smoothed over his tie, his hand rock steady. He picked up her leather portfolio.

Her mind blanked. Portfolio. Yes. The reason she was here. Zara couldn't string her thoughts together. Her brain had computed what she'd seen, but she couldn't reconcile the violence in her head. Her favorite client and congressman had been in the middle of abusing his wife?

Her coffee sloshed in her stomach, acid rising, trying hard to expel from her body as the implications scrolled through her mind at warp speed. Zara forced her feet to move. She wanted to run, far and fast. But she needed to act as if she hadn't seen what she'd seen.

There would be time to fall apart later. Time to get this trembling under control and figure out what to do next.

Xavier strode to her with that same easy, confident grace that she'd admired. She stared at his hands that she used to think were genteel and refined, but now knew were weapons of violence, as he gently put the leather portfolio in her hands.

"Glad we are continuing to work together. I look forward to your next iteration for my schedule. As a reminder, you signed an NDA that prohibits you from sharing any of our discussions and plans."

He wasn't talking about the PR plans, and everyone in that room knew it.

"Of course." She wasn't committing to anything more than an acknowledgement of his statement.

"I'd hate for Adams-Larsen to have another ding against them after all the bad press recently. They can scant afford more."

Her stomach threatened to rebel again. "Understood."

He had the power and the means to destroy ALI if she didn't keep her mouth shut. Message received loud and clear.

"I'll be in touch." She forced a small smile and hoped her face didn't convey her horror at what had happened.

Brigitte escorted Zara to the front door. She moved on wooden legs.

This whole time, since she'd moved to D.C., she had thought that she'd turned a corner. Thought she'd gotten her confidence back. That her lack of awareness about David was a bug, not a feature of her judgement. But that scene had blown up that theory.

She couldn't trust herself anymore. She'd been horribly wrong about Xavier Rodriguez.

Thud. Thud. Thud.

Her heart banged around in her chest like a lottery ball made of stone. Searching for a way to break through. White spots danced in her vision and the boulder in her chest made it hard to breathe.

She could see Jake's car parked to the side of the steps.

Jake. He'd been right about Xavier. She should be pissed.

I need to get to Jake. To safety.

His name reverberated in her head. Jake. Jake. Jake.

Since the night she met him, she'd felt safe in his presence. Even when she was pissed at him, she knew he'd never hurt her.

But what if she were wrong about him, too?

20

J ake couldn't concentrate.

He had tossed a few Black Lightning comics in the car. He pretty much always had a few lying around just in case. But instead of getting lost in Jefferson Pierce and his struggles against crime and corruption and powerful criminals, he used the time to scope out the security features of Xavier's mansion…from the car, of course.

He rolled his eyes. Rich folk. What were they worried about? He'd steal the silver?

Jake should have asked how long she expected the meeting to last.

He'd spent the past thirty minutes surreptitiously checking out the cameras mounted on the house. Careful landscaping enhanced the visual appeal but didn't leave openings for unauthorized access. The iron pigeon spikes on top of the brick wall that surrounded the acreage would also stop people of the nefarious variety from accessing the grounds.

Xavier didn't appear to have dogs. Surprising for a man of his resources.

The guard at the gate had been armed with a Beretta 92FS,

with the larger 15 round magazine, using 9x19 parabellum bullets. A favorite of the US military. The guard shack had bullet proof glass and cameras with 360 degree views.

The massively carved, over the top, front doors opened.

Zara walked toward the car. Normally, she moved with a fluid grace, but now her body lurched as if her legs and arms were on separate levers.

She opened the car door and dropped into the passenger seat. White printer paper had more color than her skin.

Jake's heart picked up tempo, banging in alarm. He didn't like seeing her upset.

"What's wrong?"

Her tight mouth quirked up in more of a grimace than a smile. "I'm ready to go back to the office."

Huh. The meeting must have gone poorly.

"Did he fire you?" Jake could only hope.

"No." She wrapped one hand around the door handle. "Can we head out?"

Jake started the car. Carefully, he pulled up to the guard gate. Zara handed him the badge to give back, her hand trembling hard.

He swooped the badge from her hand and gave it back to the guard. He needed to distract the guy in case he was super observant and noticed that Zara was one step away from freaking out.

He wasn't even sure how he knew, but he intuitively understood. Her demeanor was cool, like always, but the air in the car simmered with fear, and she was on the edge of an epic meltdown.

"Thanks for the lovely parking space. I enjoyed the view very much."

The guard ignored his sarcasm and scanned the badge. "You can go."

"Thanks, buddy." Jake continued in a stream. "You have a great day, too."

Once they were away from the mansion and had taken several turns, he pulled the car over to the side of the road.

"What are you doing?" Panic coated her voice.

"Tell me what's wrong."

"Just get me back to the office." If her voice hadn't been shaking, he might have pressed.

Then she put her hand on his forearm. "Wait. Stop." She yanked open the car door and bolted for the grassy section between the curb and the sidewalk. She puked into the grate surrounding the large shade tree currently devoid of leaves, her body jerking.

Jake whipped out of the car, ready to help any way he could.

But Zara held up the palm of her hand stopping his forward motion. "Please let me throw up in peace."

"Can I do anything?" He hated to see her in distress. The need to vanquish her problems burned in his chest.

"No." She straightened and wiped a hand over her mouth. "Let's go."

They got back in the car. Jake accelerated slowly, waiting for her to explain what happened. The silence in the car expanded filling the stifling atmosphere with a tense expectation.

"Zara." He didn't need to say anything else. She had to know he was waiting for an explanation.

"The salmon on my bagel must have been bad."

That was her excuse? Bullshit.

His worry morphed seething inside him. "I'm your bodyguard." A job he might have taken on with an unexpected paranoia, but he was beginning to realize might be more necessary than he'd thought. His concern for her safety had been worry about associates of *former* clients, not actual clients.

But something had happened inside that monstrosity of a security palace.

"I'm sure I'll be fine."

"I can't properly protect you if I'm unaware of the specificity of a threat."

Her face blanched again.

He might not have even seen it if he hadn't turned his head to check for traffic.

Anger pulsed through him, bubbling up like the crude oil that had made the Drayton family millionaires.

"Did he threaten you?"

"Why would you ask that?" She sat ramrod straight arms at her sides, as if she were actively restraining herself from wrapping them around her.

"Stating the obvious. You urped in the bushes."

She repeated her claim woodenly. "Bad salmon."

"Fuck, Zara." Jake clenched the steering wheel wishing it was Xavier's neck. "When you're ready to talk about what happened and why you're suddenly afraid of your client, I will be here."

She didn't protest his accusation, which made Jake want to rip the guy's head straight off. He clearly wasn't going to get anything from Zara. Why would she protect that asshole?

He'd *known* something was off about Rodriguez.

Maybe he was a little biased about rich people, but he knew plenty of rich people who were great. And yeah, he had a small problem with knee jerk reactions. He *expected* them to be assholes until they proved him wrong.

Yes, it was cynical. But he had reason.

They arrived at the Adams-Larsen Inc. office without her saying another word. Jake had to try one more time.

"Are you going to level with me?"

"I'm feeling off from the food poisoning." She pressed a hand to her stomach. "I'm going to head into my office and close the door for a few minutes."

"Let me help you." He wanted to wrap her up in his arms and keep her safe, stand between her and any threat.

"Nothing a little Alka Seltzer and a break from food won't cure." Her smile was tight. "I've got more work to do for my accounts."

God! Why wouldn't she talk to him? Frustration burned his chest, and his face got hot. She was shutting him out, shutting him down.

Apparently, she was going to keep working for Xavier, even though he'd clearly scared the breakfast out of her.

Xavier had done something. Or she'd seen something that upset her. Enough that she'd looked like the criminal mastermind from Black Lightning Tobias Hale's goons were chasing her to the car.

But now they were back in the office, and she wasn't going to tell him.

"So the account is more important than whatever he did?"

Her face went blank. "I'll be in my office."

Jake's frustration built. He clenched his hands into fists to stop from reaching for her.

Her gaze shot to his hands. She didn't shrink away from him, but she made herself smaller.

Shit. His body language was all wrong. "I would never hurt you."

Her wary blue gaze shifted to his. "That's what everyone says though, isn't it?"

"Zara. Public relations isn't important enough to put yourself in danger." Fuck, as soon as he uttered the words, he knew he'd made a mistake.

She stiffened.

"I've got to work on the next iteration of the proposal. Because my work is important."

"Zara, what I meant was *you* are more important than a client."

But she just turned away.

21

———

Xavier Rodriguez abused his wife.

Zara shut the door to her office and fought the urge to be sick again.

Thoughts tumbled through her brain like a rock in the dryer, clunking and banging with an ominous noise.

The scene from his office was stuck on repeat in her head like a .gif that kept looping. The rage on his face. The fear on Carolina's. Shock punched her in the solar plexus all over again. What was she going to do?

Xavier had clearly threatened her and ALI.

She should know better than to idolize anyone. They all fell eventually, then you were left with an intense disillusionment and a despair that haunted you. Goddamn, was no one a hero anymore?

Why had she ever thought Xavier might be?

Zara dropped into her desk chair. She rested her elbows on the antique desk and tilted her head forward into her palms. What did she do now?

His reluctance to do the domestic violence philanthropy

appearance made more sense. Apparently as an abuser he wasn't that hypocritical.

And she was working for him. Trying to get him elected to the highest office in the country. A man who abused a woman wouldn't create equitable policies. A man who betrayed the trust of marriage and who preyed upon those he saw as weaker had no place in the highest position of government.

But how did she stop him?

She'd figure it out. That's what she did. She needed a plan. Then she was going to take that fucker down.

First, she needed information. She needed to get Carolina alone.

Zara picked up the phone and dialed Carolina. "Hi, Carolina."

"Oh, hello, Zara." Carolina's voice was smooth, cultured. No hint of the residual violence colored her words. "How can I help you?"

Faking it. Zara knew that tactic well. Wasn't that what she had done—pretended, even in her mind, that nothing wrong had happened, nothing had shaken her world? She was Zara Cooper of Cooper Winery. She'd grown up with wealth and status. Her family was respected and revered in the Sonoma Valley. There was no way she'd be the victim of domestic violence.

The script that Carolina was likely telling herself scrolled through Zara's mind, substituting the words wife of a respected businessman and congressperson to describe herself.

"I wanted to confirm dates with you while I work on Xavier's plan so I don't suggest anything that will overlap with his schedule."

"Absolutely."

Zara pulled out her calendar and ticked through the dates. She needed to pretend that nothing was wrong.

Carolina would broach the subject if she was ready. Zara needed a plan on how to handle that possibility. "I also wanted to check in with you about possible causes to support."

"Oh, that is best left to Xavier," Carolina demurred.

"He will, of course, have final approval. But I was hoping I could avoid suggesting events that you know will be a no go for him." Zara leaned into the flattery. "Because you are integral to his platform, and if I'm being blunt, you have the most access to him in terms of what he will and won't support."

Carolina would know what his triggers were and what to avoid. Zara needed to gather as much information about the situation as possible. Any knowledge she acquired could give her more ammunition in her campaign to convince Carolina not to put up with abuse.

"You assume I have more influence than I do," Carolina said softly.

"You must have issues that you'd like Xavier to focus on. I know you were active in several charitable organizations when you lived in California," Zara pressed. "After all, if his current plan works, you would be First Lady."

Carolina laughed nervously.

"You're very accomplished in your own right. Giving up your law school ambitions to support Xavier must have been hard." Zara pushed sympathy into her voice.

"You have no idea."

But she did. She'd read extensively on abusive relationships after she'd left David. Isolate from friends and work. Take away avenues that give women autonomy and power outside the relationship.

"I am happy to raise our daughters so they will become productive, contributing members of society. It's an honor to mold the education and well-being of the next generation."

But if she continued to stay with Xavier, her daughters

were likely to fall into abusive relationships, too. The cycle perpetuated because the vulnerable continued it.

"That is an admirable outlook." No way would she criticize Carolina's statement. She wanted to stay on her good side. Wanted to keep her calm and complacent. If Zara questioned her choices or what was happening with Xavier, Carolina would likely shut down.

"You wouldn't understand because you don't have children."

Zara felt that zing down to her toes. She didn't need children to understand that abuse was wrong and that letting the guy get away with it was wrong.

But at that, her stomach twisted. She hadn't revealed David's abuse to anyone. Too ashamed of her own complicity in staying quiet, in allowing it to happen in the first place.

"You might be right," she murmured.

She needed to play this very carefully.

Fortunately, Zara had a backup list of events that might work for Xavier. She put Carolina at ease by focusing strictly on business and never even hinting that she'd seen what she'd seen. After about twenty minutes, they were finished.

"I believe I have everything I need to craft a new version for Xavier." Zara wrapped up their call. "Thank you so much for your input."

"Of course," Carolina said softly. "We all have the same goal."

No fucking way.

"I would love to take you to coffee and pick your brain about other ways to expand Xavier's reach." And to figure out how to take him down.

"It's difficult for Xavier to get away for a short meeting like that."

Carolina wanted nothing to do with that, clearly.

"Oh, I thought we could do only the two of us. Again, I don't want to take up Xavier's valuable time."

Zara chose words that minimized any kind of aggressiveness or even a hint of discussing something other than coffee and causes, couching the idea as a plan to help Xavier.

"We'll see." Code for no. Damn.

As much as she wanted to push, Zara knew it was a bad idea. She had planted the seed, now she needed patience. Grape vines didn't produce right away. Vines planted took many seasons of nurture and attention before they bore fruit.

Zara could be patient. For now.

22

He needed dirt on Rodriguez. Stat.

Jake spent the afternoon working in the ALI conference room. Worrying about what had happened to Zara at the meeting this morning.

Frustration gnawed at him. He needed more info on Xavier Rodriguez because everything he found painted the guy as a serious saint.

He'd championed workers' rights. He'd supported the military. Small business entrepreneurship. Created opportunities for marginalized communities to expand into the middle class. Fought for human rights. Supported foreign policy and business development with developing nations while a businessman. He had gone to Afghanistan last year on a diplomatic envoy. Jake felt like all the pieces were there, but he couldn't see the picture clearly.

He video-called his coworker, Kita Kim.

The petite powerhouse filled the screen. She wore a wicking tank top and leggings. This week, she had blue streaks in her hair.

"Hey, Jake."

"I like the blue."

She cocked her head and pretended to fluff the ends. "Thanks, it's Alex's favorite color."

Kita had met US Deputy Marshal Alex Saunders on a hush-hush op last fall. Jake had been out of town when everything went down. He'd been shocked to arrive back home and find Kita and Alex were an item. He'd been even more shocked when they moved in together after dating for what felt like a very short time.

"How's the babysitting?" The sympathy in her voice surprised him.

"Fine." Except that Zara wanted nothing to do with him, and he couldn't shake the idea that she was in danger. But he had no idea exactly what the threat was.

"That didn't sound fine."

He wasn't about to share his and Zara's strained relationship, or whatever the hell it was, with Kita. Ever since she and Alex moved in together, she'd been more touchy-feely. Her relationship had started the office pair-offs—like there was a love flu going around.

"They have a client that I am concerned about."

"In what way?"

"Just a feeling."

"That's not good." Kita cracked her knuckles. "Name and address if you've got it."

"Xavier Rodriguez." Jake rattled off the guy's mansion address.

Kita got up and closed her door.

She leaned toward the screen. "Uh, you want dirt on the super hot, billionaire-philanthropist-congressman whose been on an upward trajectory for the past three or four years?"

Jake swallowed his impatience. Why did everyone think this guy was so awesome?

"Wow." Kita started typing. "That's certainly disappointing."

Tension left his shoulders. She didn't ask why. She didn't argue with him. She started looking for information.

"Thanks." He forced the word out of his constricted throat. "Why is everyone so high on this guy?"

He knew he had issues about rich people but that wasn't it. In his gut, he felt like Xavier was off.

"Self-made billionaire. He didn't get his seed money from his family. He literally scrapped and clawed to create his fortune. He's involved in a lot of charities. He's brilliant. He's attractive." Kita ticked the guy's assets off on her fingers, making Jake want to punch the guy. "On the surface, he's the real deal."

"You found something?" Jake perked up.

"Nope," she said cheerfully. "But if you think there's something there, I'll keep looking."

"Thanks, Kita."

He was about to hit the disconnect button when she stopped him.

"So how is Zara?"

"Fine."

"Uh-oh. Another fine."

No one in the office knew that he and Zara had hooked up. Jill might suspect, but she wouldn't have said anything. She'd respect their privacy. "She's working."

"Okay." Kita eyed him with speculation. More speculation than when he'd accused a veritable saint of potential nefarious issues. "I would share your concerns with her."

He had. And she thought he was being difficult and paranoid.

"I tried."

"So she likes the guy?"

"She did."

"But she doesn't now." Kita shot him a contemplative look.

Who knew? She certainly wasn't sharing whatever happened in that house this morning.

"She hasn't said."

"Well, then, it's a good thing you're there watching her ass."

He must have flushed, because she rubbed her hands together. Her smile was wicked.

"Like that, is it?"

He knew better than to engage. Kita used to work for the CIA. Her radar had radar.

23

———

I t had been a long fucking day.

Zara leaned back in her chair and rubbed her eyes.

After her conversation with Carolina, she'd spent hours researching great events and causes that would *help* Xavier. Meanwhile in the background, her brain had been working on ways to expose him.

But she'd come up with nothing.

He had unlimited financial resources. Was a sitting congressman. Positive press. All she had was her word.

Since Carolina had basically punted the suggestion of getting coffee, Zara needed to come up with a way to get to Carolina. Maybe she could suggest a few events that the woman do on her own, and then Zara could casually show up.

She couldn't let this asshole get away with it. But she had to be very, very careful about her methodology.

She glanced at the clock. Eight PM. Sigh.

Everyone else had left hours ago.

Jake was in the conference room. His presence gobbled up the air, like yeast gobbling up the sugar in grape juice when making sparkling wine and converting it to carbon dioxide and ethanol.

Of course, fermentation was what produced that lovely effervescence and gave wine its heady punch.

Ugh. And if she was starting to think in wine production metaphors, it was time to head home.

Zara's phone rang. Jillian Larsen.

"Zara Cooper."

"It's Jill."

Zara could picture her in a crisp, pastel suit, hair perfectly coiffed and lipstick still bright and vibrant from the morning.

"What can I do for you?"

"I wanted to check in on your progress with the X account."

They had given Xavier's account a nickname. Besides Jake, Jillian and Marsh, no one else at the company knew that Xavier was a client.

"We had a meeting this morning." Zara felt the burn of disappointment, even though she didn't want him to succeed any more. She'd thought the program she'd put together was kick ass.

"I'm aware."

"Right." She was flustered. "He liked some of my ideas but nixed others. I've been working all day to come up with a new schedule."

"Great."

She geared up to share what happened this morning. Jillian had a right to know that Xavier had threatened to negatively impact the company if she didn't fall in line.

She'd swallowed the bile that rose to the surface. "About Xavier—"

"It would be nice to have a congressman in our corner. There have been rumblings off and on about a hearing into our business. That's the last thing we need. If Rodriguez can help stop that from happening, that would be a good thing for us."

Jillian had completely missed Zara's long silence.

"Sure would be," she said weakly.

"I'm sure you gathered from the news conference yesterday that we don't need any more bad press."

Acid tossed in her stomach. "I got that."

Creating a national incident when she exposed Xavier as a domestic abuser would be considered the height of bad press. Jesus, she was screwed.

She couldn't share about this morning, after all. All that stomach acid dropped like an anvil and settled in her gut.

She was on her own.

At least until she came up with a plan to expose Xavier without putting the company in jeopardy. Then she would come clean to Jillian.

Fatigue pulled at her as she reviewed every thought and emotion through an opaque lens, straining to find a positive solution to this morning's revelation.

Maybe she could get Carolina to leave Xavier and stay out of it. She'd have to press harder for a private meeting, without it seeming like she wanted a private meeting.

Her stomach twisted into a tangled mess like old growth vines that hadn't been pruned in years.

"Is Jake nearby?"

"Ah." Zara tried to shift gears, caught up in the worry tumbling around in her brain. "Yes?" She cleared her throat. "Sorry, yes."

"Can you hand him your phone for a moment?"

"Sure."

Zara walked to the conference room and knocked. Jake's eyebrows rose as if to say, *I thought you didn't want to talk to me?*

"Jillian is on the phone."

"Everything okay?"

She must have imagined the disappointment. He was annoyed with her. She understood why. But she couldn't tell him what had happened. He had told her he had a bad feeling about Xavier. Turned out Jake had way better instincts than she did.

"Sure."

She handed him her phone. "Do you want me to leave?"

Jake spoke into her phone. "We going to talk about anything top secret, boss lady?"

As he waited for Jillian's reply, his confident grip, his strong fingers held the device easily, caused a flutter in her belly. It was silly, and yet, she couldn't deny she was attracted to him.

He gave her a chin lift. "You can stay."

He listened intently. "No apparent follows. No harassing phone calls. Office operated business as usual."

His conversation with Jillian only lasted a few minutes. A lot of uh-huh and okays. Zara studied him as he spoke, admiring the strong line of his neck and the sturdy bulk of his muscles underneath the cotton dress shirt.

His broad shoulders straightened with tension.

"Fuck. Seriously?" Jake dropped his head to one hand. Seriously despondent. "Okay. Thanks for the heads up."

Zara tensed. What was wrong?

24

———

*F*uck, *fuck, fuck.*

Jake's stomach cramped.

"Everything okay?" Zara's question startled him.

"No." Rage surged through his body until he erupted, slamming his palm on the long wood conference table. "Dammit."

She instinctively shrank away from his violent outburst. Fear thickened her voice.

"What's wrong?"

He stood quickly but stepped back from her, trying to be less threatening. "You don't ever have to be afraid of me."

"I know." But her actions told a different story. He'd scared her. Jake stomach sloshed. She was totally afraid of him right now. Fuck.

"You aren't acting like you know." Pushing his point wasn't the way to go, and yet he couldn't drop it. She had to know. "I would *never* hurt you." He paused. "Never hurt any woman."

"What's wrong?"

She didn't want to argue with him. Check.

"The guy who killed Amancia was released on parole today."

"Oh, my gosh." She shot forward, pressed her palm to his forearm. "Are you okay?"

"Fuck." No, he wasn't okay. That asshole was free while his sister was dead and gone.

"What happened?"

Jake had gone in front of the parole board. Made an impassioned plea to keep him in prison. But he'd heard the comments from the warden and from that asshole's family. He would bet that the family had offered money to get him out early.

"They didn't listen to my warnings."

"Do you think he'll hurt someone else?"

"Odds are high. There had been rumblings about other girls he'd hurt in our small town. He hadn't killed anyone, but there'd been plenty of rumors about girls leaving town and payoffs."

Zara made a sympathetic murmur.

"His family has plenty of cash. And power." He threw his pen across the room. "They'll cover it up like they always did."

Shit. Violence was not the answer. Jake put one hand on his hip and the other grabbed the back of his neck. He needed to get his shit under control.

"Not everyone with money is a power mad jerk." Her blue eyes glittered, her words sharp-edged.

Now he'd hurt her. "I realize that."

"Do you?" She snapped, then deflated. "I'm sorry. Now is not the time to be having this discussion."

She reached for his hand and squeezed his fingers. "What can I do?"

What could anyone do?

"Nothing to do." Jake appreciated the offer though. "I'll have to let my mother know."

God, that was a conversation he didn't want to have.

"Where is your mother? Is she close by?"

"She lives in assisted living about thirty minutes from here." Another failure on his part. His mother hadn't wanted to leave her home in Mississippi, but Jake had wanted her close by so he could be there quickly if there was a problem. Although joke was on him. His mother didn't really want to see him.

He checked in with the nursing staff daily. But he only saw his mother once a month or less.

"Isn't she young?"

Too young. "My sister's death broke her." Then he'd attacked Drayton. "And then I made it worse by beating up the asshole."

"You attacked him."

"Not my finest moment."

"What happened?"

He'd been thrown in jail and nearly convicted. The army had been his way toward a better future. But he'd had to leave his mother. Not that she had wanted to see him anyway.

"In a stroke of absolute good luck, I was only seventeen. The judge granted me leniency if I agreed to join the military."

Her eyebrows rose.

"Army."

"And yet now you work for an image consulting firm doing this and that."

He wasn't touching that one.

"So she lost you both." Zara's voice was laden with sadness. "But why assisted living?"

"She couldn't live on her own anymore." Jake's chest was heavy with regret. "Her diabetes is out of control. She lost several toes and has difficulty walking and getting up and down."

"Oh, Jake."

"Honestly, she is mostly subsisting. She is waiting to join my sister and my father."

"Your father is gone, too?"

"Yeah." Jake was mentally working through what to say to his momma. "KIA in the Army when I was a baby."

"You're all alone?"

"Easier that way." Although lately he was…lonely. His sister had been gone for almost twenty years. His friends were all pairing up and in love. The sense again that he was missing something extraordinary flowed through him.

"Oh, Jake."

"Family isn't all it's cracked up to be, anyway." His family certainly couldn't withstand the tragedies that struck at the heart of their unit. "You must not be close since you moved across the country—willingly."

"My family is a pain in my ass and also the light in my heart."

Interesting.

"And yet, you moved." This was a distraction from his problems.

"I love my family." She smiled wistfully. "But a little distance makes life easier."

"Are they the reason you lost yourself?" The night they met, she'd said, *I lost me.* Had her family done that?

"What are you talking about?" She wrapped her arms around her waist. Classic defensive posture.

"The night we met." Shit, he just revealed that he remembered a lot about that night. A random pick up in a bar, and he remembered every moment of their conversation and the sex that followed.

"It was bar talk." She waved her elegant fingers as if brushing aside his question.

"Nope." Jake stalked toward her unwilling to let this drop.

Her chin lifted. "So."

"Was your family the reason?" He asked again.

"Of course not."

He took a stab at the truth so far unspoken. "Then who hurt you?"

She fell back. "No one."

Disappointment flooded him. He thought they'd been sharing. It had been…nice.

"He isn't important."

"He must be if you moved across the country to get away from him."

"I didn't move to get away from *him*." Zara refuted. "I moved to get away from the person I was when I was with him."

"Isn't it the same thing?"

"No. Maybe. I don't know anymore." Wistful. "I'd lost myself. I came here to find me."

"And is it working?"

"I thought it was."

Back to this morning again. Jake could feel it in his bones. "What happened at Xavier's?" He put his hand on her shoulder gently.

Zara curled into his chest and wrapped him in an embrace. Shock held Jake still.

She rested her head on his chest. "Can we just *be* for a few moments?"

"Yeah."

She relaxed into his arms, her body flush against his.

The boom of his heart echoed in his head. He realized he needed this contact as much as she did.

But he continued to hold back emotionally, reluctant to let down his guard. Which she clearly sensed when she said, "C'mon. The office is empty."

"I don't give a fuck if anyone sees us hugging." Maybe she cared, though.

"There isn't anything in the HR rules about fraternization." Zara rested her head in the crook of his neck.

He snorted. "There better not be. More than half the office has hooked up on ops over the last six months."

"Ops." She'd stiffened against him.

"Uh, sorry. Old habit. Cases."

"Cases you can't share with me."

"I'm a vault." But he smiled against her head. "Everyone signs NDAs."

"You like your job?"

"Yeah. We help people." He thought about it more. "I bounced around quite a bit searching for something with meaning. But I finally found my place." He was proud of the work they did. Proud that he was instrumental in protecting people. And up until about six months ago, that had been enough. But lately, he longed for more. "Yeah, I found where I belong."

Her arms tightened around his waist. "That's good."

"Yeah."

"No more violence?"

"Not if I can help it."

"The army must have worked."

He guessed. He'd become more disciplined. Less reactionary. "Women getting hurt, especially by men, is still a trigger for me."

"I can understand why." There was a flatness in her voice as she stepped out of his embrace. "Thank you for the hug. I can head home for the day."

He didn't want to leave her alone. His gut churned. Something had happened this morning and she was keeping it all inside. At least he had Kita working on getting intel on Xavier, but nothing beat firsthand experience. He wished Zara would share with him.

But whatever happened at the Rodriguez's this morning screwed him.

25

———

God, she couldn't wait to get home and fall apart.

Jake drove with both hands on the wheel, his concentration on high alert. But he'd told Jillian that everything had been normal.

He glanced in the rearview mirror again and then turned abruptly, without signaling.

A frisson of alarm shot through her. He turned again, and again, until they were driving on a street parallel to the one they had been on.

"You want to grab a bite to eat?"

Zara blinked. Analyzed the last few minutes. "Are we being followed?"

"I'll take that as a no."

"It's not a no." She liked spending time with him, and she could sure as hell use some company right now, even if she couldn't tell him why. But she was concerned that he was only suggesting it because something was wrong.

"Do you always hyper analyze a simple request to partake in food?"

"Only when someone keeps looking in the rearview mirror."

"I thought we had a tail." Jake sighed with exasperation. "But if we did, we lost them."

"Good."

Zara let the fear go, thankful he lost them. She didn't want anyone following them to her house.

He pulled up to the curb outside her brownstone. He glanced around, looking at the cars on the street. "But we need to be on guard for unfriendlies at your house."

"Fortunately, my address isn't easily found."

"Why is that?"

"Woman living alone in a big city." She hesitated. No need to make it easy for her ex to track her down. Not that she was running away from him, but she had no desire to see him ever again. "Plus…family money."

The silence was less comfortable now. "Would you tell me if you were hiding?"

"I'm not hiding," Zara confessed. "I'm avoiding."

"Is he dangerous?"

"No." She laughed. David was a preppy, trust fund guy with a high intensity job in high finance he got through his godfather.

"Name?"

"Nope."

He tapped his fingers on the steering wheel. "I have ways of finding out."

"Why would you want his name?"

"If we're ever in the same space, I can … caution him about treating women properly."

"I can fight my own battles, Jake."

He said fiercely, "But you don't always need to."

Her heart melted. "I'll consider it."

Jake and Zara exited the car at the same time. His previous words caused a chill to skitter down her spine. Zara searched the shadows for any threats. She wasn't ready to be alone.

"Let me change, and we can get food," she said impulsively.

Jake kept close behind her as she opened the door. The remnants of their conversation lingered in her mind. She didn't want to talk about David. But maybe if she did, it would help him understand his sister.

The door closed with an ominous thud. Jake reached out his hand as if to touch her then pulled back. As if he had a line into her brain, he said, "Help me understand?"

Zara curled her fingers around his in a show of trust. His hand was warm and solid beneath hers, giving her the courage to share. Maybe this would be cathartic for her, too.

"I was more upset with myself because I stayed after he hit me." Shame cascaded through her.

Looking back on that time, she could objectively recall how he had belittled her in subtle ways. But he'd also weirdly been a cheerleader for her. The constant see-saw of derisive criticism, then praise, kept her off-balance. The comments were subtle at first, but the longer she allowed him to cut her down, the more frequent they got. Then the first time she'd rejected advice that seemed more like a demand, he'd hit her.

Jake's confusion was transmitted by the taut muscles in his forearm, his fingers tense beneath hers. "Why did you?"

"The first time it happens you're…stunned." The shock of that punch still took her breath away.

David's fist had plowed into her solar plexus. The pain sang up her body and reverberated in her head.

She'd grown up in a loving, accepting household. It hadn't been perfect. Of course, her parents had raised their voices.

And of course, she and her brothers fought. But she'd never been physically assaulted before.

Right after, he'd been so contrite. So *sorry*. That she'd believed him when he said it was an accident. It would never happen again.

Until it did.

"And then it happens again, and you're sure it was an accident. A rough day at the office. He was under a lot of pressure at work."

She'd believed him. She'd believed that he was sorry. That he hadn't meant to hit her. That he'd been frustrated with work and other things, and he'd lashed out. But then it happened again.

The next time she'd told him it was unacceptable.

He agreed. She should have left then but she hadn't. She'd believed him again.

"But it keeps happening. Attack and remorse. In this cycle until suddenly it's a pattern of abuse."

"You left him, though?"

"Yes. Fortunately, I have resources and a loving family. But not everyone does."

"I loved my sister." As if in defense.

"I know you did. But you need to forgive your sister for staying." Zara urged him. "No one ever believes that it's intentional, that it's going to continue."

"You left."

"I did. But not right away." The fourth time she was done. But she harbored a deep shame because she'd allowed him to abuse her. "And it haunts me."

The words burst from him. "Why didn't she tell me what was going on?"

"Because she was ashamed." Her voice wavered.

Jake said fiercely, "The shame was his. Not hers."

"That's not how it feels when it's happening to you." She hunched, instinctively shying away from the pity he must be feeling.

So much for the burgeoning feelings she'd been having. Weakness was like a disease, catching.

"God." Jake breathed. "I want to touch you so badly."

Shock jerked her head up. Pity wasn't in his gaze. She saw compassion and need.

She remembered the first time she'd met him. She'd been flying high with the triumph of taking back her power. Of releasing from the chains of shame that she'd bound herself in.

She'd been sure that he was her moment to step into her future with an open heart and an optimism that had been missing for a while.

"Can I hug you?" He vibrated with pent up need.

Consent. His request for it was sexy but still she hesitated.

"Shit. I don't want to scare you." He fell back quickly. "Never mind."

Zara took a tentative step toward him. "I would like that very much."

Jake held out his arms, letting her make the first move.

Zara stepped into his embrace. He enveloped her in a cocoon of safety and acceptance, his muscled chest solid beneath her ear. The steady, calm beat of his heart soothed her frazzled nerves. Once again, he'd shown her that her judgement wasn't completely blown.

They stayed there for awhile, her body slowly relaxing as he continued to give her comfort.

"Rather than go out, let's eat in," Zara said impulsively. "I'll cook."

"You know how to cook?" Jake teased.

26

"Of course." She flushed. She knew how to cook a few things. "Sort of."

She had a repertoire of a few easy meals. She'd probably need to triple the recipe so she made enough to feed him.

"Sounds…good."

The back of her neck prickled as Jake followed her into the kitchen.

She chattered away, talking about nothing, trying to fill the silence. She opened the fridge and pulled out chicken, some gorgonzola cheese, and a variety of produce, lettuce, shredded carrots, cucumber, and put them all on the island.

She hadn't looked at him since the hug.

"Zara," he said patiently. "I don't need to stay."

"What?" She whipped around, her eyes wide. "Why would you say that?"

"You seem nervous."

She shrugged with a little bit of embarrassment. "Well, I did share something incredibly personal." Total honesty. "Just trying to lighten the moment."

"I'm not judging you."

Whether he was or wasn't, she was flustered. "I know, how about a glass of wine? Red or white?"

He smiled. "Red is fine."

"Fabulous. I have a reserve cabernet that I think you'll love." She headed to the wine rack on the end of the island and pulled out one of Cooper Winery's best. She handed him the bottle and a corkscrew.

"If you open it, we'll let it breathe for a few minutes. It has a nice bouquet and a soft finish. The gorgonzola will pair well with it."

His lips quirked in a small smile.

"What?" She asked.

"Talking about wine seems to calm you down."

"Yeah, completely easy subject for me." Zara pulled out balsamic vinegar and oil and some herbs and whipped up a quick marinade for the chicken. "We'll let this marinate for about half an hour and then it can go in the oven."

Jake used the corkscrew easily then glanced around the kitchen.

"Wine glasses are in that cabinet." She jerked her chin toward it.

Jake pulled out two Riedel glasses etched with the Cooper Winery logo.

"This is you?" he asked.

"Well, my family."

He poured the dark ruby wine into the goblet and handed her one. "You didn't want to go into the family business?"

She paused. Shook her head. "No."

"How come?"

Forget about letting the wine breathe. Zara swallowed a large gulp. "I wanted to do something that would make an impact."

The wine sloshed in her stomach. Things weren't going well in that regard. But she couldn't tell Jake.

"PR will do that?"

"Sure," she said. "I wanted to do something positive."

"You say that as if positive isn't a given. What kind of negative PR is there?"

"There are big and small examples. For instance, you've probably never heard of it, but there was a large scandal a few years ago when a British PR firm, Bell Pottinger, basically influenced South African citizens. They were hired by a corrupt family to cover the family's business ties to the current government and to hide their illegal influence in government policies. Bell Pottinger created a smear campaign and used fake news to convince the public that the corrupt family was being discriminated against by a monopoly of elite white business owners. The campaign ended up inciting riots and influencing politics. When journalists exposed the scheme, Bell Pottinger was vilified for unethical practices."

Jake pressed his mouth together. She figured he wanted to bring up Xavier. But he didn't.

"On a smaller scale, there was Edward Bernays. He basically coined the term public relations in the late 1920s. He understood the human psyche because he was influenced by his uncle, Sigmund Freud. He used fear to sell products. For Dixie cups, Bernays launched a campaign to scare people into thinking that only disposable cups were sanitary. As part of this campaign, he founded the Committee for the Study and Promotion of the Sanitary Dispensing of Food and Drink and then convinced people that paper was more sanitary than glass."

"You don't want to do something like that," he said.

"No, I want to make a difference in a positive way."

"Give me an example." He smiled, encouraging her. "You're passionate about this."

"Yes."

"It suits you."

Pleasure bloomed in her chest. She wanted to matter.

"Okay, I was working on a brand campaign in San Francisco for a female founded venture capital firm. We partnered the firm with a nonprofit that helped women prepare for job interviews. The campaign highlighted the growth of women in tech and inspired girls to pursue STEM careers and created a culture of empowerment."

"So PR isn't all about corporate, or other, greed?"

If he'd been accusatory she might have been annoyed, but the question was clearly curious not judgmental.

"No, of course not. But if you can create a campaign that both inspires and makes money it's a win-win."

They worked together seamlessly, moving around the kitchen in a slow dance. Jake assembled the salad while Zara prepped the rest of the chicken recipe.

After putting the chicken in the oven, Zara said, "We can sit in the living room while we're waiting for the food to be done."

Jake sat in one of the big end chairs and assessed her over the rim of his wine glass. He paused and she braced waiting for a question she didn't want to hear. Instead he asked, "You couldn't do all that in San Francisco?"

She sighed. "In San Francisco, I'm Zara Cooper."

"You're Zara Cooper here, too."

"Yeah, but in D.C. nobody knows me, or my family, so I can be judged on the merit of my actions, not on the fact that my last name is Cooper."

"Being a Cooper is bad?"

"No! But people assume one of two things. Either I got the

job because of nepotism, my last name is Cooper and I may be decent at PR but I took the job from someone else who needed it. Or I am incompetent, but I got the credit because my last name was Cooper. It didn't matter how much work I put into anything. My accomplishments were discarded and diminished because of my last name, and I was tired of it."

"I get it. I understand the weight of expectations. I was an angry teenager after my sister started dating Drayton. In my hometown, I wasn't ever going to lose the label of angry Black man because I attacked him—even if it was justified. I had no intention of living down to their negative expectations."

The weight of other's expectations could be crushing. They shared a moment.

Her face softened as the tension left her body. Their connection swirled between them. Zara leaned toward Jake.

The timer went off, breaking the odd camaraderie.

After serving their plates, they sat at the kitchen table. "Can you tell me more about your sister?"

Jake sighed and closed his eyes. "Yeah," he said softly. "She was beautiful. As I told you before, she was a dancer. She was obsessed with Misty Copeland."

"The ballet dancer?"

Jake stared out the dark windows. "Yeah, she wanted to be the next Misty Copeland."

"You were close," she said.

"Oh yeah," Jake replied. "My mom was a nurse, a single mother. She worked a lot of nights and weekends. Better pay in those off hours."

Zara nodded.

"Cia and I spent a lot of time together. I had to go with her when she went to the dance studio—which she did a lot. And she got me hooked on comics so I wouldn't be bored."

Zara sipped her wine, waiting for him to continue. The love in his voice caused a lump in her throat.

"We were inseparable until she started dating him. She got quiet and sometimes she was really sad, and I couldn't fix it for her. It killed me. I didn't understand why she wouldn't just leave him."

She wasn't about to interrupt this memory.

"How did they meet?"

"She worked at the country club as a waitress. She was stunning. She could have done anything."

Zara's chest was tight.

"When she danced, the world stopped. She was so beautiful and so graceful. She wanted to go to New York." Jake put down his fork and poured more wine. "But she refused to leave Mississippi until I turned eighteen."

Zara reached out her hand and placed it over his clenched fist. "Don't think what you're thinking."

"If she'd left, maybe she'd still be alive."

That certainly backfired.

"It's why I try not to think about her." He drank his wine like a general heading into battle.

"Give me another memory. A good one."

"She was going to go to some gala with Drayton. For all her ballet dancing and hip-hop training, she wasn't super comfortable with ballroom dancing. So she taught me and I helped her practice." Jake's eyes softened as he visualized that memory. "Some days I think she was the best part of me."

"She would be proud of you."

"I like to think so. She's the reason that I protect people, that I do what I do."

"That's beautiful." Zara's heart ached with a combination of sorrow and joy. He had loved his sister so much.

Jake cleared his throat, and his gaze cut away from hers, as if embarrassed at how much he'd shared.

"I am so glad you had seventeen years with her."

"That's...a good way to look at it." He tilted his head. "I never thought of it that way."

He gripped the wine glass with his strong fingers. Fingers that could bestow tenderness.

That thought burbled up inside her, her brain tripping on his tenderness and skill in the bedroom.

"What's that for?"

"What?" Heat flooded her cheeks. Why did she react like a horny college girl around him?

"That blush."

She eased away and started clearing the table, but he followed prowling like a cat, his gaze considering.

"Did I blush? It must be warm in here."

"Zara," Jake replied patiently.

She wasn't about to admit that she still lusted after him. They were coworkers. The last time they'd had sex, he'd backed away faster than a cockroach from a pesticide.

She said brightly, "Are you interested in dessert?"

"I'd rather talk about that blush."

She knew how to spin things; she was a master at her job. But all her intellect rushed from her head when he trapped her between his arms and the kitchen counter.

Her heart thundered, the boom echoing in her ears as her face heated even more. Was it hot in here? Zara licked her lips.

Jake's gaze dropped to her mouth.

Her breath caught, stuck, as she raised her gaze to take in the blazing heat in his eyes. He let everything he was thinking show. And it appeared he was thinking the same thing she was.

"I'm hungry for something other than dessert."

God, so was she.

The first few times they'd gotten together had been about sex, but this was more. Desire rolled through her in a slow wave. This was deep, intense longing.

She wanted to comfort him and be consumed by him.

"This is a bad idea." *Right?*

Jake leaned closer. The inferno from his body lit her up like a firecracker fuse ready to explode.

"But is it?"

27

What a way to wake up.

A warm, naked Zara, all sleek skin and soft angles, snuggled in his arms. She had a runner's body and angles that should have felt sharp, but her personality smoothed those edges.

A subtle lavender scent wafted in the air like a halo enveloping his senses.

Her butt wiggled experimentally against his growing erection.

Every time they hooked up, the sex just got better. It didn't seem possible, but it was the truth.

He liked her. Her sharp wit, her compassion, her vulnerability. She'd let him in in ways he hadn't been expecting.

He wanted to hold on and hold tight.

Never let her go.

Jake jolted at the thought. He wasn't cut out for a relationship. He would have to keep things from her. Then he thought about waking up every day like this, and his chest filled with happiness and light.

She knows some of your secrets. A little voice whispered in his head. He wouldn't completely have to lie to her.

But he would still have to lie.

She deserved better.

All those conflicting thoughts rambled around in his brain.

Before things got weird, and it was trending that way, at least in Jake's head, the doorbell rang.

Zara stiffened.

"Are you expecting a visitor?" Maybe it was time for him to clear out.

"No," she said slowly. "Very few people have my address. None of whom would stop by unannounced at…" She peered at the clock. "…six AM on Saturday."

"Maybe it's your family."

"Not a chance."

She leapt from the bed, pulling on a pair of loose joggers and a zip up hoodie. "I'll be right back." She rushed from the room.

Not quite what he was expecting. If anything, he'd have thought she'd suggest he get his things on and leave.

The doorbell rang again, the sound transmitting impatience.

Jake didn't like this.

He pulled on the sweats he'd retrieved from the go bag he kept in his trunk last night, but didn't bother with a shirt.

He padded down the grand staircase lightly, listening. Zara unlocked the door, so she clearly knew the person on the other side. Jake turned to go back upstairs. Her next words stopped him cold.

"Congressman. Did I forget we had a meeting?" Her voice was firm, but Jake heard the underlying note of fear.

Congressman. Shit. What did Rodriguez want? Jake had known that something seriously wrong went down yesterday.

He should have pushed harder so he could take care of this problem now.

"Let me in." The smooth, polished tones of an up-and-coming politician were gone.

"It's a little early for a visit." But the door squeaked open. Dammit. Why was she letting him inside?

Jake wanted to burst down the stairs and muscle in front of her. Protect her from whatever this was. But she'd opened the door, so he had to trust that she knew what she was doing.

What he didn't do was go back upstairs. He lingered in the curve of the landing where he could listen in while staying out of sight.

The door slammed shut with an ominous thud.

Jake would bet that was deliberate. He really didn't like this guy.

"I believe we had a miscommunication yesterday morning." Rodriguez's frigid voice was sharp. Cold, like the bastard Jake had sensed beneath his polished exterior.

"I understood you weren't happy with the events I'd planned. I spent yesterday afternoon working up new ideas."

"You called Carolina to set up a private meeting."

"Well, I called her to go over the new ideas, but I also wanted to pick her brain about adding to your schedule before wasting your time."

That sounded logical but…a tone underneath that easy reply had his senses tingling. That wasn't why she had called the congressman's wife. Why would Zara want a private meeting with Carolina Rodriguez?

"I warned you."

Jake had to strain to hear the words, low and filled with menace. What the actual fuck was happening right now?

He wanted to rush down the stairs, but he held back.

He peered around the corner, saw the grip Rodriguez had

on Zara's bicep. His fingers were white, his mouth pinched, and his eyes narrowed with rage.

She stood frozen, as if afraid to move.

"I can make life very difficult for your employer," he hissed.

Zara whimpered.

That was it.

"Hey, babe. What's taking so long?" He bounded down the stairs and stopped at the bottom as if surprised by the man in her entryway.

Zara's shocked gaze shot to him, trying to warn him away. Yeah, not happening.

"Mr. Brown." Rodriguez nodded.

"Hey, buddy." He purposely used the casual address, knowing a guy like Xavier would hate not being shown the respect he thought he deserved. Another question…how did Rodriguez know Jake's last name? The guard yesterday must have reported to him. Although why would Rodriguez concern himself with petty details like a visitor's driver's name? "A little early for a work visit."

"I could say the same." Rodriguez finally, *finally* stepped back from Zara.

Jake sauntered over to Zara and curled his arm around her shoulders. Her body stayed stiff beneath his quasi embrace.

"Smart guy like you, I'm sure you've figured out that we're a little more than workmates."

"In the future, I expect you not to bring your boyfriend to meetings." Rodriguez's mouth tightened into a cruel, thin line.

Oh, no, he didn't. "Oh, I'm also her bodyguard. I am very good at multi-tasking." He put a lot of innuendo into the words, the urge to needle this guy like a burr under his breastbone.

He wanted Rodriguez to know that Zara wasn't vulnerable. That he had her back.

"Thank you for the visit. I will get to work on your suggestions right away." Zara pretended that Rodriguez hadn't been threatening her, but no one could miss her strained voice.

"See that you keep everything under wraps. You can't afford for your work to get out." That threat hit, and the color drained from Zara's face.

He couldn't wait until this asshat left so he could find out what was going on.

Fuck.

"I'd offer coffee, but we're out." Jake made it sound like he was always here. He wanted to make sure that Rodriguez wouldn't stop by again unannounced. He also wanted to punch him in the face, but assaulting a US congressman wasn't a prudent move. Jake had passed the point in his life where he solved things with his fists, even if he did believe that hearing the crunch of this guy's nose would be a great pleasure.

"I'll get back to you in a few days with the updated schedule." Zara's smile was tight as she broke away from Jake's hug and walked with Xavier to the door.

Xavier leaned close to Zara and whispered in her ear. Jake couldn't hear what Xavier said, but the way her face blanched clued him in that it was another threat.

He strode out with an extra swagger in his step.

The sidewalk outside was dark. The discreet sedan a few doors down at the curb didn't have an official license plate that designated a member of Congress.

Clearly, Xavier hadn't wanted anyone who noticed a strange car on the street to remember that detail. It was a nondescript Honda Accord, similar to the office cars that ALIAS used.

As far as Jake could tell, Xavier had come without a driver. With his security protocols, that was a huge red flag.

Jake watched until Xavier was in the car and driving away. Something seriously whack had gone down, and Zara had yet to say a word.

The silence in the grand entryway was oppressive and heavy as he fought to get his frustration and annoyance under control. Nope. Wasn't going to happen.

He turned to Zara.

"What the fuck was that?"

28

———

J ake didn't yell.

As a matter of fact, his voice was low but menacing. His body language screamed with pent-up aggression.

"The timing for a home visit is a little unusual, but he's a big client." She forced the words out like she was talking through marbles.

Inside, she felt like she was going to shake apart. Questions pinged through her brain, ramping up her terror. How had Xavier known that she'd suggested meeting Carolina for coffee?

Thankfully, she hadn't said anything incriminating when she'd talked to his wife. Xavier couldn't possibly know that she'd planned on trying to convince Carolina to leave her husband. To tell the world that the congressman who championed the underdog, who was an economic representation of the American dream, was an abuser.

"Don't fucking lie to me, Zara." He appeared to bulk up before her eyes, like a modern-day Hulk.

She couldn't tell him. Xavier had been very clear on that.

A fine trembling started in her body, her hands and feet

tingling with cold. Air trapped in her chest, and she couldn't seem to pull in more breath, like a parasite plant, cutting off her oxygen supply and draining the life out of her.

"I can't." She wanted the words to come out forceful and strong, but they were little more than a whisper.

"What just happened?"

"I can't."

"You have to." Jake's voice gentled. "You understand he was threatening you."

"I know!" But he was also threatening Adams-Larsen.

"Let me help you."

God, she wanted to lean on him for a moment.

"If you won't let me help, then let's get Jill in here. Or better yet, fire him as a client." Jake threw out solutions that would only make things worse.

"I can't." Xavier wasn't the kind of client, or man, you walked away from.

"What's he got on you? What could he possible hold over you that is making you so scared?"

Zara trembled, unable to stop shaking.

"C'mon, Zara. You can tell me." Jake cajoled.

"He threatened the company."

Jake blinked, tilted his head. "The guy is smart."

That was his response?

"He already figured out that threatening you was a nonstarter. You're more likely to protect other people." He tapped his chin. "What was the meeting with his wife about?"

"I suggested we meet for coffee so I could run campaign suggestions by her before I presented them to him."

"It was more than that." Jake frowned, his frustration obvious. "You really are making me work for it."

It wasn't like that. "I'm trying to protect you!"

"I can protect myself." Jake brushed aside her fears. "Let me help you."

Did it really matter if she told him? "If I tell you, you have to promise not to say anything. I signed an NDA."

"I refuse to make a promise like that." Jake said, "But I give you my word that I won't share with anyone else without your permission."

She wanted to tell him, but she was trapped.

Xavier had come to her residence early in the morning on the weekend, without any witnesses, and threatened her. She hadn't shared where she lived with him. Her driver's license that the security guard had was her California license. She didn't have a car here. She hadn't made the trip to the DMV to get a new license because it was low priority. It was on her to-do list, but what did it really matter?

Xavier's demeanor had done a complete one-eighty. If she had been alone, what would have happened?

He'd frightened the shit out of her. Thank God Jake had been here.

"He hit her." Her voice was barely audible in the tense air. Acid rumbled and gurgled in her stomach as she ruthlessly suppressed her turmoil.

"What?"

"Please don't make me repeat it."

"You're saying that he hit his wife?"

"Yes."

Jake's fists clenched. "I *knew* there was something off about him."

"Not helping right now."

"My instincts were right, though."

Hers were apparently horribly broken. Her shoulders slumped as she curled in on her body.

He pulled her into his arms. Zara thunked her head on his

bare chest and breathed in the scent of Jake and sex, but not even that could distract her from her despair.

"I didn't see it."

"Literally millions of people didn't see it." He cupped her head in his big palm and tilted her face so he could talk to her. "Do not beat yourself up."

"My morality radar is broken." She avoided his eyes, her gaze darting around the room as she searched for a way to make sense of the past day.

"It isn't broken."

"I'm zero for two recently." Between David, her ex, and Xavier, she'd made horrendous mistakes.

"What about me?"

"Jury is still out."

He snorted. "There's no way you would have had sex with me if you didn't trust me, at least on some level."

"I picked you up in a bar." Her voice rose to a shout.

"Sure, the first time," he countered mildly. "But what about the second, third, and fourth?"

Her brain got stuck on one detail. "There wasn't a fourth."

"Not yet." He grinned, his teeth white and his topaz eyes sparkled. "But I'm hopeful you'll come back for more of my mad skills."

This conversation would be interesting if her world wasn't imploding in front of her. What was she going to do?

Zara broke from his arms and went into the kitchen. She paced around the island, her hand to her forehead as if the answers were in her palm.

"Why were you trying to meet with Carolina Rodriguez alone?" he asked again.

This time she answered truthfully. "To see if I could convince her to tell people what is happening to her."

He looked at her steadily. He didn't berate her or tell her

that was a dumb idea. Maybe she'd feel better if he did. And yes, that was totally contrary to the strong, competent woman she affirmed to her mirror every morning. She was complicated, dammit.

"Yes, I know it was a long shot, but he wants to be president of the United States!" Acid churned in her stomach. "We can't have a man who abuses women in charge of national policies that affect fifty percent of the population."

She recalled Xavier's dismissal of the women's shelter promo op.

"How did he know about your talk with his wife?"

"I…don't know. Maybe she told him. Or maybe he is monitoring her calls."

"Recording them?" Jake tapped his chin. "Or was he recording you?"

"I have no idea. Would it be legal for him to record me?" And did it matter? He was a bazillionaire. She was not.

"In D.C., it's legal to record yourself having a conversation, but it is *not* legal to record two people without their knowledge," Jake mused.

She didn't even blink that he knew that off the top of his head.

"I wonder if she gave him permission to record her."

"Even if she did, it's not like I said, hey, you need to tell the world about your abusive husband." Zara threw up her hands and began to pace. "I literally invited her for coffee to go over my ideas for his media plan."

"Maybe she told him?" Jake continued hypothesizing.

Did it matter? How was she going to get Carolina alone now?

"What the hell am I going to do?"

"You're going to rely on your team to have your back."

"I don't have a team!"

"Of course you do."

"But…"

"He's trying to isolate you and make you fear him," Jake said patiently. "We got this."

The tension that had knotted her neck since Xavier had threatened her yesterday began to loosen. Jake seemed so positive that things were going to be okay. But they were talking about one of the most powerful men in the country.

"What do you think *we* can do against one of the most powerful men in the country? Possibly the world?"

29

Jake braced for pushback. This wasn't going to go well.

"We're going to have a meeting with Jill and Marsh and let them know what's going on."

"No." Panic, fear, shock chased across her face. She wrapped her arms around her waist.

"They need to know about the threat." He meant to her, but he knew she'd be thinking about everyone else.

"I can handle this."

"We're literally trained for conflict." Jake then pushed the button he knew would work on her. "They deserve a heads up that Rodriguez is threatening Adams-Larsen. We can be better prepared with advance knowledge. You don't want blowback because they were blindsided by him."

Because a guy like Rodriguez wasn't going to let this drop. Once Kita gave Jake more info, he'd have a better picture of how this asshole operated, but he'd bet that Rodriguez would use Zara and then find a way to neutralize her. Impotence. He needed her impotent so that she couldn't ruin his plans.

Zara's shoulders slumped. "You're right."

"Damn straight." Jake would prefer to take her back to bed and revel in making her lose her mind. But this couldn't wait.

"Okay, first thing Monday morning…"

Jake put his mean face on. He could be a scary mother trucker when he wanted to be.

"We'll give them an hour to lollygag in bed with their partners then we'll meet at the office."

"It's Saturday."

"It's critical," Jake said. "We need to jump on this. I would bet while we sit around, he's doing oppo research, looking for more ways to handicap you. We need a game plan ASAP. Right now, Xavier doesn't have a clue what Adams-Larsen can do." They needed to keep him in the dark as long as possible.

"Neither do I." Her voice rose.

Jake wanted to tell her what they were capable of. Wanted to share all that ALIAS had done and could do, but he let that drop. It would be up to his bosses to decide how much to share with her.

An hour later, after an extended SDR—since he wouldn't put it past Rodriguez to have surveillance on Zara—they pulled into the parking lot at the ALIAS office.

She stared at the elegant brownstone that appeared benign from the exterior.

"I've never been here." Her nerves were on display as she squeezed her fingers together.

"I assume that was deliberate on Jill's part."

Jake drove into their underground parking lot. He went through the entry protocol for the office. Biometrics from his handprint, eight-digit password, and visual recognition from the mounted camera to whoever was in the security booth. The alarm system beeped as he waited for entrance to the building.

"Why does this feel like I'm entering the bat cave?"

Jake snorted.

Dwayne's deep voice came over a speaker in the small foyer. "You're clear."

Zara jumped and then looked around, searching for the camera. Jake pointed to the small high-tech device in the upper corner covering the entrance.

Jake tried to reassure her. "Someone is always in the office, watching the doors. Ever since the shooting with Sergei Polzin."

She frowned at him. "I read about that in the paper. I thought it was random happenstance."

"That was a crazy situation that resulted from Jill doing a favor for a friend."

"I didn't realize favors came with weapons."

"We take our client's safety very seriously."

"You were protecting a client?"

"Not that time."

Jake caught the unease on her face. He could practically see the wheels turning.

"So all those questions thrown during the press conference had basis in truth?"

"I can neither confirm nor deny."

She looked like she'd been punched.

The door opened, and Jake ushered Zara inside.

"Hey, man." Dwayne's pacific islander descent was on display as he grabbed Jake's hand and then pulled him in for a hug. "Nice work pulling the bosses in on the weekend."

"Couldn't be helped." Jake gestured between them. "Zara, this is Dwayne. He's the guy in the booth today."

Zara gaped at Dwayne as he took her delicate hand in his giant paw. Jake didn't typically think about how attractive his co-worker and friend was, but he couldn't help but notice her reaction.

Dwayne's muscles strained against a performance wicking

shirt and showed off his tattoos and serious muscles. He wore mesh gym shorts low on his narrow hips. He smiled widely, his teeth white in his swarthy face.

Zara dazedly shook his hand. "Hi." Her voice was breathy, soft. In a tone he'd never heard from her.

Jake scowled. "Where's Maria? Your *girlfriend*." Dwayne had been a confirmed bachelor and king of the one-night-stand until he and Maria decided they were soulmates on a job a few months ago.

Dwayne shot Jake an amused glance. "She's out shopping with my mom and sisters."

Jake winced. Dwayne had five very opinionated, very strong-willed sisters, but fortunately, Mama Lameko loved Maria.

"Jill and Marsh are up in her office." Dwayne waved. "Nice to meet you, Zara."

"You, too."

"Good luck."

"We're going to need it." Zara's smiled disappeared.

30

—————

Wow, that man was seriously hot.

Dwayne's gorgeousness had taken her mind off the worry churning in her stomach.

As they ascended the fancy staircase of the converted brownstone, her nerves and anxiety came rushing back.

Jake led her into a large office that reminded her of her father's study at their house in Sonoma. Bookcases lined the walls, a commanding desk dominated the far end, and a formal sitting area designed for casual conversations filled the large space.

Jillian Larsen and Marsh Adams sat at the grouping of wing chairs and settee. Jillian had a ball of pale yellow yarn in her lap. She loosely held a pair of circular knitting needles, while a cup of tea steamed at her elbow.

Wouldn't have pegged her as a knitter. Zara was always fascinated by people and their life choices.

Marsh was dressed more casually than his partner. This morning, he wore a pair of hole-y jeans frayed at the cuffs and a waffle knit Henley with three-quarter-length sleeves. His hair flopped over one brow, and something that might have been paint was splattered on his pants.

They had both left careers at the US Marshals to start Adams-Larsen. Jillian had been involved in a high-profile error that probably would have ended her career, anyway. But Marsh had been an up-and-coming agent in witness protection.

Zara was also an example of doing the unexpected. She could have gone into the family winery, but her brother loved the business. She liked the end result, but at the end of the day, she wanted to have a bigger effect on the world than a fleeting enjoyment of a bottle of wine. Not that creating wine wasn't a noble endeavor.

However, farming was a profession that ceded control to the elements. You could plan and plant and tend to your vines, and then a fire or drought or flood could impact an entire year's harvest. The vagaries of factors outside of her control had always frustrated her.

Plus, she preferred to impact people rather than crops.

She longed to create a media campaign that had the kind of impact that Dove's Real Beauty had on women everywhere. Fostering positive self-esteem in women and girls and encouraging body confidence and body positivity. Designing media that both inspired and made money for the client.

One reason she enjoyed public relations was because she could game out every single action/reaction to determine the best way to approach a client's situation.

Sure, occasionally you dealt with clients whose motives weren't pristine and the random client with moral gray areas. One reason she loved working for Jillian and Marsh was they had given her full rein, and she was free to decline working with clients who didn't align with her values.

Which was why she'd been so excited about working with

Xavier. He appeared to stand for the things that she was passionate about. She had loved the idea of helping Xavier because he was going to impact millions of lives if he became president. But now that was all obliterated.

Asshole.

"Have a seat." Jillian began knitting. "What's so important that you called us in early on a Saturday morning?"

Jake gestured to her. Shit. Her mind blanked.

She drew in a deep breath and released it slowly. Pretend like this was a briefing.

"Yesterday morning at the Rodriguez house, after our meeting, I realized I forgotten my portfolio, and when I went back into his home office, I witnessed Xavier Rodriguez hitting his wife."

The clicking of the knitting needles stopped abruptly.

"Oh, fuck," Marsh blurted out.

Jake nodded grimly.

"No wonder you were so tentative on the phone last night." Jillian eyed her curiously. "You could have told me."

"You wanted an ally in congress and thought he might be it." Zara wasn't going to spin this. "So I kept it to myself."

"What made you change your mind?" Curiosity lit Jillian's gray eyes.

Zara's words balled in her throat.

"Because that's not the worst of it," Jake finally said.

Jillian raised one brow.

Jake made a 'go on' gesture with his hand.

Zara threaded her fingers together and clasped her hands, her fingers squeezed so tightly it hurt.

"He, ah…" She cleared her throat. "He threatened Adams-Larsen."

"What a tool." Marsh relaxed back into his chair.

"Interesting." Jillian set aside her knitting. "Tell us exactly what he said."

Zara repeated as much of the threat as she could. Her words warbling as her reaction to the menace in his demeanor squeezed her throat.

"I guess we won't be using him to help us in Congress." There was a cool amusement in Jillian's voice.

How could they be so calm?

Jake interrupted, "The bigger problem is he showed up at her residence this morning at six AM, and he was far less ambiguous in his threats."

At that, both Jillian and Marsh straightened. They'd been fairly chill about the threat to the company, but when they heard he'd threatened her personally…they were pissed.

"Safe to assume it wasn't a social call." Jillian crossed her legs. Even on the weekend, her style was country club casual, with a wool skirt and a collared cotton shirt in a gingham check. But she'd left her white blonde hair down rather than in the customary twist.

"We won't ask why you're intimately familiar with the interaction." Marsh threw in the comment, basically letting them know he understood that Jake hadn't been there in his official capacity at the time.

She could feel the flush spread from her stomach up into her cheeks.

"Not the point, boss," Jake drawled, a hint of south in his words.

"None of our business." Jillian tilted her head to the side. "You didn't give him your address."

"No. And it isn't easy to find. I own the rowhouse under an LLC." Zara rubbed her palms together, a chill skittered down her spine. "And I haven't updated my driver's license since I don't have a car here. It's been on my to-do list."

"He came alone and parked the car down the street. He didn't use his official government vehicle," Jake continued. "Didn't appear to be a driver or security with him."

"No official record." Marsh nodded.

"He'd already made his point, why show up this morning?"

"Intimidation. Showing he can get to you anytime, anywhere. He's trying to take away your sense of safety," Jillian explained.

"He's succeeding." Zara's voice shook.

"Anything else we should know?" Marsh leaned forward, and Zara saw paint spatters in his hair.

She told them about suggesting to Carolina that they meet for coffee. "But I mentioned it in the context of talking about his events."

"We think he listened to the conversation," Jake interjected.

"What was your plan?" Jillian started knitting again.

"I didn't have one. I thought if I could get her alone…"

Jake shook his head. "He's not going to let you mess up his perfect life."

"Carolina deserves a perfect life, too," Zara said fiercely.

Jake held up his hands in surrender. "I'm not disagreeing with you."

"Have you had any tails this week?" Jillian asked.

"It's been pretty quiet." Jake rubbed the back of his neck. "Once or twice, I thought we were being followed, but when I turned off, they kept going."

"No follows. That's good." Jillian unrolled more of the yarn. "Any issues at the office?"

"No," Zara said slowly. Were they going to hang her out on her own? Her heart clenched. What if they abandoned her?

"On a scale of one to ten, how threatened are you?" Marsh asked.

She went for complete honesty. "One hundred."

"Can we get Viktor to shadow her?" Jake leaned forward in his chair. "Our caseload is pretty light right now. I'd like Vik to be on our six when he's back from vacation."

"He isn't coming back," Jillian said.

Jake didn't move. "What?"

"He needed a change after Sasha…died, and he decided to pursue other interests."

"I'll give him a call. Maybe he'll make an exception."

"He's requested that we give him time." Jillian's rejection of the idea was firm. "And we are going to abide by that request."

Jake didn't seem inclined to let it drop. Zara tried to break the sudden tension in the room.

Oh, that's right, she remembered they had mentioned that before. That was so sad.

"How did his boyfriend die?"

Marsh snorted. "Good thing that mofo is dead. Moscow frowns on men with boyfriends."

"Sasha was a Russian enforcer," Jillian said.

A Russian enforcer?

"He isn't coming back?" Jake suddenly smiled. "Really?"

That seemed to make him happy. Which was even weirder.

"Looks like you're on your own," Marsh said.

They were hanging her out to dry. And he seemed far too pleased with himself.

Jillian said, "Jake, you're on Zara. Treat her like a client."

He subtly relaxed.

"We'll get Kita on Rodriguez. We need ammunition."

Jake ducked his head. "Ah, I already asked her to dig into him."

She didn't know Kita, but she got the gist of what he meant. Anger and frustration bubbled up inside.

"You were investigating him?"

"I was concerned for your safety."

"You just wanted to be right." Zara was breathing hard, her irritation rose obscuring rationality. How dare he try to work around her? "Not everyone with money is a bad person, Jake."

"I am well aware of that," Jake shot back. "But you were wrong about Rodriguez, and I didn't trust him."

Jake had leaned forward in the chair until they were only a few inches apart.

Jillian cleared her throat. "Ah, you appear to know each other *much* better than we were aware."

She turned to look at her bosses at the same time as Jake

"Is this going to be a problem if Jake is your bodyguard?" Marsh asked her.

"She doesn't have a choice," Jake growled. Damn her body, she reacted to his rough insistence by getting turned on.

"I make my own decisions." Desire tinged her knee jerk response.

Marsh and Jillian watched the verbal back and forth like a tennis match, heads swinging as she and Jake verbally tussled.

"I'm trying to protect you!"

"Then ask me, don't tell me!" Zara shout-whispered.

"Fine," Jake gritted out. "It isn't going to be a problem, as long as you agree to listen to the security expert, *me*, when discussing your safety."

Zara's tried to slow her heart rate. Security expert. She needed a security expert. Her life felt out of control careening toward disaster.

"We good?" Marsh smiled. Did nothing ruffle this guy's calm?

"We can see about getting someone else to take over," Jillian offered. "But we are shorthanded at the moment."

"It's fine." Zara didn't want anyone but Jake, so why was she arguing? Because she was done having a man tell her what to do.

"I have files on Rodriguez as well. But what can we do? He's a billionaire with unlimited money, and he's a congressman with access to government power."

He could make life hell for Adams-Larsen.

"We aren't without our own resources," Marsh said.

"Would she leave him?" Jillian asked suddenly.

"I don't know." Zara tried to imagine Carolina standing up for herself. "She was a teacher and very accomplished in her own right before they had children. But he's got the resources and the power."

"You of all people should know only she can make that decision," Jake said softly.

Shame rolled through her. "I know."

"Is there anything else we need to know?" Jillian asked.

"What did he say when he whispered to you?" Jake asked. He apparently hadn't heard Xavier's last words.

"He said he has assets that I couldn't even begin to imagine, and that I would never see them coming, and no one would ever know it was him behind it."

Everyone straightened at that.

"Assets." Jillian leaned forward. "He used the term assets and them?"

"Fuck." Marsh lost his laidback demeanor.

Jake's fists were clenched.

Zara didn't understand why everyone was so alarmed.

"Uh, yes. I figured he meant money."

"He could have meant money, but it could also be something more sinister."

"What else does an asset mean?"

"Shit," Jake muttered. "If he's dirty, as well as an abuser, he's hiding it very well. He's the champion of the underdog."

"We need to know about every deal his businesses have been involved in. We also need to study the committees that he is a member of," Jillian snapped out.

"I'm not sure I understand." Everyone was talking in a foreign language that she didn't know.

"Assets can be people who spy on others or carry out clandestine operations."

She didn't like the idea of being spied on. "What kind of operations?"

Jake grimaced. "Assets can be hitmen, enforcers compensated with untraceable payoffs. Especially with bitcoin. The ability to hide payments to illegal entities is much easier."

Hitmen? Enforcers? What the fuck?

Marsh grimaced. "I can ask my father if he has heard any rumors about him."

The judge?

"Maybe Kita would be willing to ask Alex and Shep if there's any rumors," Jake said.

Alex and Shep?

"Kita's boyfriend is a US Deputy Marshal," Jillian explained.

"This is an all-hands-on deck situation," Marsh said.

Zara felt like this whole thing had spun out of control. "What am I supposed to do?"

"You keep being appropriately fearful of him and working for him." Jillian tapped a finger on her lips. "I wonder if we could get a bug in his study."

"No." Jake shook his head violently. "He's already threatened her. We are not going to put her in danger in a hostile environment."

Last few minutes felt as if she'd been dropped into the Twilight Zone.

"Do we need a safe house?" Marsh said.

"Safe house? Bugs? Assets? Hit men?"

Holy shit. *What had she gotten herself into?*

31

———

"This all seems far outside the realm of reputation management." Like in the next fucking galaxy outside of it.

Suspicion crowded her brain. Events were moving at warp speed, flowing past her as she stood still, while she processed this whole conversation in slow motion.

"Our division of Adams-Larsen handles more atypical cases."

No shit. She'd figured out that much on her own after the press conference. Her head spun with all the terms they'd thrown around.

But what mattered was finding a way to neutralize Xavier Rodriguez.

"I want to help," Zara insisted.

"Absolutely not."

"My job literally entails research and creating programs to benefit the client based on that research. I've been studying Xavier from the standpoint of helping him run for president. But all that research could now be put together to find a way to take him down."

"She has a point," Marsh said.

Jake dug in. "I don't want you in danger."

"A public relations expert's best assets are curiosity and creativity." Zara crossed her arms over her chest. "I'm the perfect person because all research is critical to my job. No suspicion at all if I'm digging into things."

"That is the perfect cover." Marsh eyed her with consideration.

"Protecting Zara is the mission."

"Taking down Rodriguez is the mission," Zara shot back. "Besides, don't take away my right to help with this."

"I'm not trying to take away anything, I'm trying to keep you safe." Jake's voice got lower and lower. That meant he was pissed. Good!

"I need to participate in this. He took away my safety by threatening me." Zara didn't want to battle with Jake. "Don't make me fight you, too."

Jake deflated. "You're right."

"Thank you," she whispered. "I *need* to be involved."

Jillian's phone rang. She glanced at the screen and then ignored it. It stopped.

Jake turned to Jillian and Marsh. "What next?"

Before either could answer, the main number at the Adams Larson office rang. A moment later, Dwyane paged Jillian.

"Jill, I've got Xavier Rodriguez on the line."

Jillian raised her eyebrows and glanced at Zara. "Well, this is interesting." She very deliberately set down her knitting and sauntered over to her desk.

After pressing a button on the main office phone, she said, "Congressman Rodriguez, what can I do for you?"

Zara tensed as Jillian muttered a series of ahas and uh-huhs. Jake and Marsh seemed relaxed, but she was a ball of nerves. Why would Xavier be calling her boss? After a few minutes, Jillian very deliberately hung up the phone.

She sauntered back over to the grouping of chairs and sat down. Zara couldn't stand it any longer.

"What did he say?"

"He was calling to make a complaint about Jake."

"What?!" Zara's heart pounded in her chest so hard that she couldn't hear over the thundering beat.

Jillian smirked. "Apparently, the congressman felt threatened by Jake's attitude this morning. He made it clear that he wants you reprimanded, or he would make life difficult for Adams-Larsen."

Oh, shit. This was it.

Jake was going to be angry with her. Jillian and Marsh would wash their hands of her, and she would be on her own. She supposed she could just quit and go back home to California, but she didn't want to.

She didn't want Xavier to get away with this, with any of it. And she couldn't leave Carolina, knowing what she did. But what could she do?

"Consider yourself reprimanded." Jillian's gray eyes twinkled.

Zara was so confused. What in the heck was happening?

Jillian and Marsh exchanged a fraught glance. "Perhaps we need to be more punitive. Jake, we're going to suspend you indefinitely while we investigate this matter."

What! Zara jumped to her feet. "You can't do that to him! This isn't his fault. This is all Xavier."

Jake grabbed her hand and squeezed. "Zara, it's fine."

"No, it's not. They can't punish you for that amoral, madman's asshole actions. He can't get away with this." She paced.

Marsh regarded her with what she used to think were kind eyes, but now she was re-thinking things.

"Zara, have a seat."

She sat back down and mulishly crossed her arms.

Jillian said, "We're not actually suspending him."

The crushing anxiety that stopped her breath eased. "Then what *is* happening?"

"We're going to let Xavier *think* I'm suspended. It's another way to isolate you and me," Jake explained.

Okay, okay. But she didn't understand.

"This gives us breathing room while we investigate him," Marsh said.

"He thinks he's winning. And now I'm with you in my capacity as your boyfriend, not as your bodyguard from ALIAS."

"ALIAS?"

"That's our fun code name for Adams-Larsen Inc and Associates."

"Huh."

"This way, he'll think the official protection is over."

"It won't be." Marsh tried to reassure her.

Jake rolled his beautiful topaz eyes. "He believes I'm far less of a threat without the company behind me."

"But you'll be at risk," she said.

"Don't worry." Jillian picked up her knitting again, as if it were no big deal instead of the screws tightening. "We'll have people watching you both. We are not going to let him get away with this."

Zara shivered at Jillian's tone. "Aren't you worried?"

"If this were a normal company concerned with profits rather than people, he would probably be right. But Rodriguez doesn't understand the way ALIAS works." Jake bared his teeth in a smile that she wouldn't want to be on the receiving end of. "And that will be his downfall."

Marsh rubbed his palms together. "Now, let's see that research."

A couple of hours later, they were done.

"What do we do now?" They'd been over everything she had on Xavier. With every comment they made about her research, she realized that she had been working for a company she didn't even know.

Zara tried not to let her resentment show. She felt betrayed and lied to. Even worse, she began to doubt her own judgement again.

She'd been completely taken in by Adams-Larsen.

"Now, you go about your day. Jake, let them find you. Go do couple-y stuff. Get a coffee, go for a run, whatever you would do if you were dating."

A flush started in the pit of Zara's belly and worked its way up to her face. Even though she was mad at Jake, she knew what she'd be doing if they were a couple.

Marsh seemed to read her mind. "Do something in public. Let them find you."

"See if you've got a tail. Don't lose them, but don't make it too easy." Jillian directed. "See if they report back to anyone."

"Ten-four," Jake confirmed.

"And then we will very publicly suspend you later today."

Even though the day felt long already, it was only mid-morning. Wound tight from nerves, she was on the verge of snapping.

"Let's go for a run." Maybe she could run off the anger and disillusionment swirling in her gut. She had to spend the day with Jake.

Her heart clenched, making it hard to breathe. Their entire

relationship felt like a see-saw, wide open connection, and then contracting to a tiny little ball of suspicion.

She hated that ball.

32

———

If only they were actually a couple.

Running through Rock Creek Park, they had fallen into an easy rhythm.

His feet pounded the paved path, the contact sang up through his legs, his heart pumping, pushing out the frustration at Xavier and at himself.

He'd watched Zara's growing disillusionment while they'd discussed her research on Xavier. The understanding in her eyes as they went over his programs and companies and tried to come up with ways to use the information against him.

No fucking way was he going to let Xavier hurt her.

They finished the run. Zara's cheeks were flushed, and her eyes sparkled with pleasure. She seemed to have forgotten for a bit that she was pissed at him.

But he knew it wouldn't last.

"What do you want to do now?"

"Take me to the coffee shop where you got that amazing coffee."

Jake started the car and headed to the coffee shop. He did

an SDR and then took a direct route. He'd glanced in the rear view mirror a few times.

"You lied to me," she said. The glow of pleasure from the run had worn off.

"I didn't have a choice," he answered patiently.

"What about now? Do you have a choice now?"

He waited a beat. "There are still things I can't tell you. But ask me a question, and I'll answer if I can."

It was the best he could do. He had to hope she'd forgive him.

Zara smiled grimly. "Okay, but coffee first."

Jake drove to the coffee shop where he'd found the amazing coffee. She kept checking the mirrors, looking for anybody who might be following them.

"We want to be followed." It was as if he could read her mind.

"Anything?" she asked.

"I've seen several tails. I think we have a team following us. They are switching off, so we need to make sure we act normal."

Normal. What the hell was normal anymore?

"I know you're angry with me, but you can't let it show when we're in public."

"I am. But at the moment, you're the only one standing between me and Xavier."

The place was full, which made sense for a Saturday morning. It was one of those hip places that served coffee twenty different ways as well as chai tea, and jazz music was piped in. Funky art deco posters hung on the bright white walls. Black bistro tables and chairs were full.

The clientele was a mix of college students and young professionals, people in running gear and others with infants in strollers. A group of women in yoga pants clustered around one long communal wood table.

Normally, Jake would have thought this place was all style and no substance, but the coffee was top notch. He didn't care about atmosphere; he cared about taste. And this was the best.

"Look for a seat while I grab our order."

Zara found a table in the back corner near the bathroom. The location was perfect. He couldn't have picked a better one. He'd be able to see the customers and the door. She fidgeted with her phone and tucked her hair behind her ear as she studied the people in the shop. Jake could feel her paranoia, but he didn't think anyone else would notice.

Jake sauntered over with their coffee order and squeezed himself into one of the little bistro chairs.

"These things were not made for a guy my size," he grumbled.

"Not much is made for a guy your size," she teased.

"It feels like you were made for my size." His wicked grin reflected his thoughts. But he wanted to apologize. "Sorry."

Zara took a sip of the coffee and moaned. "Oh my God, this is good."

God, he wanted to hear her moan like that again while they were in bed. He wanted to do dirty things to her. He wished he could. She opened her eyes and noticed that Jake was shifting in his seat.

"Everything okay?" she asked.

He glanced around the shop, avoiding her gaze. His erection strained his joggers. "Nothing a little bit of time won't cure."

Suddenly, he stiffened as the bell on the door rang. "Oh shit," he muttered. He turned to face her.

"What?"

"Don't look." One more of those things that he'd kept from her walked through the door. Ben's parents were here.

Jake stared at Zara. This was a clusterfuck.

Out of the corner of his eye, he watched Ben's parents move through the line to get coffee. This couldn't be a coincidence. His mom clutched a picture in her hand and showed it to the people in line.

When they got up to the counter, she asked the people making coffee if they had seen Ben.

Zara hunched over her cup. "How did you find this coffee shop?"

Jake shrugged. How had he found the coffee shop?

"I don't remember."

She leaned closer. "Was Ben a client of yours?"

Thank God he could answer with total honesty. "No, he was not a client of Adams-Larsen."

Ben's parents grabbed their coffees and started around the room, showing the picture to anyone who would talk to them.

"They're going to see us," she said.

"I am aware," he replied. *Fuck.* This was going to become a problem. With everything else going on, he'd forgotten about Ben's parents. He'd had an asset send Ben's parents a postcard from California saying he was fine and not to worry about him, that he loved them.

Clearly, that contact hadn't assuaged their worry. Ben's parents stopped short when they saw Jake and Zara.

"What are you doing here?" his mother asked.

Jake didn't want to brush off their suspicions. "We are close to our residences," he said.

"You said you didn't know Ben."

Does anyone ever really know anyone?

"What does this coffee shop have to do with your son?"

Jake needed more information, and this was the only way he was going to get it.

"He was coming here almost every day before he disappeared," Ben's father said. "We traced his credit card purchases."

Jake wondered what else ALIAS had missed when he'd let Layla convince him to reconnect her with Ben. This was becoming a huge problem.

"I find it strange that you're here," Ben's dad said.

"Would you like us to leave?"

"You know something about Ben," his mother accused.

If Jake didn't know anything about Ben, what would he do?

"Hmm. Can I see his picture again? Just in case."

His mother shoved the photo of Ben at Jake. He shook his head, again very careful with his words. "I've never seen him here, but I typically grab my coffee and go."

Ben's parents weren't going to back down easily. "You're sure you haven't seen him?"

"I'm sorry," Jake said gently.

His mother started to cry. Tears trailed down her face.

Jake's phone buzzed. He had a text from Jill.

Get to the office now.

Deep sorrow for Ben and his parents filled him. They clearly loved him so much.

"We have to go. My boss needs me."

"You're welcome to have our table." Zara grabbed her cup and Jake stood. "Good luck. I hope you find him."

33

They headed to the car in silence.

"Did you know him?" she finally asked.

"I got a text from Jill. I have to head to the office. This is probably the public suspension. You're going to have to come with me because I can't leave you alone."

"I noticed you didn't answer."

"I promise I will never lie to you." That was also not an answer.

"And there it is." Zara sat back in the passenger seat and crossed her arms over her chest. "You know that kid."

God, his poor parents. And Jake had intelligence that would ease their anguish. But telling them where Ben was would put everyone in danger.

The drive to the office was silent. Zara simmered with a frustration that filled the interior of his truck. Jake continued to glance in the rearview mirror. They had a tail. But Jill hadn't said to lose anyone, so he let them follow.

When they got to Adams-Larsen, the parking lot was full.

Zara glanced around. "What is happening?"

"Looks like a company-wide meeting to put me on suspension."

"Maybe I should just stay in the car."

"Nope. Where I go, you go. Until this is resolved, I don't want you going anywhere alone. Or at the very least, anywhere without protection." He wasn't letting anything happen to her.

After going through the entrance protocol, they headed to the conference room.

The conference room used to be a dining room when the brownstone was a residence. Now it was outfitted with a large oval mahogany table, a sideboard laden with a silver coffee urn, a hot water urn for tea and hot chocolate, and white ceramic coffee cups with the Adams-Larsen logo.

Lately, they were also treated to Maria's confections. Today's cookies were heart-shaped like those old Valentine's Day candies, decorated with cutesy slogans like, Be Mine, Kiss Me, Sweet Pea, You and Me, Sweet Talk, True Love, Soul Mate, and First Kiss.

Jake grabbed two cookies and handed one to Zara that said, *Kiss Me.*

She grunted after reading it. Guess that answered that.

"Good. Jake is here." Jill gestured to the table. "Everyone, have a seat."

The room was loud with camaraderie as Kita teased Dwayne and Maria. Alex and Shep stood in the corner, looking slightly uncomfortable. Hamish, Jill's Scottish boyfriend, was munching on a cookie and chatting with Marsh.

The only people missing were Shep's girlfriend, Dr. Mila Patel, and Marsh's girlfriend, up-and-coming artist Ayesha Brown.

The conversation around the table stopped. Jill made the introductions.

"Everyone, this is Zara Cooper. She runs Adams Larsen Inc., our PR branch in Arlington."

People eyed Zara speculatively.

No one said a word. They didn't talk about clients in front of strangers, and Zara didn't have the clearance to know about active cases.

"What's going on?" Maria asked, shooting a shy smile at Zara. She had come out of her shell quite a bit, but she took a while to get comfortable around new people.

"I'm going to make this quick. We've got a problem. Congressman Xavier Rodriguez is threatening ALIAS." Everybody straightened, looking surprised.

Alex, Kita's boyfriend, dropped his head into his hands. "Not again," he muttered.

"We've prepared a dossier on Rodriguez, but we need more information," Jillian continued. "The purpose of this meeting, though, is to reprimand Jake and put him on suspension."

The room erupted in noise.

"What?! You can't do that!" Zara cried.

The cacophony of 'no ways' and 'that's not going to happen' from his friends warmed Jake's heart.

The last few months had been rough. He'd been feeling slightly disconnected and as if everyone was passing him by. Everyone had paired off except for him. Even Viktor, their perennial bachelor, had fallen in love. And now, Viktor was gone.

In that loneliness, he felt isolated and frustrated.

Jillian stood, held her hand up. "Relax. This is all for show. Jake is going to continue to protect Zara."

"Jake is on suspension and informally protecting Zara until we can find a way to shut down Rodriguez's threats. Marsh already contacted his father and is waiting to hear back from him regarding any intelligence he might have."

"Uh, I'm not sure why we—" Shepperd Gaffney wagged his finger between him and Alex. "—are here."

Jillian said, "I know you don't work for me, but I would appreciate it if Mila puts her ear to the ground and lets us know if she hears anything regarding Rodriguez's family."

Shepherd Gaffney frowned. "What about his family?"

"Any kind of off-the-books medical care for accidents involving his wife or children."

Alex straightened. "Are you saying that Xavier Rodriguez, the congressman from California who is rumored to be eyeing a run at the Oval Office, hurts his wife and children?"

"Cannot confirm the children." Zara finally spoke up.

"Bollocks," said Hamish.

"Kita, I want you to continue to dig into Rodriguez's finances and background."

"So far he's come up clean." Kita grimaced.

"We have Zara's research to add to your file."

"Okay. Cool."

"Nobody threatens ALIAS," Jill said fiercely.

"Absolutely."

"What can we do?"

"We've got your back."

Affirmations of support filled the air as everyone chimed in.

Jake was happy everyone was on board.

"Dwayne and Maria, I want you to follow Rodriguez and see what you can find out, but do it discreetly. See if you can get a copy of his official schedule and then observe any deviations. Also, make note of every person he comes into contact with."

"He's got an army of security professionals, and they aren't slouches," Jake cautioned.

"Kita, keep digging."

"On it."

Jill said, "I'm going to see if I can casually bump into Carolina Rodriguez at a fundraiser that she's going to be attending tonight. Fortunately, Marsh, Ayesha, Hamish and I already had tickets."

"Zara, you continue to pretend to work for him. Jake, you can stay with Zara while we focus on investigating. Your job is to keep her safe."

"Can't you give me another job to do as well?" Jake didn't like being hamstrung.

"Technically, you're suspended." Marsh handed him a cardboard box. "I want you to throw a few things from your desk in this. We'll have someone escort you out. Head back to Zara's house. Be very glum and stomping around as you leave."

"Everyone else needs to leave in waves. We don't want to all leave at once. Rodriguez has to believe that Jake is on his own," Jill directed.

"Sorry, mate." Hamish slapped him on the back.

"If anything comes up, call me. Otherwise, we'll meet again on Monday morning for our weekly staff meeting. We'll find a way to conference in Jake and Zara. That's it."

"Before we disband…" Kita stopped Jake and Zara from leaving. "Can I pick your brain for a few minutes? You likely noticed details that aren't in the file that might be crucial."

"Sure. Although I keep meticulous notes, and I turned them all over."

"I'm talking about things you noticed when you met with him and his wife." Kita snuck a glance at Alex. "You know, things that aren't in the official record."

Her live-in lover shot her a dark look.

"I don't know what else I could tell you."

"We'll get started." Dwayne and Maria headed out.

Shep Gaffney waved goodbye. "We'll let you know if anything comes up."

Alex pressed a kiss on Kita's head. "See you later."

And then it was just Jillian, Marsh, Jake, and Kita at the table with her.

"Tell me anything that surprised you when you were interacting." Kita leaned closer to Zara.

"Well, he shot down an appearance at a battered woman's shelter, saying he didn't want to piss off half the voting pool."

"Asshole." Kita clenched her fists.

Yeah. That had been the first red flag.

"At the time I was surprised, but then figured it was more Carolina's interest. Years ago, she had mentioned domestic violence in her family."

"Based on your new information, apparently, supporting a women's shelter when you're whaling on your wife is a little too hypocritical." The keys clacked as Kita entered more stuff in her files.

Zara snorted. "Although it isn't funny." She wanted to take the fucker down. To strike a blow and claim victory for women everywhere. Xavier Rodriguez did not deserve his exalted position and power by claiming to work for the regular working-class families when he was abusing his own.

"Nope. Have you been to his house?"

"Uh, yeah," Zara said. "That's how this whole mess started."

"Describe it. Give me your impressions."

"Crazy security," Zara commented. "I know he's a billionaire. But I know plenty of rich people who don't have the kind of security that he has."

Jake piped up, "Gate house. Biometric screening. Identification checks. We checked in via iPad at the gate. Those entry logs could be a gold mine. RFID badges worn at all times."

Kita raised her eyebrows. "Interesting. But also, he and his family are kidnap risks. He might have something to hide, but he may also just be cautious."

"I want to take this fucker down." Zara burned with that goal. "I'll do whatever it takes." She was tired of men getting away with abuse of power.

"Sing it, sister." Kita high-fived her. "What else?"

"Ostentatious. The whole place looked like he was trying too hard to impress."

Kita pounded on her keyboard.

"Books that looked like they hadn't been read, giant partner desk that was way too clean to be used, and the rare Persian Gazelle head mounted on the wall from a crazy, exotic mountain hunting expedition in Iran."

Jake stilled. Jillian and Marsh looked shocked. That entire room fell silent. What was that about?

"Iran? Are you sure?" Jake asked urgently.

"Apparently he's a big hunter, and they only issue a few permits to this special mountain where he caught an endangered animal."

Jake closed his eyes as if he were counting to ten. Then he looked at Jillian and Marsh.

"We need to talk."

"Not without me." Zara jumped to her feet.

"This is regarding confidential client information," Jillian said gently.

"What the hell?" Zara clenched her fists. Why was she being left out? They wouldn't even know about Xavier if she hadn't brought him in as a client.

Of course, their business wouldn't be in jeopardy if she hadn't brought him in as a client. Her shoulders slumped.

"We're talking about putting someone's life in danger, Zara." Jake reached out as if to touch her then pulled his hand away. "You can't be privy to the information."

"If it helps, I have no idea what they are talking about." Kita glanced between her bosses and Jake.

"In my office." Jill pointed at Jake. "Now."

34

———

Jake followed Marsh and Jill back into her office and closed the door quietly.

"What are the odds that the Iranians are involved with another one of our cases?" Marsh asked.

"Let's not get ahead of ourselves at this point." Jill paced the office. "It could be coincidence."

"But what if it isn't?" Jake grimaced. "Speaking of the Iranians. We've got another problem."

"Another?" Marsh frowned.

"Ben's parents."

"I thought you were able to distract them," said Jill.

"I thought so, too." Jake paced around the office. "But we ran into them at a coffee shop today, and they were showing pictures of Ben."

"Didn't we send them a postcard saying not to worry and that everything was fine?"

"We did," Jake said. "Apparently, they're not falling for it. They accessed Ben's credit card statements and have been going to all the places he went in the last few weeks before he disappeared."

"That's not good."

"Hopefully, they can't get ahold of any security tapes from the coffee shop," Marsh said.

Jake's heart iced.

"If they exist, we need to get those tapes and destroy them before they see pictures of Layla."

"I'll have my contact at the CIA look into that."

Jillian's contact, to whom they had given all their evidence about the Iranians.

"We need to explore this connection between Xavier and the Iranians. Maybe there's more to his "special permit,' than just a special permit to hunt." Jake's heart revved. If Xavier was connected to the Iranians, this was worse than an ambitious guy wanting to be president.

"Favors from a guy in Congress? Relaxing sanctions? There are a hundred different ways Xavier could be helping the Iranians." Marsh ticked options off on his fingers.

"We also need to shut up Ben's parents because we don't want the Iranians finding a connection between Layla and Ben."

"How are they?" Jill asked.

Jake wasn't supposed to know. It figured that his boss understood that Layla was different. Ever since he helped Layla disappear, she'd been more like a little sister than a client. They weren't supposed to get involved with their clients. Jake felt a little testy.

"They are doing well."

"I trust that you aren't putting her in any jeopardy."

"I would never do that." Jake couldn't help but add, "If you recall, I thought helping her was a mistake."

Of course, he'd changed his mind once he'd gotten to know Layla. And if ALIAS hadn't helped her, she would be dead.

The Iranians had blown up her house and hunted her, believing that she had information and pictures regarding the perpetrators who had killed an Iranian scientist.

Layla had, in fact, had the pictures. Jill had turned them over to the CIA.

"Is there any word about the intelligence that Layla gave your friend?" Part of Jake hoped that Layla would be able to come out of hiding soon.

"You know I don't have any idea. I may not ever know." Jill grimaced. "We shouldn't have relocated Ben with her."

"I agree. But they were going to be together, no matter what we did. This way, at least they're safe. I had hoped that the Iranians would let it go once Layla disappeared."

"But that doesn't seem to be the case," Marsh continued. "I've checked in with a few friends, and there hasn't been any change on the FATWA."

Jill's phone rang again. Initially, she ignored it. But when she noticed the number, she raised her eyebrows. "It's Xavier again." She put him on speaker. "Good afternoon, Congressman Rodriguez. What can I do for you? I've got you on speaker so my assistant can take notes."

Xavier said smoothly, "I trust you have taken care of my problem."

Jill replied, "Jake Brown is currently on suspension while we investigate his conduct. He's gathering his things as we speak."

Jake's stomach swirled at the conciliatory note in her voice. Damn, she was good.

"I won't outright fire him until I am convinced that he has behaved inappropriately. But in the meantime, he's on leave."

"What about Zara Cooper's security?" Xavier asked

smoothly. Pretending that he was worried about Zara. Fucker just wanted to know if he could get to her.

"We had been ready to pull Jake, anyway. There hasn't been any fall-out from our press conference. The original detail was precautionary."

"Excellent. Glad to hear it."

Jake wondered what exactly Xavier was glad to hear. That Zara was safe? Or that she was no longer being guarded? He wanted to punch the smug SOB in the face.

"I would hate to have anything happen to my favorite consultant."

A direct threat. Jake burned. He wanted to take this fucker down.

"I have intelligence that you might be interested in," Xavier said.

Jake straightened. *What the fuck?*

"I had my security team dig into Jacob Brown's background."

Jillian raised her eyebrows. "We do a very thorough vetting of our employees, but if you have concerning information, I would be interested in seeing it."

Divide and conquer. The oldest trick in the book.

"I thought you would," Xavier replied. "I'll have it couriered over to you."

Jill said, "That would be great. I'm at the office now, waiting for Jake to leave. My team has been advised not to have contact with him while we are investigating your complaints."

"Excellent." The satisfaction in Xavier's voice turned Jake's stomach. Asshole.

"However, Mr. Rodriguez, I must tell you that I cannot dictate how Jake spends his free time while he's on suspension. He and Zara Cooper are close. If he continues to spend time with her, I can't stop him."

"Understood," Xavier said.

Jake's stomach curdled. No way would he leave Zara alone. He couldn't save his sister, but he damn well wasn't going to let anything happen to Zara. She would be protected, no matter what.

"It would be unfortunate if we had to open up a hearing on Adams-Larsen's activities over the past few months."

And there it was, the direct threat.

"Are you threatening us?" Jill asked.

"Not at all," replied Xavier. "I'm just letting you know that it would be perfectly within my purview as a United States congressman, if I were concerned about a private company's actions impacting national security."

"I am aware. Thank you for your time, Congressman." Jill jabbed the button on her phone. "Asshole."

"We'd better get to work," Marsh said.

Jake hesitated. "Can I talk to you for a minute?"

Marsh raised his eyebrows. "Me?"

"Yeah."

"Not me?" Jill asked.

"My question doesn't apply to your circumstances."

Marsh made a go-ahead gesture with his hand. "Sure."

"How do you...handle not being honest about ALIAS with Ayesha?"

Marsh sat back in his chair. "Like that, is it?"

He was trying to navigate this thing with Zara. "Maybe." He was conflicted. She deserved more than he could give, but... "I can't leave her alone until this situation is resolved."

And worry was tearing him in two.

"It's a balance. Share what you can as long as it doesn't put our clients or you in danger."

"ALIAS is full of secrets. That's never going to change." A particular despair washed over him.

"That's true. She needs to figure out if she can live with that," Marsh said.

He had no idea what he was going to do next.

Jill rubbed at her temples. "Jake, you're suspended. Get some stuff from your desk and get out. Use your acting chops and look mad." In case Xavier was watching.

Even though he knew it was fake, anxiety balled in his chest, constricting his breath. ALIAS was his life. He'd slowly let all his other relationships fall away. He wasn't close to his only living family, his momma, and his friends were his coworkers.

What if this suspension became real? Who was he, if he wasn't a protector of the innocent?

35

Jake flipped his laptop shut with a bang.

He had studied the info they had on Xavier, combing through all the details. Searching for anything that they could use against him. He had set up in Zara's sunroom with his computer and headphones.

Zara had disappeared upstairs after they'd gotten home. She'd shot him an annoyed look as she went up the steps.

He got that she was upset with him, with them, but he couldn't tell her anything else. The fact that Xavier had been to Iran and received a special permit from the government had five alarm fire bells going off.

There were no coincidences, but how did it all fit together? The doorbell rang. Jake stiffened. He headed for the front door as Zara came down the stairs.

"Are you expecting anyone?" They needed to be extra cautious until this situation with Xavier was resolved. He would need to know her schedule and vet any visitors before they arrived. He needed to start treating her like a client and not a lover. But they could go over that once they dispatched with whoever was at the front door.

Zara shook her head, her eyes wide with apprehension. Dammit, he hated that she was afraid.

The protector in him rose. "Why don't you go into the kitchen, and I'll see who it is."

She straightened her shoulders and marched toward the front door. "I'll get it."

"At least let me see who it is before you open it." He hoped it wasn't Xavier, even though typically a guy like that didn't do his own dirty work. Jake couldn't assault a sitting congressman, no matter how much he wanted to, and he wasn't that guy anymore.

Jake peered through the security peephole. "There's a guy on your porch, slicked back blond hair, kind of preppy-looking, in a lightweight pea coat and a scarf tied around his neck."

Zara grimaced.

"You know him?"

She pushed him out of the way. "Let me see." She peered through the hole, then sighed. "It's my ex."

Jake didn't like this. "Didn't you say that you made it hard to find your address?"

She nodded. "Yes, but he can be particularly persistent."

"I'll get rid of him," he said.

"No. He's my problem. I'll take care of it." She hesitated. "But if you wanted to stay for moral support, I wouldn't object."

Jake nodded, wanting to be her knight in shining armor but understanding that she needed to do this. He didn't like the fact that this guy had showed up all the sudden. There were too many distractions and complications being thrown at them both. He wondered cynically if Xavier had something to do with this as well.

Gah, now he was being paranoid.

Zara opened the door.

"David, what are you doing here?" She had only opened the door crack, putting her face through the sliver. At the moment, Jake was hidden.

"Zara, darling."

Jake hated the guy already. What should have been affectionate came across as smarmy. Of course, he might be a little bit biased.

She didn't go on the defensive. She didn't ask how he found her. She just said, "I don't want you here."

"I came to throw myself on your mercy and say I'm sorry." He pushed against the door lightly. Instead of holding her ground, Zara let him in.

Jake frowned. Why was she letting him in?

The guy pushed the door closed, a triumphant smile on his face. Until he realized Jake was there. The smile dropped away.

"Who the hell are you?"

Jake slung a casual arm over Zara's shoulder, letting her know he'd back her up any way she needed. "Jake. You are . . .?"

He might be a little rough around the edges, but he knew his manners. His momma had taught him well. He deliberately didn't hold out his hand.

He knew how to put people in their place without verbally putting them in their place.

David sputtered. "I... I... I'm Zara's boyfriend," he said defiantly.

"Ex." Zara and Jake spoke at the same time. They turned and looked at each other, her grin matching his, completely ignoring this asshat.

David puffed up his chest. "Not if I have anything to say about it."

Jake wanted to interrupt, but he didn't. He let her speak.

"Not interested, David. Please go away."

"I saw your press conference yesterday. This company you've gotten mixed up with is bad news. You need to quit."

"First of all, you know nothing about Adams-Larsen. Second, you don't tell me what to do." She narrowed her eyes. Her body vibrating with rage. "Don't push me."

"But Zara, it's a mistake. Besides, it's not like you need the money."

Jake rolled his eyes. This guy knew nothing about her. She could care less about money. He straightened as if a light bulb had gone off in his head.

Shit, she didn't care about money. She cared about *people*. David was right about one thing. She didn't need the job. She'd be perfectly fine without it. But instead of quitting in the face of threats, she dug in and was ready to fight.

She was amazing.

"Wow," Jake drawled. "You really don't understand her at all, do you?"

David shot him a contemptuous glance, his gaze skimming down Jake's workout sweats and wicking shirt. He hadn't changed after their run.

"Slumming, darling?"

If he thought that kind of insult was going to get to Jake, he was sorely mistaken. Instead of defending himself, he smiled at Zara, pressed a kiss to her temple.

"You've got this. I'll go make us coffee."

Zara blinked, understanding rolling through her gaze.

"Thanks." Her gaze softened. Jake hoped that look meant she was on the path to forgiving him for keeping things from her.

Then she turned to David. "Third, and finally, if you don't leave me alone, I will tell the world why I left you, most especially your bosses."

"Are you threatening me?" David fumed.

"This is not a threat," Zara said. "It's a promise."

"You wouldn't dare."

"This is me taking back my power. This is me telling you that hitting women is not okay. This is me telling you that if you continue to harass me, I will let the world know what kind of scum you are."

David sputtered.

Zara opened the door. "You need to leave, and don't come back."

36

—————

amn, that felt amazing.

Zara turned the deadbolt. Elation rose in her chest, fizzing and bubbling along with a sense of relief and peace.

She finally let go of the shame that had been dogging her for the past year. And Jake, Jake had let her handle it.

He didn't take over. He recognized she needed to do it on her own and that she was capable. He trusted her to take care of it.

He *trusted* her.

God, that felt good.

She needed to forgive him for keeping secrets from her. She needed to acknowledge that she understood that he couldn't tell her certain things. He had encouraged her to take control. He encouraged her to finally break that last filament of shame.

She rushed back into the kitchen. He was preparing her cup of coffee. She couldn't help but compare Jake and David.

What had she ever seen in David? She'd been vulnerable. Frustrated with life and her job. She'd been passed over for promotion *again* at her old firm—because they knew she didn't need the money. It had gone to a perfectly nice man with a wife and three kids who didn't have the skills that she did. In about ten years, he would be ready. But she hadn't wanted to do his job for him while he found his way.

David had come along at just the right time. Originally, he'd said all the right things and seemed to understand her and appreciate her. But his support had eroded slowly.

She wondered about Carolina. What had happened that created the situation she found herself in now?

She had been a teacher supporting her husband while he went to law school, accomplished in her own right when she had married Xavier. What had happened to her? Maybe that was the key to figuring out how to take down Xavier. What had Carolina's tipping point been? Carolina Rodriguez's choices were a puzzle for later.

Right now, she needed to thank Jake for supporting her. "Thank you."

"You're welcome." He didn't pretend to not understand. "You have no idea how hard it was to leave the room."

He was a protector to his core.

"I can imagine, yet you did it anyway, for *me*."

"I did. But if he comes around again, the conversation is going to be very different and I'm going to have a chat with him and let him know that I will destroy him if he comes near you again."

A bubble of gratitude expanded in her chest. David was a douchebag. She had definitely traded up. It was time to admit, even if just to herself, that Jake was amazing. He was kind, strong, principled, confident enough to let her lead when appropriate.

He reached out to hand her the steaming mug of coffee.

"You need to put that down," she said.

"What?" Confusion skittered across his face.

She took in the wicking shirt that clung to his chest. The track pants slung low on his hips, her gaze lingering on the bulge in front of his pants. She was attracted to his physique—who wouldn't be? She'd had his gorgeous body all last night.

But even more attractive were his mind and his heart.

"I'm really attracted to your heart."

"Okay."

"Put the coffee down." She skimmed her gaze back up to meet his. Zara licked her lips.

He nodded slowly, beginning to understand.

"Not just my heart."

"Yep." She took two giant steps and wrapped her arms around his neck and jumped up, climbing him like a monkey, curling her legs around his hips. He didn't even flinch.

He held onto her tightly.

She cupped his face in her hands, admiring his smooth, dark skin, tracing over his features, his high, proud cheekbones, his flat, regal nose, his mouth.

She squeezed his cheeks. "Thank you." Then she pressed her lips to his.

The kiss began softly, a quiet exploration, a tender gesture.

Jake staggered to the counter and pulled her tight against his body.

What started out soft quickly became intense. He cupped her small breasts as she locked her ankles around his back.

She poured gratitude for this amazing man into every kiss, clinging to his broad shoulders.

He pulled away, pressed his forehead to hers, staring deep into her eyes.

"Are you sure?"

"I'm sure I want you *right now.*" Just in case he wasn't getting her urgency.

"There are still things I can't tell you."

"I know," she said. "But you've shown me who you are. You're a protector, but you raise people up. You allowed me to advocate for myself. Even when you can't tell me exactly what's going on, you trust my intelligence rather than treating me like a fool."

"I've done things that I'm not proud of."

"Haven't we all?" Zara countered. "One mistake doesn't define you."

Her breath caught in her chest. *One mistake did not define you.* If you kept doing the same thing over and over, then it was an issue.

"I used to communicate with my fists. He dropped the words as if waiting for her to pull away."

"Have you ever hit a woman?"

"No, and I never would." But he hesitated. "Recently, there was a situation where a woman thought I was going to hurt her, and I let her believe it because we needed information."

"Jake, I know you. You would never hurt a woman. You would never hit a woman."

"But she believed I would. Isn't that just as bad?"

"I assume that the situation was dire."

"Lives were in danger," he said. "We didn't have much time. We needed to find someone before they hurt anyone else."

"At some point, I'd like to understand exactly what you do, even if you can't give me everything. Maybe you can tell me something."

He barely hesitated. "I already talked to Jill and Marsh," he blurted out. "I can't give you specifics because that's not the way we work. But maybe I could tell you more about our methods."

"I would appreciate that."

"But there are things I will never be able to tell you."

Her heart trilled. He was speaking as if they had a future.

"As long as you don't keep anything from me that relates to me, I will understand."

A future. She wanted that, with him.

They had to get out from underneath the threat from Xavier first. But Zara was beginning to think they would be okay.

Jake carried her up the stairs, stopping every few steps to kiss her.

When they got to her bedroom, she laughed when he tossed her on the bed.

"Thank you."

"For throwing you like a circus acrobat?"

She giggled. "For trusting me."

She spread her legs, and he crawled between them. "I'm too heavy."

"You're fine."

He rolled so that she lay on top of him. "Nope."

Zara bent her head to kiss him, all those delicious feelings slammed into her. She went from completely sober to drunk on him in thirty seconds—like a high alcohol content port wine hitting her bloodstream.

Jake drew her dress up, skimming his fingers along the outside of her leg, leaving a trail of desire in his wake.

When he reached her pink lace boy shorts, he traced the outline, rubbing his callused finger along her belly.

"Have I mentioned how much I enjoy your underwear?" he murmured against her mouth.

He rubbed his thick finger along her slit, barely penetrating her.

His scent, an understated musk with that hint of pine, perfectly captured his personality. Cautiously wild.

Jake made her forget every bad decision she'd ever made,

overwhelming her with his sheer physical presence, lifting her to new heights. He added another finger and pumped inside her in a slow, erotic rhythm.

She pushed aside the elastic waistband of his joggers and reached for his hard cock, wanting to pleasure him like he was pleasuring her.

Jake lifted her dress over her head, exposing her lace clad breasts. "You are so fucking gorgeous." He nipped each hard bud, then gently pushed her back so she spread out before him on her comforter.

Zara arched against him, tilting her head and exposing her neck. He sucked on the sensitive skin. She was ensnared between his fingers and his mouth. Jake pressed wet, open-mouthed kisses down her neck, taking his time, running his tongue along her collarbones, before dipping his head to suck her hard nipple into his mouth.

The sensual assault zapped a line between her breasts and her clit.

"Oh, my God."

"Nope. Just me," he rumbled against her breast.

"I need you."

Jake's heart expanded at her desperate plea.

But he didn't want this to be over too soon. He rolled Zara so her back was to him.

"What are you doing?"

"Worshipping you." He palmed her breast, smiling as her nipple hardened against his hand. He licked a path from the base of her neck to her earlobe. Triumph spilled through him when she shivered.

Zara's breath quickened, her chest lifting, her breast pushing into his palm.

Jake spread his fingers wide and captured both breasts in his hand, plucking the nipples like a delicate instrument.

He nipped at her earlobe eliciting a soft groan.

His erection grew, throbbing in time to her quickening breath.

"You are a wizard." A pink flush spread over her skin. Jake wondered what that was about. But rather than ask—the blush was enough of an ego stroke—he kissed his way down each vertebra of her spine. His hands held her in place as she tried to turn.

The scent of sex filled the room, and a heated warmth surrounded them in a cocoon as his desire grew.

"Jake."

God, he loved that breathy moan.

He nipped the globe of her tight ass.

"Let me turn."

"Nope."

"Pretty please."

Instead, Jake nudged her so she rolled onto her stomach. Then he pulled up her hips, so she was on her hands and knees in front of him. His cock was painfully full now, and his breath caught when he brushed against her. Zara stretched like a cat, arching her back and sticking her ass in the air.

"You want me this way." He ground out the words in a guttural voice as his palms shaped her hips and ass. He dipped his fingers into her channel again and found her slick and ready for him.

He pulled out his fingers as her body desperately tried to suck him back in. She was so fucking tight. Every time, he needed to ease into her, because her grip was intense and incredible.

He rubbed the head of his cock along her sex lips.

Zara's fingers fisted in the sheets.

"You ready for me?"

"Always."

He wanted to plunge inside her. "Condom."

She yanked open the drawer and grabbed a fistful, tossing them at him. "Hurry."

The packet hit him in the abdomen. He wanted to see his Black cock disappearing into her pink lips. Jake rushed to roll on the latex.

He pushed slowly inside, pausing to let her body adjust around his length.

Zara's breath caught, and she tensed for a moment, then relaxed into his invasion, giving him her trust.

"Every damn time," she moaned.

He slid one hand around to play with her clit as he eased inside her, reveling in that grip as if she couldn't stand for him to leave her.

Her clit was sensitive. They'd gone at each other multiple times last night, each time insatiable.

Jake watched his cock power into her, her hips shaking, her breasts bouncing as she thrust back against his invasion. His heart thundered, a swell of lust and something more, something deeper filled his chest.

His balls drew up, tightening.

"Get there." He pinched her clit. Zara threw back her head on a long moan, her body quivering, arms shaking. Sweat dampened the curls against the base of her neck as she shuddered beneath him.

As soon as she orgasmed, Jake let go. He pulled her ass against his groin, his cock buried deep inside her as he emptied into the condom. His orgasm went on and on, pulsing in hard jets.

His heart shattered, his vision splintering into shards of light, filling him with pure energy. He wanted to scoop her up and never let her go.

The moment hit him with the force of a sledgehammer. He didn't want to let her go.

He dropped his forehead to the curve of her shoulder, his heart slowly returning to normal. But would anything be normal again?

She softened around him, her body holding him tight, as he wanted to do with her.

Zara curled into Jake's side, reveling in the warmth of his body as she lazily ran her fingers over his arms, shaping his muscles with her palms, savoring his smooth skin.

He was a generous lover, and it was tempting to hide away in her bedroom for the afternoon.

"We should probably get up and get back to researching Xavier." The pit in her stomach returned.

"We need to follow the money," Jake said.

"I don't think that will work this time. That's one of the appeals of Xavier. He funded his own campaigns."

"He never took a dime from any PACs so that he could appear above board and people would trust him," Jake mused.

"That would be my guess. I certainly believed it," Zara confessed. "It was refreshing to have a politician not beholden to donor money."

"What about his businesses? They would have to be in receivership while he served in Congress."

"In theory, but it wouldn't surprise me at all if he has back-door communications with his various CEOs." Zara wondered how to find that out.

"He probably uses an app that has untraceable messages like What's App or Telegram."

Zara raised her eyebrows. "Is there a way to hack those?"

"I'll ask Kita, but I don't think so."

"What if he is taking favors from foreign governments?"

"But what kind of favors?" Jake stared at the ceiling with intense concentration.

Xavier had interests all over the world. His businesses were global. But she didn't think that's where Jake was going.

"You're thinking about Iran," Zara said.

His body stiffened ever so slightly. "Yes."

She waited.

"The Iranians are connected to a case we worked on a few months ago," Jake finally said.

"That doesn't sound like PR to me." The pit in Zara's stomach grew. The types of campaigns that she knew about relating to public relations were about promoting French wineries or German cars. They were also never referenced by their country of origin, but their brand. The fact that Jake was talking about a client and the Iranians was terrifying.

"You're better off not knowing."

"I'm not sure how to respond to that," she said.

"I still think we should dig into public records regarding his campaigns. There must be something somewhere that we can use."

A particular despair rolled through her.

Xavier was a billionaire with unlimited resources. "How are we ever going to protect Adams-Larsen?" She burrowed her head into the curve of his neck. His arms tightened around her.

"We'll find something. I'm positive."

Zara sighed. In the meantime, they would all be living

under the threat of what Xavier could do to them personally and to the company.

"I guess we should get up." Even though it was tempting to stay in bed and forget the world.

Before he could answer, her cell rang. It was her mother's ringtone.

"I have to get that. It's my mom. I haven't spoken with her in the last couple days."

"You're close, yes?"

"Yeah." She pulled on her robe. She couldn't talk to her mom naked, that would be weird. "We are."

She answered the phone. "Hi, Mom."

"Hey, honey, how are you?"

"Pretty good."

"Listen, do you have any plans for this evening?"

Zara's gaze cut to Jake's naked body. Only partially covered by the sheets.

"Nothing formal," she said.

"Well, I have a favor to ask."

Zara settled into the wing chair by the window, letting the soft afternoon light in. "What do you need?"

"It's so weird. Have you heard of Xavier Rodriguez?"

Zara's heart stopped. She took a minute to get under control. "Sure, everyone has."

"Well, he called your father a few weeks ago, and he's been pestering us to sell him the winery."

"What?"

"I know, right? As far as I know he's never had any interest in viticulture before."

Zara could barely hear over the thunder of her heart.

"I don't know why he chose us. The Iron Trail Winery across town has been on the market for a while. But he's very persistent."

Zara knew exactly why he had chosen her family's winery.

It was such a strange move, though. "You're not going to sell, are you?"

"Of course not." Her mother laughed. "However, in the course of our conversations, he recommended a charitable organization that raises money for families dealing with childhood cancer."

Incredible. If it had been anyone else, she might have believed the intention was purely philanthropic.

"There's a gala tonight."

Zara hesitated. It couldn't be coincidence that he had talked her mother about the gala this evening. It had to be the same one that Jillian was going to.

"What's the name of the event?" Zara forced the words out through a tight throat.

"I'll send you the information. He sent us a ticket and asked if a representative could attend."

"Only one ticket?"

"Yes. Just one. Apparently, it's sold out, so I don't think we could get you another one," her mother said slyly. "Is there a reason you want a second ticket?"

Sure. But not the reason her mother thought. Jake was going to flip. Clearly Xavier wanted to get Zara alone.

"I hate going to those things alone."

"If I called the people in charge, they might be able to make it happen."

There was no way Jake would let her go to this event alone. There was no way she *wanted* to go to the gala alone.

But Jillian would be there with her boyfriend, Hamish. Marsh Adams and Ayesha were also supposed to attend. With both her bosses in attendance, she should be safe.

"I think my boss is already going to that. Maybe I can see if I can sit with her."

"How wonderful," her mother gushed.

Wonderful. Yeah. That's what it was. Jake was going to lose his shit.

Jake sat up when she'd mentioned Jillian. He shook his head no, his face thunderous.

Zara turned away from him. He understood immediately that she was talking about the fundraiser that Jillian referenced.

Zara finished out the conversation with her mother, viscerally aware of Jake studying her intently. He'd pushed up so his back rested against the ornate headboard. His arms crossed over his chest, showcasing his magnificent pectorals.

Zara wanted to be distracted, but she knew the next few minutes were not going to be pleasant.

"What's up with your mom?"

She traced the edge of her robe with her finger avoiding his gaze.

"Zara," he said patiently.

"Xavier got to my parents."

37

Jake paced around the ALIAS disguise closet.

The closet was an old bedroom that had been converted to hold everything needed to transform clients or themselves. They had full wardrobes of clothes, men's and women's, in multiple sizes, as well as shoes, hats, belts, scarves, watches and jewelry.

Another wardrobe held wigs, makeup, and even hair dye. One bureau held burner phones, purchased in bulk and loaded with minutes, high tech listening devices, button cameras, surveillance cameras, prepaid credit cards, and actual cash in several currencies.

A large gun safe held weapons and ammunition, although they rarely needed them.

However, the person working the security booth was always armed.

ALIAS believed in being over-prepared.

Zara sat in the cosmetologist's chair. The trifold mirror with the makeup lights emphasized her wide blue eyes as she took in the scene around her.

"I don't like this." He couldn't shake the feeling that something bad was going to happen.

"Jake, we've got your girl covered," Marsh said.

Maria helped Zara with the large fake diamond studs that hid a listening device.

"He's not going to do anything to her in a public place." Dwayne clapped his hand on Jake's shoulder. Jake fought the urge to shake off Dwayne's hand. He knew that, but he didn't like it.

He strode over to Zara, held her hand. "You don't have to do this."

"It's fine," she said.

It wasn't fine. He decided, spur of the moment.

"I'm going to be there."

The room erupted.

"What? You can't be there."

"We don't have a ticket for you."

"There's no place for you."

The negatives came from all sides.

"Xavier wants her separated from you." Jill's tone was way too patient for his state of mind.

"I won't go into the event, but I'll be at the hotel, ready and willing if you need me." He wanted to protect her. Even more importantly. He *needed* to protect her.

He wanted to wrap her up in his arms and not let go. She was precious, and he refused to allow Xavier to hurt her.

"I'll stay out of sight, but I'm at the hotel." Jake refused to take any answer other than yes.

"If you need to be there," said Marsh. "You need to be there."

"Don't worry, man," Dwayne said. "We've got her covered."

Dwayne was going to drive the car that dropped Zara off.

Jill had made a quick call to the people in charge of the event and gotten Zara a seat at their table.

ALIAS made a last-minute donation of a large PR package for the live auction, and they'd been happy to accommodate her.

Zara had been quiet until now. "I'm worried about my family."

Everyone stopped.

"We can offer them protection if you feel like they need it," Jake burst out, then looked to Marsh and Jill for confirmation.

Zara blinked. "Protection?"

"Sure, we occasionally protect our clients." Marsh waited for her reply.

"They can pay for their own protection if they need it. I'm afraid that he's got sinister plans that we can't see. He's brilliant."

"Yeah, but you know what he doesn't have? He doesn't have us." Jake wrapped an arm around her shoulders. "We're not going to let anything happen to your family."

"I'll give Jack a call and see if he can do a security assessment." Jill picked up her cell. "It wouldn't hurt to have eyes on your parents for the next bit."

"Jack?" Zara blinked.

"Jack Stone. He runs a consulting business out of Monterey, California. We occasionally coordinate on jobs."

Maria's brown eyes softened.

"I know Jack Stone from Monterey." Now Zara looked confused. "His family attends my family's foundation fundraiser every year."

Zara rubbed her palms over her biceps, in a move that signaled she was trying to self soothe.

Marsh said, "His wife, Bliss, used to work with us."

Zara's eyes narrowed.

"What would Jack Stone and his family know about protection?" Zara squinted at them. "They run a philanthropy organization."

"They also do consulting, in more…security related situations," Jill replied smoothly, attempting to distract Zara's excellent brain from making the leap about Jack and Stone Consulting. "He owes me a favor."

But the damage had been done. Jake could see Zara mentally putting the pieces together along with the revelations from this morning.

"I don't want my parents to be worried," Zara protested.

"What if we have the Stones invite Zara's parents to their place in Lake Tahoe?" Maria smiled softly at Dwayne. They had begun their relationship on an op there. "Easily defended and beautiful scenery."

"Great idea." Jill picked up her phone and dialed.

Jake didn't know Jack well, but he'd worked with Bliss for years and she was solid.

"You have nothing to worry about."

38

———————

Jake paced the living room of Zara's rowhouse, waiting for her to come downstairs. Dwayne and Maria had brought her home while Jake swung by his apartment and picked up his suit. With this latest threat from Xavier, no way in hell was he leaving her alone.

As far as he was concerned, someone from ALIAS was going to be with her 24-7 until the situation resolved. He hated the anxiety that simmered beneath his breastbone. He wished he could go into the event with her, but logically he knew that would create more problems than it would solve.

He paced around her living room again. He turned as she came down the stairs.

She was stunning. Her hair was sculpted high and away from her face. She'd done something to her regular bob, and it looked much fancier.

She wore a strapless coral dress, highlighting her sleek shoulders and sculpted arms. The skirt belled out and hit her legs at mid-calf, and her shoes matched her dress.

She looked like a princess, with diamonds adorning her ears, throat, and wrist. The jewels glittered against her alabaster skin. He knew the earrings were listening devices from ALIAS, but the other jewelry must be hers.

She wore more makeup than normal. She'd done something with her eyes that made them look mysterious, and thick brown lashes framed those phlox blue irises, accenting her face.

She was totally at ease in the fancy dress, elegant and graceful as she descended the stairs, and Jake realized he was seeing Zara Cooper of Cooper Winery, not just his Zara.

She got to the bottom of the stairs, and he strode over to her.

"You look stunning."

"Thank you," she said softly, staring up at him with faith and trust.

"I'm sorry I can't be there."

"Just knowing you'll be in the hotel helps."

"I have complete confidence you can do this." Jake took her hand in his, the delicate bones fragile in his large palm.

"Oh, I know I can." She pressed her other hand to her stomach. "But I wish I didn't have to."

She glanced around the room, as if looking for a way out. "I guess I should go."

Jake was monitoring Dwayne's progress, and they had a few minutes.

"There's something we need to do first."

"What? Do we need to check my equipment?"

He snorted. "I'd like to check your equipment, but we don't have time."

Zara laughed, relief and gratitude softening her worried gaze.

Jake connected his phone to her stereo system. He put on *Waltz of the Flowers* by Tchaikovsky, then crooked his fingers at her.

She raised an eyebrow. "Yes?"

"Ms. Cooper, would you do the honor of dancing with me?"

"Why, Mr. Brown, I would love to."

Jake took Zara in his arms, his left arm wrapped around her waist, his right arm up as she threaded her fingers through his. Slowly, they began to waltz around the room, dancing closer than was traditionally appropriate.

They didn't speak, just stared into each other's eyes as Jake tried to convey his support and admiration.

"I love this song," she confessed breathlessly as they whirled around the living room. "My parents used to take us to the Nutcracker ballet every Christmas."

"My sister performed Clara when she was sixteen." He'd seen the show so many times. He'd endured months of practices, listening to the songs on repeat while Cia rehearsed the intricate steps.

The past blended with the present, each offering him a gift.

They fell into an easy rhythm as if they'd danced together for years. Floating through the one-two-three steps and holding each other in their arms as the music crescendoed.

As the song was winding down, he twirled her around, took her in his arms, and dipped her.

"I'd like to kiss you now."

"I thought you'd never ask," she whispered.

He scooped her up and wrapped her in his arms. The kiss was gentle, sweet, reverent.

"Don't worry about tonight. We've all got you."

"I only need you," she said.

He wouldn't let her down.

39

Zara walked into the ballroom. trying to project an air of confidence, ignoring the butterflies in her stomach. Xavier was here, and knowing that he would be watching her was unsettling.

He had an ulterior motive in getting her here tonight. She felt like she was playing chess but was three moves behind him. Everyone else had been chill about this event…except for Jake.

Jillian and her boyfriend, Hamish, were already here. Marsh and his girlfriend, Ayesha, were on their way.

She draped the faux fur stole over the back of a chair at their table.

Jillian said, "Zara, you remember Hamish."

Sure, they'd met earlier today, but in a sea of people. "Nice to see you." She had on her polite public smile.

"Pleasure to see ya."

Oh, she bet his deep Scottish brogue made women swoon.

"He's going to be a new addition to our office as soon as we get his immigration and visa paperwork taken care of." They smiled at each other, wrapped in an invisible world that only they inhabited.

She wished she was part of a world like that.

Marsh entered with his girlfriend, Ayesha. He introduced Zara to the artist.

Ayesha Brown was stunning, slender with a large afro and a slinky dress in a deep purple. Zara had read the piece that Allison from the *Sunday Magazine* had done on Ayesha. Zara had gotten that interview set up and thought it had gone really well.

Zara said, "It's a pleasure to meet you. I was sorry I missed your show at The Promise Gallery."

"Zara is the PR person who put your plan together," Marsh said.

"As opposed to the person who gave me the plan." Ayesha's smile sparkled with mischief.

"Yep." Marsh smiled right back.

"Nice to meet you." Ayesha looked perfectly put together until Zara noticed the dab of coral paint behind one ear and splatters of purple that matched her dress on her fingers.

Ayesha laughed and held up her hands. "Oops."

Marsh slung a casual arm around her shoulders and pressed a kiss to the side of her head.

"You wouldn't be you without paint somewhere on your body."

They shared an intimate look full of heat.

Zara wished that Jake were inside the ballroom. The two couples seemed so at ease together, and in love, and if this were any other situation she might enjoy the evening.

The fundraiser was for a great cause, and she loved to dress up.

The event was carousel-themed. Pastel pinks, purples, blues and teals accented with gold decorated the ballroom.

The space glittered with shiny ribbons and bouquets of balloons. Whimsical miniature horses on poles set on a bed of spun translucent tinsel created the table centerpieces. In one corner, a life-sized carousel that must have been thirty feet in diameter sat idle. The lights around the top crown twinkled, and a line had formed along outside the fence surrounding the party feature.

Two other corners held bar setups.

Zara had been to a million of these in her lifetime. At least it felt like that. But she'd never had this rock of anxiety sitting in her chest.

She inhaled slowly and blew out a slow breath.

"Be yourself, and act naturally. You'll be fine." Jillian handed her a flute of champagne.

She could schmooze with the best of them. She'd grown up in this kind of world. Sweet-talking wealthy people out of their money for good causes. The Cooper Family Foundation donated millions every year to various charities, so she'd also been sweet-talked out of her family's money as well. These things were a give and take. Members of society being seen with a generous heart and goodwill for people. They got to look good, and the charitable causes got their money, and the papers and magazines promoted the event bringing even more attention to charitable causes. That was the trade-off.

She couldn't just show up. She needed to put in the research on this Childhood Cancer Foundation and see if it was a good fit for the Cooper Family Foundation. They tended to focus on the environment and hunger; as farmers they understood the importance of good nutrition and being good stewards of the land. But their portfolio had grown in recent years, and the money with it.

They were considering branching out.

So she'd best get to speaking with the principals involved in the organization.

Zara took a sip of the champagne, a demi-sec to appeal to a wide variety of drinkers. She swished the liquid in her mouth, noting the feel, the grapes maybe an assemblage of several varieties, with hints of apple and honey blossoms. Not bad.

"Can you introduce me to the person in charge or any board members you know?"

"Absolutely," Jillian said. "I can make that happen."

"Thanks."

"You don't have to cave to Xavier's pressure to work while you're here," Jillian murmured.

"My family's foundation might be interested in adding this charity to their portfolio."

Jillian nodded. She knew Zara's family had money. They had discussed the fact that she was moving far away from her support network during her interview when she had assured Jillian that it would not be an issue. And so far, it hadn't been.

She certainly hadn't expected a billionaire to threaten her family. That radically changed the dynamic.

She didn't know anything about Jillian's family life. But her boss had been quick to agree to protect Zara's parents, which she appreciated.

Zara gulped the rest of the champagne for fortification. "I might as well kill two birds with one stone."

She had a feeling that Xavier wouldn't be expecting her to do anything but be here. This was an intimidation ploy, but she was going to turn it back on him and get something done.

Jillian led her over to a well-preserved older woman in a sleeveless, one shoulder, vintage Dior in pale pink. The evening dress had one bare shoulder with the other draped with abstract flowers that trailed across the bodice.

"Zara, meet Candace Witherspoon. She's the genius behind this very worthy organization."

"It's a pleasure. We've heard so much about the Cooper Family Foundation." She extended her hand and clasped Zara's fingers in a half-shake.

"I'll leave you to it." Jillian sauntered away.

Zara chatted with the woman about the particulars of their charity, how they raised money, how they distributed money, how they decided who was worthy. Were they local? Were they national? What kind of overhead and expenses did they have? Her family was very careful to donate only to charities where the majority of the money went straight to helping people and not for administrative costs. Of course there were administrative costs that were unavoidable, but they vetted their recipients very carefully.

"Ah, Candace, I see you've met Zara Cooper." Xavier glided up so quietly, Zara jumped. She'd been engrossed in the conversation with the engaging woman.

She was impressed with the organization and their mission.

"Thank you for the introduction, Xavier," Candace said. "After talking with Zara, I'm excited for the possibilities." She glanced at Zara. "If the Cooper Family Foundation decides to invest in our program."

"I thought you would be a good fit for each other. I'm absolutely thrilled that it's working out."

If Zara didn't know any better, she would believe him. She would believe that he was a philanthropic billionaire connecting donors and recipients to serve the greater good. Xavier smiled. Maybe only Zara thought it was oily, but she really wanted to shower off the stench.

"Childhood cancer is a scourge. The children are our future."

"Absolutely." Candace beamed.

"We need to protect our future at all costs," Xavier parroted lines he'd used in his last campaign.

Who knows? Maybe he really did believe that. Maybe in his mind, children were the future. But the women who birthed them were only vessels to carry future generations, not worthy of their own autonomy or their own thoughts and feelings?

A particular rage burned beneath her breastbone, and she smiled tightly.

"Thank you very much for the introduction, Xavier. The Cooper Family Foundation will definitely be discussing this wonderful organization at our next board meeting."

Zara sat on the board of their family foundation. She'd missed the last quarterly meeting since she'd been getting settled in D.C., but she wouldn't skip the next one.

Xavier nodded, clearly pleased with her answer.

Maybe something good could come out of this situation. Zara was trapped right now, needing to appease him, but she vowed he wouldn't get any closer to her parents.

She would protect them at all costs.

"Thank you for the introduction. My family appreciates it." Zara inclined her head at Xavier. Not deigning to fawn over him like Candace. But that wasn't fair to the woman because she understood that for Candace, a benefactor like Xavier could make or break an organization.

"We're very careful about who we invest in, making sure that they are truly supporting the greater good. We don't like to be scammed."

The band started playing.

"Zara, I have another person I would love for you to meet. May I steal her away?"

"Absolutely," said Candace. "It was a pleasure meeting you."

"I look forward to talking with you again." Zara nodded politely and let Xavier lead her away. She decided to pretend that nothing was wrong. That he hadn't actively threatened her this morning.

His fingers tightened on her bicep. He'd gotten the message about being scammed. Maybe she shouldn't have thrown subtle shade, but she'd been unwilling to subdue the need to poke at him.

"Did you have someone else that you needed me to speak with this evening?" Zara asked. She would love to get away from him. Jake was probably losing his mind about now.

She realized for a moment she'd forgotten he was listening in. But now, the thought that he was there, only a room away if she needed him, eased her tension. Her shoulders relaxed.

She had this.

Jillian caught her eye. Sending the silent message. *Do you need rescuing?*

Zara gave a slight shake of her head. She could handle him. Besides he wouldn't do anything that would jeopardize his reputation in front of all these people.

Xavier, completely unaware of her backup, said snidely, "You need to be careful who you associate with."

She snorted. "No kidding."

"Your boyfriend is dangerous."

Zara blinked. This was a new tactic.

"His last girlfriend disappeared."

"Excuse me?"

"Layla Habib, a little young for him if you ask me, disappeared after they had been dating."

Static filled the space between her ears. *Disappeared?*

"Not sure what you're implying."

"Oh, I'm not implying anything." Xavier attempted a concerned look, but now that she knew what lay beneath his exterior façade, she saw the calculation. "She disappeared. Her house blew up."

"Blew up?!" She didn't have to feign shock at that one. Her house blew up?

"The last person she was dating was your boyfriend. Perhaps you should do your homework better next time."

She couldn't help another small dig. "Apparently, I need to work on my research in more than one area."

"He has a history of violence. Be careful who you associate with." He repeated the warning.

"Believe me, I've learned that lesson." Zara desperately wished she hadn't drunk that champagne as it sloshed in her stomach, threatening to come back up. "Thank you for the information. I'll look into it."

"See that you do." Xavier glided across the room toward the bar. "I'd hate for your personal life to get in the way of our business relationship."

"I am a professional," Zara forced the words out. She wanted to punch him. But that wouldn't further their cause. She had to be pleasant even if she did want to puke all over his bespoke tuxedo.

"I'd like to schedule a meeting to go over the schedule. My house, Monday morning, before I head to the Hill. Can you accommodate that?"

Jake would lose his mind. But Jillian had said to keep Xavier placated. "I should be able to make that meeting. I've got a new plan ready to go."

No way was she going to help this guy get elected. She would find a way to sabotage him if Adams-Larsen couldn't.

Xavier's bodyguards had been keeping people at bay. Zara had noticed them running interference as he spoke with her, making sure they were uninterrupted.

He handed her a flash drive. "I gave this information to your boss as well. Read it. Consider who you are hanging around with."

She'd take Jake over this...miserable excuse for a human any day.

Maybe Zara could stop working for him. She had to try. Maybe the threats against Adams-Larsen could all just disappear.

"If you're unhappy with my performance, then perhaps we should part ways."

He smiled benignly. "Of course I'm not unhappy. You're doing a great job. Will continue to do a great job." Was there a threat in there?

"There was no need to get Jake in trouble for defending me," she said mildly. "I'm sure it will all be cleared up soon."

"I wouldn't count on that." Xavier inclined his head toward the USB drive Zara clutched in her palm. "Read it."

He walked away.

The urge to see what was on it was intense, but she was going to have to wait until she got home. But that sick feeling wouldn't go away. What did Xavier have on Jake?

Clearly, he thought the information would be a dealbreaker for her. Would it?

40

———

Jake was jonesing to see Zara again.

They had agreed to go back to Marsh's place and discuss what had happened during the fundraiser. He left a few minutes before everyone else.

Even though he knew she was no longer in Xavier's presence, Jake couldn't shake that low-level anxiety swirling inside him. Xavier had resources beyond normal rich people. He could pay people to track her. Jake didn't trust anyone else to watch out for her.

Not even his bosses.

After the initial discussion, Xavier had left her alone. Jake had been sweating it while listening to her conversations. Logically, he knew that Xavier wouldn't do anything to Zara in public, but fear wasn't rational.

Zara was with Jillian and Hamish. Jake took an extended SDR back to Marsh's in case he was being followed by Xavier's goons. Marsh and Ayesha were right behind him.

They needed to check for any kind of bugs or tracking device in the flash drive that Xavier had given to Zara. He was a little worried about what was on that drive. He didn't have anything to hide, but still, Xavier was rich enough to manufacture things against Jake.

Marsh had given Jake a key, so he let himself in to the condo on the eighth floor and headed for the fridge. He grabbed a bottle of water and began to pace Marsh's penthouse, ignoring the masculine space with spare lines, sleek furnishings and walls scattered with plenty of art.

Marsh and Ayesha were about fifteen minutes behind Jake.

They walked into the condo. Marsh took one look at Jake and said, "Babe, why don't you go change? I'll be right there."

Ayesha glanced between the two of them. "Sure."

"You okay?" Marsh asked.

"Getting there." Jake paced jerkily. "How do you handle it?"

Jake hated that Zara was out of his sight.

"By giving her the tools to take care of herself." Marsh joked, "I may have researched panic buttons."

"Seriously?"

"Jake, loving someone means giving them the space to be themselves. I don't know Zara well, but she seems solid. And she knows you've got her back."

Love? That seemed premature. But the word induced panic. Love meant weakness and vulnerability. Was he ready for that?

After their talk, Marsh had disappeared into the bedroom to change out of his formal wear.

And then Zara arrived with Jill and Hamish.

Jake wanted to pull Zara into his arms, but the moment she walked in, arms around her waist, shoulders slightly hunched, he figured she wouldn't want him to touch her. Jake had been going over her brief conversation with Xavier, looking for any kind of clue as to what Xavier might have planned.

Right now, Xavier believed his divide and conquer to

isolate her from Jake and to isolate Jake from Adams-Larsen was working. They had to tread carefully to stay ahead of the billionaire.

Thankfully, after the initial contact, Xavier had left Zara alone.

That didn't mean Jake didn't sweat the entire time, worrying about Xavier coming after her, worrying about what else he would say, worrying about what was on that flash drive. As soon as Xavier had mentioned Layla, Jake wanted to storm in and carry Zara out of there. Before tonight, the Iranian connection was a thin thread, potentially a coincidence, but they now knew that Xavier must be connected to the Iranians.

The situation with Layla had happened months ago.

The only people who would know about his association to Layla were the Iranians and Jill and Marsh. No one else at ALIAS had been involved. The relocation had been weird and unusual from the get-go.

Hamish puttered around the kitchen and put the kettle on to make tea. Jill had removed her shoes and padded on the hardwood floors to sit properly on one side of the modern sofa. It was the most relaxed Jake had ever seen his boss. Even in the office, she maintained a straightlaced demeanor.

Hamish brought Jill a cup of tea, then sat on the arm of the sofa next to her, and she smiled softly at him. So weird to see. There hadn't been a visible soft bone in her body before she and Hamish had gotten together. They leaned toward each other, as if a light duty magnet drew them together.

Then Marsh and Ayesha came back into the living room, walking close together, holding hands.

Jake wanted what his bosses had.

He wanted that quiet intimacy, that serene attraction, that feeling that he and Zara were together in a sea of uncertainty.

She could count on him to be her raft, to hold her up and carry her.

Jake wanted desperately to claim Zara, to touch her for reassurance that she was okay.

But her body language screamed, *Back off and leave me alone.*

Zara huddled into the opposite corner of the boxy, modern sofa, just as stunning as when they'd danced in her living room. Her matching high-heeled pumps lay on the floor in front of her. She looked so far out of his league, he couldn't believe she had ever even touched him.

"Your last girlfriend disappeared?" She shivered, her body shaking.

He hated that hint of fear in her eyes before her gaze skittered away from him.

"She wasn't my girlfriend."

She had curled her legs and tucked her feet under the skirt of the gown.

"You're cold," he said. He shrugged off his jacket and placed it around her shoulders. He'd worn a suit to the hotel, attempting to try to fit in. But he wasn't all that comfortable in fancy clothes, and it showed.

"Thank you," she said softly. "You didn't answer my question. She disappeared?"

For Layla's safety, Jake had relocated her and Ben. Because the Iranians had wanted her dead. They'd been rather persistent about it too.

He couldn't lie to her. He nodded. Anything he said would make it worse.

"Should we check for a tracker on the flash drive?" Jake diverted the attention.

"We weren't followed." Marsh dropped into one of the armchairs next to the sofa. "So it stands to reason there might be a tracker on it. However, it's logical for Zara to come back here for a post-event glass of wine."

"Anyone want wine?" Hamish asked.

No one said yes. Hamish grabbed bottles of water from the fridge and handed them out.

"We have to assume that Xavier has files on all of us." Jillian stared off into the distance.

Marsh plugged the USB into an old laptop that wasn't connected to the internet in case there was a Trojan horse or other surveillance device embedded in the coding. Camera on the laptop was turned off and covered.

"Let's see what's on this." He pulled up the pictures.

Shock punched Jake's heart. There were pictures of him at Layla's back door and of him and her in one of the ALIAS Hondas that they used for transporting their clients. Shit. So Xavier didn't just have information; he had actual photo evidence.

Marsh muttered, "Dammit."

"This was a loose end," Jake said. With everything else that had gone on when they'd been relocating Layla, they had forgotten that the Iranians had thought Jake was Layla's boyfriend. He'd let that stand because he hadn't wanted anything to happen to Ben.

"The problem here is these pictures are from months ago," Jake reiterated the bigger issue. "We don't know how Xavier and the Iranians are connected, but they are definitely connected."

Did Xavier give the Iranians his name and picture? How did they make the leap?

"He said she disappeared." Zara shivered beneath his coat. "What happened to Layla?"

Jake glanced at Jill and then at Marsh. They shook their heads.

"We can't tell you," Jill said.

"Hey, Ayesha, why don't you show me your brilliant studio?" Hamish smiled tightly.

"Oh, uh, sure. Great idea!"

Hamish and Ayesha headed for what used to be Marsh's guest bedroom.

"I'm assuming you didn't kill her." Zara's voice was rock steady, but Jake caught the slight tremor in her fingers.

"She wasn't my girlfriend," Jake said. "Let me make that perfectly clear."

Zara blinked.

"We don't kill people!" Marsh practically yelled. "This is troubling. We need to find the connection between Xavier and the Iranians. That is priority number one."

"What makes you think these pictures are from the Iranians?" Zara asked. They didn't answer. "Are you guys going to tell me anything, or am I going to sit here in the dark the entire time?"

Jake had been hoping Jill and Marsh would come to this conclusion without him needing to press the issue.

"We need to read her in."

"She doesn't have clearance," Jill said.

"Fuck clearance. This is her life." Jake's clenched his fists. "We cannot put her in danger without her understanding what's happening."

"It's a huge security risk," Marsh said patiently.

"She deserves the truth." Jake wasn't going to back down.

"Are you sure this isn't because you want her to know who Layla is to you?" Marsh said.

Jake snarled, "Xavier isn't above making her disappear to make me look bad."

"What?!" Zara's mouth rounded in shock.

"It would get rid of two problems at once. Zara is the one

who saw him hit his wife, and he would essentially neutralize ALIAS." Jill tapped her French manicured finger against her lips. Her tone was way too casual for his dread.

"This is about making her understand her life is in danger."

Shit. He shouldn't have blurted that out.

Zara asked with a measured tone, "Are you saying you think he will kill me? He's a businessman and a congressman, not the mob."

"I think we should put her in a safe house." A desperate fear rocked his body. He couldn't let anything happen to her.

Neither Jill nor Marsh objected, which amped Jake's fear even higher.

"There are more pictures on this drive. Let's take a look everything he's got and *then* figure out our game plan."

Then they needed to explain to Zara.

Jill made a go on gesture with her fingers, and Marsh clicked on the next picture.

"Do you think they are after her?" Now he was talking about Layla. She'd become far more than a client. She was the little sister he had been able to save, unlike his real sister.

Marsh said, "Maybe this is an attempt to find out if she's alive?"

After the press conference, maybe Xavier had started to put things together, especially if he connected the photos of Layla and him to her disappearance. Maybe this was about giving the Iranians intelligence.

Marsh clicked on the next file.

Aw. Crap.

41

____

What in the hell was happening?

Zara was so confused. She was in a fun house of terror with things happening so far outside her realm that she couldn't make sense of anything. Safe house, Iranians, Jake's old girlfriend disappeared?

Now everyone was staring at the picture on the screen in horror.

The face of a battered woman filled the screen. Jake had frozen.

The picture wasn't the same woman as the girlfriend.

Jillian bent down and peered at the screen. "Is that...?"

Jake rubbed his eyes with the heels of his hands. "Fuck, yes."

"Does somebody want to fill me in on what's happening?" Zara said.

Marsh right clicked on the picture and pulled up the information. "It was taken with a smart phone, but there's no other data."

"We need to see if Kita can recover the timestamp on this picture." Marsh picked up his phone and dialed.

"Marsh," Jill interrupted.

"Give me a minute." Marsh held up a finger.

Zara could hear Kita on the other end of the line. It was eleven o'clock on a Saturday night, but Marsh hadn't even hesitated.

He hung up. "She's already on her way."

"If you'd let me finish, I could have told you that I called her on the way here. Just in case." Jillian rolled her eyes.

"Maybe Kita can find a location." Jake put one hand on the back of his neck, the other on his waist and began to pace. "How the hell would he know about this?"

Jillian glanced between her and Jake. "Zara, why don't you go get yourself a cup of tea?"

Frustration and anger bubbled up inside her, making her throat tight. "Since this directly involves me, why don't I *not*?"

Zara stared at the woman in the picture and flinched. Bruises covered her face and upper body. She looked like she might be part Asian, but it was hard to tell.

One eye was swollen shut.

"Keep going." Zara forced the words through her tight throat. This whole thing had escalated into crazytown. "Look, there's nothing to tie this woman to Jake, so why did Xavier include it on the drive?"

"Because he wants you to think I beat up women."

Another form of divide and conquer.

Someone knocked on the door with three hard raps. Instantly three weapons appeared. Jake, Jillian and Marsh. Zara's heart ramped up. Guns?

Marsh checked the peephole. "It's Kita."

"Look at you guys all dressed up!" Kita blew into the room like a whirling dervish and stopped dead at the picture on the screen. "Is that...?"

"We think so."

"Oh, that's not good." Kita was shaking her head.

"Is that *who*?" Zara yelled in frustration.

"That situation has been resolved. How would he have gotten those pictures?" Jake stared at the floor, his face a blank mask. But she could feel his frustration seething beneath the surface.

"Look at the background. See if there are any clues," Jillian ordered.

"Do you think he has her?" Jake asked.

Kita nudged Marsh out of the way. "Did you check for malware or viruses on the drive?"

"No."

She sighed and did some quick typing. "Looks like it's fine."

"There's no way to track that drive, right?" Jake asked.

"As far as I am aware, there isn't any GPS tracker capability on thumb drives." Kita held up her hand. "Doesn't mean it doesn't exist. It means it isn't common knowledge."

Okay, one good thing.

"Besides, flash drives are typically an inefficient way to store data. Too easily lost and breached."

"Okay." Even if Xavier had tracked the drive here, he wouldn't know they were looking at the information.

"Let's focus on one problem at a time. She was supposed to stay put." Kita began tapping on the keyboard and pulled up the location. "Those pictures were taken right here in D.C. Dammit."

"What's the date?"

"Two days ago."

"She looks terrified."

"I bet they are coercing her to say Jake is the one who hurt her."

Fuck.

"We need to let the Marshals know she's here."

"Now this is interesting," said Jillian. "These pictures were not in the information that Xavier sent me. He sent me the info about your army discharge. He also sent me old news about your interaction with your Amancia's killer."

"Don't candy-coat it. I beat the shit out of him," Jake said. "But that was years ago. I've changed."

"He's clearly setting you up to make it look like you hurt women."

"Would someone please explain to me what's happening?" Zara was done.

"If anyone interviews her, she can directly ID me as someone who threatened her," Jake said miserably.

"Is this what you were talking about the other day?" Zara was worried about the misery on his face. She knew he didn't hit her. "You said you didn't hit her."

"I didn't."

"But I'm sure if they interview her, with clever editing they could make it sound like I did. And with pictures like these, I'm fucked." Jake straightened.

"The bigger question right now is, where is she? She was fine when we left her. That was months ago."

"We always knew long-term, she'd be a flight risk. She didn't want to leave in the first place." Kita rubbed her wrist. "She was a hostile witness."

"And someone could pay her to say *you* did that…" Marsh left the rest dangling.

Jillian's tone was calculating. "He thinks you're out on your own now."

Zara didn't like the look on her boss's face. "You need to protect Jake." Her heart thudded slow and heavy in her chest. She might be pissed at him, but she didn't want him hurt.

"I'll be fine. I'm not leaving you unprotected." Jake was adamant.

"The question remains. How did he know about her? The Russians? The CIA?"

Russians? Now there were Russians involved. Holy moly. Every new revelation moved Adams-Larsen further out of the realm of reputation management.

Jillian's phone rang. "I need to take this. No one leave."

As if they would.

42

———

"Hello, Allison."

Zara straightened. The reporter they'd used for Ayesha's Sunday feature? Strange time of night for her to be calling. Didn't seem like the appropriate hour for a call from a reporter who worked on feature articles.

There were a lot of uh-huhs. Jillian said thanks for the heads up and pressed the off button on her phone. She held her smartphone in her hand and stared at a striking landscape over the fireplace for about ten seconds.

"Are you going to tell us what she said?" Marsh asked.

"There's going to be a very unflattering piece in Monday's paper about Adams-Larsen."

Zara's stomach sloshed. Xavier had already started.

"Fuck," said Jake.

"She couldn't give me the specific details, but suffice it to say that it's highly likely we're going to be subpoenaed to testify in front of Congress about stories that have been in the paper recently."

Zara blinked. Wow, this was crazy.

The room was silent as if they were all grasping for what to do next. This was literally her area of expertise, the one she'd been trying to get them to listen to for the past hour. Except no one would tell her anything, and no one took her seriously. Suddenly she'd had enough.

"I quit."

Jillian barely reacted. "If that's what you need to do, but I don't think it will make your problem with Xavier go away."

"We're not leaving her out in the cold," Jake said.

Marsh didn't say a word.

"I have ideas on how to combat this. Techniques that will work to minimize the impact of the article. But you have to trust me," Zara said. "So either read me in, or I quit."

Jake's eyes lit up and his smile could power the entire city. "There she is."

Jillian studied her, crossing her arms over her chest.

"I'll consider it."

Zara thought about taking that win but then decided—nope. "No considering. Either yes or no."

Jillian's pale eyebrows rose. "All right. You're in."

Marsh piped up, "She needs to sign an NDA."

"Already did when you hired me." Zara was done sitting on the sideline like a damsel in distress. *Time to take control.* "We need to start a crisis campaign for ALIAS." To get ahead of this issue.

"Crisis campaign?"

Jake didn't like the sound of this.

"We can't outright attack Xavier. He would bury us." Zara shivered. Hopefully not literally. "We need a two-pronged approach. But there are plenty of PR techniques that can slant the coverage in the right direction."

"Explain."

"Whenever you're dealing with a negative story, the first

recommendation is for an organization to immediately admit fault, accept responsibility."

"Doesn't that defeat the purpose?"

"Not if you spin it that you were working for the greater good."

"Will that be effective?"

"Not on its own." Zara shook her head.

Jill sipped her tea. "We can't violate our NDA with him. But we can point a journalist in the proper direction."

Marsh snapped his fingers. "We promised Allison a news article. She's been wanting to break out of the lighter pieces. Can we give her a direction to start?"

"She needs to understand there will be heat and pressure from Xavier. It could backfire on her. I can pitch it to her with the understanding that there could be negative consequences," Zara said. "And that she needs to research quietly."

"Have him get hit from every side." Jillian smiled.

"I can give her all the research on Xavier that I used to formulate his plan," Zara thought out loud. "We also need to be able to use multiple sources to boost the algorithm to promote the negative stories when they start showing up."

"That would be my area of expertise." Kita grinned.

"It's possible he used astroturfing to create his incredible popularity." Zara's brain considered and discarded several options.

"Explain astroturfing."

"Astroturfing is where there is press that looks like grass-roots support for a cause, but in actuality, the support is from someone who will benefit from the cause."

"You think Rodriguez used this technique?"

"If you remember, he had always been in the news for his business exploits, but there was a sudden boom of stories when he ran for office. Stories of support that looked like they came from various sources, but what if they were from people with a stake in the outcome of the story?"

"What kind of stake?"

"If Xavier used the support of foreign countries, like Iran, for influence, and they boosted his popularity through what looked like impartial articles. He didn't take political contributions, but he took their aid to help him get elected."

Kita clacked away on the computer. "We need to analyze who has been supporting Xavier in the press and in Congress recently. These are the people who covered up his misdeeds for their own gain."

"See if it correlates to him using his influence to benefit foreign countries," Zara agreed.

"We've had restrictions on Iran since 1979. The type of sanctions has varied over time, but many are still in place."

"What if he is working to get those lifted or lessened?"

Kita listed it off like she was reading a report. "We have very limited trade with them, but lately, there have been rumblings that the restrictions should be lifted. Besides oil and gas, they export iron and steel, which would come in handy for the large infrastructure bill passed last year. Shoring up the US railways would utilize both. They also export certain organic chemicals."

"So we need to search for any other links to Iran." Marsh tapped his fingers on his knee.

Jillian mused, "And then we could expose this astro-turfing."

"We're talking about a years' long investigation." Jake's frustration bled through his words.

"It won't happen overnight," Zara cautioned. "Instead, we need to reverse astroturf him. Very carefully, gently, push a few journalists toward negative articles."

"How?"

"In this case, getting the negative stories about Rodriguez out there into the internet, from our friends and associates, multiple sources, who then get others to amplify those stories to create negative buzz about Rodriguez," Zara explained.

"But we, the original source, actually have a stake in the outcome." Understanding dawned on Jake's face.

"Yes. This tactic can also be used to turn public opinion against someone. There was a recent case of a PR firm tarnishing the image of an actress so the public turned against her. It worked extremely effectively."

"And we are going to do that?" Jillian seemed to be contemplating the idea.

"We do the same thing to him. Start the process and slowly begin to generate articles and plant seeds." Zara let her anger burn. Xavier deserved every bit of what they were planning.

"That's my expertise." Kita rubbed her hands together. "I can seed the internet with questions about Xavier. Then as things heat up, we can bump the articles so that when people search for him, they see the questionable stories first."

"You can do that?" Zara thought about all the implications of being able to manipulate news stories. "Is that legal?"

Silence.

"Sometimes it's better not to ask."

Did she find anything in her research that she ignored because it didn't fit with his profile of the philanthropist?

"I wonder if we can find bills he voted for that benefited his business interests."

"Let's run an algorithm to look at his votes in the House and corresponding articles right prior to those votes. There may be a pattern that isn't obvious at first." Kita pounded on her keyboard. "I can also start tracing the source of the positive articles about him and see if there is any correlation between Iran and Russia."

"You can do that?" Zara was amazed.

"Kita is a genius."

She beamed at Jake. "Thanks, man."

"According to his website, his business is in a receiver-ship," Zara countered.

"Do we really believe that?" Jake's sarcasm was on full display.

"Huh. How would we find out if he's been in contact with his company CEOs?"

Zara wracked her brain. "I wish there was a way we could get ahold of his visitor logs from the house."

Kita smiled broadly. "Didn't you say everything is logged via iPad?"

"No," Jake said before Zara could answer.

"If we could get close enough to clone it, we could get that data. There might be other visitors who would tie to the good press he's gotten."

"No, no, no, no, no. It's too risky."

"Could you teach me how to do it?" Zara asked Kita.

"Sure."

"Great."

"I don't want you anywhere near him." Jake's heart iced.

"I don't have a choice," Zara said softly. "I've got a meeting with him early Monday morning at the house."

"Let's meet tomorrow, and I'll give you the tech and explain what you need to do." Kita grinned, cackling with glee. "This is going to be fun."

Jake had completely lost control of the situation. He didn't want Zara anywhere near Xavier. But he also understood her need to be involved.

"We need to put security protocols in place. Tracker on the car and your person. Listening device in your ears again. And another on your person, maybe a button in your shirt, and a pen. The devices will all transmit to your phone and then upload to a cloud." Jake bulleted out points. They even had a tracker they could put in a shoe heel.

"Seems like a bit of overkill."

"I can't be in the car with you, but I'll be around the corner." Jake paced. "I want another backup also around the corner."

"He'll think I'm vulnerable." Zara nodded. "But he'll be wrong."

Everyone looked so pleased. But Zara was still in the dark about so much. That changed now.

"But first, you're going to explain about the women." She gestured to the laptop. "Or I walk."

"It's late," Jillian said. "Jake, can you explain about Layla? I trust you to keep as many top-secret details to yourself as possible. Don't share anything that would put her new life in danger."

New life… Zara was finally going to find out exactly what was going on.

"Who's Layla?" Kita's gaze swung between her coworkers. "Uh."

"Oh, crap." Kita held up her hands. "Okay. No need to say anything else."

"Yeah." He rubbed his hand over his face.

They were all exhausted.

"We'll reconvene tomorrow morning at the office."

"I need Zara protected." Jake's voice was hard.

Jillian said, "I think you two need to have a public break up."

Jake shook his head. "Zara would never break up with me publicly."

"We need to make sure whoever is watching you sees it," Jillian insisted.

He didn't want her left alone.

"I know it can't be me, but she needs a bodyguard when she's out of the house." And when she was home, he would be there. That was non-negotiable.

"Let's meet tomorrow to go over our plan. We also need to follow the trail to figure out how Xavier got this information," Jillian said. "Everyone, go home and get a good night's sleep."

"I need to have a counter release ready for the article in Monday's paper," Zara reminded them.

"Good point. We'll work on it tomorrow."

Tiredness overwhelmed Jake. He wasn't convinced the danger to Zara was over. He'd make damn sure she was protected. Xavier would have to go through him to get to her.

43

J ake parked behind her rowhouse, then traversed the
back alley to access the rear of Zara's house. He'd
checked his truck for any kind of tracker, keeping a
balance between not hiding that he was at Zara's but
not making it too obvious. Let Xavier work for it.

Jillian and Hamish were driving her home right now. He let
himself in through the back door in the sunroom.

The security system didn't beep. Jake frowned. It should
have been on. But maybe Zara forgot to set it in the rush to get
ready for the fundraiser tonight. That seemed out of character.
Quietly, he pulled his SIG from the holster at his waist and
listened carefully.

The house felt empty.

Zara had left lights on throughout the downstairs.
Carefully, he opened the French doors that separated the
sunroom from the rest of the house and entered the kitchen.
The light over the stovetop cast a warm glow over the sleek
appliances and quartz where Jake had lain her down and—

Fuck. *Focus, Brown.*

The kitchen seemed undisturbed. Jake took a moment to text Zara.

"Don't come in until I tell you it's okay. Your alarm system wasn't engaged. Ask Jillian if she has any kind of bug detector with her. And whatever you do, don't give away that you've already seen the pictures. We need to pretend until we're sure that there are no surveillance devices in your house."

He set his phone to silent.

Jake stalked past the circular staircase into the living room. Another light on an end table cast more glow and shadows. Jake searched the darkness for an intruder. He paused, listening, but the house felt empty.

He cleared each room, looking behind the doors, behind the curtains, searching under the furniture for an intruder. He headed upstairs and cleared each bedroom, searching the closets, under the beds, and the attached bathrooms.

The house was clear.

But the intruder could have planted bugs. Jake turned on the lights, picked up the remote, and turned on the television.

Then he prowled the living room looking for any kind of listening device. Behind a ceramic otter on one of the pale wood bookshelves was a small transmitting bug.

Fuck.

They needed that bug detecting equipment. At least they'd be able to have their public fight—not in public.

Zara let herself in.

Jake plopped on the stuffy sofa and propped his feet up on the glass coffee table. "Hey, babe."

"Hi." Zara closed the door softly and removed her faux fur.

"I missed you tonight."

Jake typed a message into his phone and held it up for her to see. *Don't say anything important. Someone was here and put a listening device in your living room.*

Zara's eyes widened, her gaze darting around the room.

Act like you would if you and I were really dating and you got bad information about your boyfriend.

Shit. The silence had lasted too long.

"How was the fundraiser?" Jake asked.

"It was really good. It's a great organization, and I think it would be a good fit for my family's foundation."

Jake snorted.

"Look, I know you have issues with my family's money, but we do good things with it."

"Yeah, yeah, I know." He kissed her softly. "Let's not fight about this tonight."

"Yeah, hold up there." She put her hand on his chest.

"What?" Jake asked. "What's wrong?"

She pulled the flash drive out of her purse. "Well, I saw Xavier at the fundraiser tonight."

"I don't like that guy." Jake grumbled.

"You've made that abundantly clear."

"So what is this thumb drive thing?"

"He said your last girlfriend disappeared."

"Disappeared is sort of right."

"Her name was Layla? Apparently, she was really young." She did a great job with the accusatory tone.

Jake blew out a breath. "Come on, do we really have to talk about this tonight?"

"I'd like an explanation."

"We had a very short, quick thing. Her family was in trouble. She was being stalked and harassed."

By the Iranians after they hired her father to do surveillance on an Iranian scientist who had defected.

"Stalked and harassed!" Zara cried. "That's terrible."

"Yeah," Jake said. "There wasn't really anything I could do

about it. I suggested she disappear for a while." *Adams-Larsen helped her.* He shrugged. "So she did."

"Well, where is she now?"

"I have no idea. She said she was going to take off, and one day she left. How would Xavier know about that, anyway?"

"I don't know."

"What's on that thumb drive?"

"I don't know. I haven't looked at it yet."

"Then how did you know about Layla?"

"He told me she disappeared."

"Yeah, I hope wherever she is, she's safe," Jake said.

Zara eyed him suspiciously. "You're sure you don't know where she's at?"

"Not a clue." *I really don't know.*

He smiled at her. "Want to hit the sheets? Or you want to look at whatever's on that drive now?" He kissed her again softly. The kiss turned heated.

"I'll take a look in the morning," she said breathlessly.

"Let's go to bed."

"Okay. But I'm not going to forget about this."

Zara handed him the bug tech from Jill.

"I'll clean up the kitchen and turn off the lights. You get ready for bed."

Jake prowled through the house scanning each room carefully. He'd found another one in the kitchen.

He finished with her bedroom and found one there as well. That fucking pervert.

Jake put his hand over hers and held up a finger.

"Zara, do you really have to turn that thing on?" He texted in his phone. *Bug in the bedroom.* She read it.

"I've told you I can't sleep without the white noise."

He sighed as if heavily put upon. "The things I do for you."

Jake turned on the white noise and set it near the listening device in her dresser lamp.

"You want to fool around?" he asked, shaking his head no.

"I'm exhausted. It's been a really long day. Can we just cuddle?"

"Sure, babe. Whatever you want." Jake carefully opened the door to the bathroom and gently tugged Zara inside.

Once the door was closed, he wrapped her in his arms and whispered in her ear, "I'm sorry."

She hugged him back.

"What are you sorry for? None of this is your fault."

"I just wish you weren't caught up in this." Jake promised, "I'll keep you safe."

44

Zara woke up slowly. Jake's arm was wrapped around her belly, and his warmth snuggled up behind her. His morning erection pushed into her butt. She moaned softly and rolled over.

"Good morning," she whispered. But the sound of the white noise penetrated her consciousness. Someone was listening.

"Hey." Jake's raspy voice tingled over her senses. No way was she having sex with him right now, because what if they heard? She stared into his topaz brown gaze, trying to transmit without words that she was behind him, that she believed him, and that they were not going to let Xavier win.

Jake cupped her face in his hands. The pads of his fingers traced her features.

With tender strokes, as he transmitted right back, *I've got you.*

She stared into his eyes, realizing that this was more than sex, that he'd breached her castle walls and stormed the keep. Her defenses were down.

"You want coffee?" His deep voice rumbled.

"Yeah, that would be great."

He kissed her once softly, then whispered in her ear, "Don't forget they're listening."

She nodded solemnly. She wasn't likely to forget.

Jake tugged on a pair of loose joggers. She admired his broad shoulders, sculpted arms, the long, sexy line of his back. The joggers rode low on his hips, emphasizing his ass. Desire stirred.

Nothing she could do about it now.

She dressed quickly. Even knowing that there were no cameras, only listening devices, she felt naked, raw, exposed.

Her throat tightened, and she swallowed with difficulty. Anxiety balled in her chest as she turned off the white noise. A few minutes later, she wandered downstairs, dressed to go into the office in jeans and a blue sweater that matched her eyes, very consciously aware that she and Jake were not alone.

"Hey," he said. "I was going to bring this upstairs."

She looked at him steadily and mouthed, *I'm going to start yelling at you.*

"Yeah, I'll drink it down here," she replied in a frosty voice.

"What's wrong?" he asked.

"I looked at what was on this drive."

"Okay. And?" Jake sipped his coffee. "How bad could it be?"

"Well, I'm assuming this girl with you in the pictures was your girlfriend." She thought about how hurt she would be if these pictures were real and infused that hurt into her voice.

"I already told you it was no big deal."

"She looks like she's twelve."

"She was over eighteen." His voice was defensive. "I was helping her when she needed a friend."

"A friend? Is that what we're calling ourselves now? Friends?"

"Come on, don't be like that. She wasn't anything."

"So it doesn't mean anything when you have sex with people?"

"Ouch. That's harsh, don't you think?"

"Not really. Did it mean anything when you had sex with me?" She mouthed, *I'm sorry*. But she must have put a little bit too much reality in her voice because there was a crinkle between his brows.

"Of course it did. Don't be like that."

"Yeah, well, maybe I could get past her, but who was the woman who was beat up?"

"Beat up?" She could see Jake's heart pounding hard. "That's crazy. I would never hit a woman."

She knew that but the panic in his voice sounded real.

"I don't know what that's about. And honestly, there's nothing that would tie me to this woman."

There better fucking not be. She wished they could get their hands on the article that was coming out about Adams-Larsen. It would be really nice to know what the journalist had dug up and whether it was true or not and whether Jake was impli-cated. And whether those pictures would be part of it.

"Look, babe, I don't know who that is."

"I think we need to take a break." Her voice wobbled.

Jake set the mug down on the counter with a clatter. "What? Why?"

"I need space right now."

"I *told* you. I didn't have anything to do with this woman." Now his voice was angry. Zara shivered at his harsh tone. "I don't hit women."

"Okay, but I want to know who this woman is, and I still think we should take a break."

"You want a break? Fine." He stomped toward the stairs, brushing her fingers as he walked by, giving her silent reassurance that it was all going to be okay.

She certainly hoped he was right.

45

The plan was to meet at the office.

Jake took a roundabout route back to his apartment to change. Then he left again and then he took the metro three stops to Kita's place. Kita unlocked her car door, and he slid inside so he could hide in the back seat, covered by a blanket.

Jake jolted when her boyfriend, Alex Saunders, got in the car with them.

"Hey, Alex." His voice was muffled from underneath the blanket. "What are you doing here?"

"I don't like what's going on right now, so I'm providing unofficial backup."

Jake was quiet the rest of the ride into the office. Kita pulled in underground, and once they were free of exterior cameras, Jake flipped the blanket off.

Jake had felt a low-level anxiety ever since he'd left Zara's earlier. She should be safe. Marsh was going to pick her up, and he trusted his boss to take good care of her.

But fear wasn't rational, and they could not predict what

Xavier was planning on doing next. When they reached the conference room, Zara was already there.

He didn't care what anyone thought. He grabbed her and gave her a big hug. His disquiet eased as soon as they touched. He took an easy breath for the first time since he left her place.

"Sorry about everything."

"It's all good." She wrapped her arms around his waist and hung on. "I knew you didn't mean it."

Their fight had set off a foreboding within him that he didn't like. His brain knew it was fake, but his heart had been struggling not to freak out.

"Everyone, have a seat." Jill sat at the head of the table, Marsh to her right.

They convened in the conference room to go over next steps. This time, Alex sat at the table.

"I don't like that she's going to Xavier's house." Jake didn't waste any time making his objections known.

"I don't have a choice. We need to act like he's winning, and part of that is going to his house and pretending to fall in line. I already broke up with you."

Zara hadn't seen enough bad things in her life. But Jake had. "I'd prefer you didn't go alone."

"I think going alone will show that I feel comfortable. And that I'm not a threat."

Jillian pulled up a picture of Jake and Layla outside her house.

Jake froze. "What's happening?" They never revealed their clients. And definitely not in such an explicit manner. Last night was one thing, because Jill, Marsh and Jake had known about Layla. And they needed to explain to Zara. But now they were showing these pictures to Kita and Alex?

"We need everyone on the same page."

"This is highly unusual."

"Xavier Rodriguez is a threat. Everyone in this room needs context." Jill gestured to the table at large. "Jake, you go."

Jake said, "This is Layla Habib. She was being stalked by the Iranians after her father was murdered in prison. He was a private investigator who unknowingly did work for the Iranian government, surveilling a dissident Iranian scientist, Dr. Ghorbani."

If Jake hadn't been watching, he would have missed it, but he saw Alex twitch.

Jake put things together at warp speed. Alex, Kita's boyfriend, the US Marshal, who worked in witness protection, recognized the scientist.

"What was that?"

Alex's face was blank.

No one else had seemed to notice Alex's response. Jake stood.

"Saunders, what was that?"

"What are you talking about?" Kita frowned at him.

"Your boyfriend just jolted in surprise."

Alex crossed his arms over his chest. "Were you guys involved with Habib's disappearance?"

Jillian said slowly, "She was in danger, and the US Marshals declined to protect her."

"I'm confused." Zara glanced from person to person, clearly not picking up on the significance of Kita's US Marshal boyfriend recognizing the scientist.

Jake continued, "They believed she had intelligence, pictures, on who had bombed Dr. Ghorbani."

Alex blinked, sat back in his chair. "You relocated Layla Habib," he said slowly.

"Holy shit, he's not dead."

"What?" The room erupted.

Jake said evenly, "Ghorbani's not dead, is he?"

"I can neither confirm nor deny that statement."

Jake's gaze shot to Jill. "You knew."

Jill didn't say a word, but the truth was written all over her face.

"Ghorbani's alive?"

"Irrelevant to our current problem, which is figuring out how our billionaire client got a hold of photos that we know were taken by the Iranians."

Alex's mouth dropped open.

"Did she actually have intelligence about who bombed his house?" Alex asked.

Jake said snidely, "We can neither confirm nor deny."

"Holy shit, she did. What happened to it?"

So many security breaches happening right now. He thought his head would explode.

Jake was pissed at Jill. "We let her believe that her father was partially responsible for Ghorbani's death."

"I didn't have a choice," Jill said.

"We all have choices." Jake shot back. "She's just a kid."

"She's not your sister, Jake," Jill said.

"Fuck, that was low."

"You're right, it was. But you need to get your head on straight. We protected her."

Marsh finally weighed in. "She's safe. Now we need to deal with this new threat."

"This whole thing is crazy. We need to protect Zara."

"We have to figure out how Rodriguez and the Iranians are connected." Jill tried to get the discussion back on track. "Also, are these pictures a fishing attempt to find out if we know where Layla is?"

"Fuck." Alex's phone pinged. He pulled it out of his pocket and stared at the text. "Uh oh."

There was a significant pause. Jake couldn't wait any longer. "What?"

"Mina treated Carolina Rodriguez for a broken arm this morning." Alex rubbed his hand over his face.

Zara pressed a hand to her stomach.

"She told Mina that she slipped on the pool deck."

Everyone in the room knew that wasn't true.

"He's escalating," Jake pointed out the obvious. Who knew what he would do next?

Kita said, "I've got the programs running to flag any social media posts or articles that could demonstrate a tie between the Iranians and Rodriguez. In the meantime, I need to teach Zara how to clone an iPad."

The bottom dropped out of Jake's stomach. "I don't like this."

Marsh gave him a sympathetic look. "Noted. But she's got to go to his house, and we may as well try."

Zara had watched the whole exchange silently.

"It may not work." Kita shrugged. "Besides, nobody's going to suspect the PR person of espionage using tech. She's perfect."

46

<hr>

She was living in a spy novel.

Zara pulled up to the security booth outside of Xavier's mansion in one of the office Honda Accords. She had so many tracking devices on her, it was a wonder the air around her didn't shimmer.

Jake had gone full overkill on making sure she was safe. "Pulling up to the booth now." She rolled down her window.

"Name," the guard said tersely. The guy's muscles had muscles, and he had a thick neck, a shaved head, and an unsmiling mouth.

"Oh, hi." She gave him her best smile, trying to disarm him. "Haven't seen you here before."

No smile. "Name."

"Oh, uh, Zara Cooper? I'm with Adams-Larson Inc." She smiled nervously, hoping that he'd think the nerves were because he was so abrupt. She'd already set the phone on the dashboard and pressed the button. "I do public relations."

Nothing.

"Ah, hopefully it's okay that I told you that." She fluttered her hands. "I mean, you work for him, too."

Hopefully, Kita's program was doing its magic. He was close enough to the car that she should be in range.

The guy said, "Mr. Rodriguez is expecting you."

He handed her an RFID badge. Zara let the badge slip through her fingers, so it dropped outside the car on the ground. "Oh my gosh, I'm so sorry."

As the guy grunted and bent over, he held the iPad in his hand. Hopefully, the logs and data from the device were transferring to her phone.

"Had a little too much wine last night, you know?" She laughed.

It didn't help that she knew everybody could hear what she was saying, which made her even more nervous. They needed time for everything to transfer—a minimum of two minutes.

She needed to distract the guy for a little longer. She wished that she'd been able to put an earpiece in so she could have Jake's voice in her ear, but they decided that that was too dangerous. The guy handed her the RFID badge. This time she held onto it.

"Please clip this to your shirt. Do not take it off."

"Oh great, thank you so much," she said. "You know, the last time I came, I had a driver, so I'm not sure what I'm supposed to do with my car. Can you tell me?"

She leaned out the window, smiling, sort of trying to flirt, but not really. She didn't want to be too obvious.

The guy's face did not crack. "Pull around the fountain and park right off to the side."

"Oh okay, that's great." Fuck, she needed more time. "Um, do I leave my keys in the car or take them with me?"

He nodded. "Leave them."

"Fantastic," she said. "I'm a little early. Is that okay? Do I need to wait until my appointment time?"

"You can go on in, ma'am."

Crap, she needed a few more seconds.

A catering van parked off to the side caught her eye. "Oh, are they having a party? I'm always on the lookout for new vendors to use. I'll have to ask Mrs. Rodriguez what she thinks of that company."

"You need to move along through the gate and park now, ma'am."

"Sure, sure, thank you. Have a great day!" she said gaily.

Zara carefully refastened her seat belt, tilted her head, and smiled at the guard and waved. He used a 'get moving' gesture, and she knew she had to go. Hopefully, it had worked.

As she drove around the fountain, she murmured, "Guy was less than friendly, as I'm sure you all heard, but I think we got it." She put the car in park in the same spot that Jake had parked the other day and left her keys in the ignition.

"There's a catering van here. District Catering." She rattled off the license plate number.

"Not sure if that's important, but all information is knowledge that can potentially be used, right?"

She laughed nervously. "Hopefully nobody's paying attention to the fact that I'm sitting in the car talking to myself."

Zara took a deep breath, looked at her phone and sighed. They'd gotten the logs. Now it needed to be transmitted to the office. "All right, I'm leaving my phone in the car so this can send to you, Kita."

She set the phone in the console, looked around the car to make sure she wasn't missing anything else and took a deep breath. "I'm ready."

She could hear Jake's voice in her head telling her to act normal and don't worry. It's just a meeting. He wasn't going to let Xavier hurt her.

She hoped he was right.

Jake sat in one of the office Hondas around the corner.

He'd followed Zara at a discreet distance. He wanted to be close in case there were any issues. The worst thing was he was still too far away.

He jiggled his leg, his heart jittering. He hated this.

Jill was on the other side of the mansion and down the street, so she'd be able to monitor the comings and goings from the guard gate.

"Got the logs," Kita's voice crowed over his comms. She was back at the office, working her magic. "I'll start searching for anything."

"Run a check on that catering company," Jake said. "It's a little weird that they're there this early in the morning."

It was barely 6:30 AM.

"Will do," Kita said.

Jake sighed heavily.

"She's going to be fine," Jill said. "She's got a backbone of steel, and I have confidence in her."

"She isn't used to covert missions. What if she gives something away?"

"Your girl knows how to spin things and she's quick on her feet. She'll be fine." Marsh was also listening in from the office. He was trying to reassure Jake. But Jake wouldn't feel better until she was back in her office and in his arms.

Once she returned to the office, she was going to have to craft a press release regarding the article in the paper. Fortunately, it was mostly suspicion and innuendo. He was surprised they'd run the piece. There hadn't been anything about the sex worker and Jake, which had been his main concern. Or the disappearance of Layla. But he had to assume that neither the Iranians nor Rodriguez wanted a spotlight on the missing woman.

He hoped she was all right. Jake's cell phone rang. Shit was never good when your phone rang this early.

He looked at the screen. "I have to take this. It's my mom's assisted living facility."

"We've got her. Go ahead."

Jake answered the call quickly and listened to the nurse on the other end. "Mr. Brown, your mom has a visitor, and she seems to be very agitated."

A visitor this early in the morning? "How did he get in?" His heart iced.

"I'm not really sure. Normally, we don't have visitors this time of day, but as you know, family is allowed anytime."

"We don't have any other family. It's just me and my mom."

"Oh dear, he said he was your brother-in-law."

"What? My sister's dead." Jake had a bad feeling. "What does he look like?"

"He's a tall White man, dark hair parted on the side, blue eyes, looks like his nose was broken. Dressed nicely, in a navy suit with a blue button-down shirt."

That could be anyone. Could Xavier have gone after his mom? Not content to smear Jake? That seemed excessive since as far as Xavier knew, he had neutralized Jake.

"What did he say his name was?"

"Let me look." She consulted the logs. "Edward."

Fuck. Drayton was at his mom's assisted living.

He spoke to the nurse. "We have a restraining order against the man." Jake had filed it as a precaution the day Drayton had been released. He never actually thought they would need it.

Jake's heart thudded hard. He needed to protect his mother, but Zara was counting on him.

Jake muted his phone and spoke to his teammates. "Drayton is at my mom's assisted living facility. I need to go deal with this."

"Don't worry about it, Jake."

"We've got this. She should be fine. Go take care of your mother," Jillian said.

Still, he couldn't let go of the feeling that he was abandoning Zara when she needed him.

"We got this," Marsh repeated. "I'll head out and take your cover spot."

Jake's tension eased a little.

Jake unmuted the phone and said, "Call the police. I'm on my way."

"Thank you, Mr. Brown. So sorry to bother you." Jake hung up.

Zara would be okay. She had to be, right? God, he wished he'd been able to talk to her before he abandoned her. He quickly sent Zara a text. What a shitty way to leave her.

Fuck, there was no good solution here.

He raced away from his surveillance spot towards his mother's assisted living. He couldn't leave his mother with Drayton. He didn't want to leave Zara with Xavier.

It was his worst nightmare.

47

———

*D*rayton *is with my mother. I have to go.*

Jake's text came through right as she was about to get out of the car.

Of course you do. She texted back, her hand trembling. *Go take care of your mom. I'll be fine.* She set her phone in the middle console. She'd brought along one of Jake's comics, with a picture of Luke Cage bursting out of a graphic of fire. She dragged her finger over the illustration for good luck.

He had to take care of his mom. He'd never forgive himself if something happened to her. She knew that. But disappointment rolled through her, and her heart sunk.

In the back of her mind, she'd taken reassurance that Jake was around the corner, which was silly. There were several hurdles to get through the guard gate anyway. Of course he needed to make sure his mom was okay, but the timing couldn't have been worse.

She left the keys in the car and headed to the front door, carrying her portfolio with her. The doorbell played a long chiming song.

Zara clutched her portfolio to her chest and waited for the maid to answer.

A few minutes later, Carolina Rodriguez, instead of a maid, opened the door. She was perfectly put together in another demure skirt and twin set, but the sling with the cast on her left arm and the deep shadows beneath her eyes told a different story.

"Good morning, Carolina." Zara breezed in, pretending that everything was fine. She couldn't afford to fuck this up and she couldn't afford to let Rodriguez know that they were working against him.

She had to pretend like everything was normal.

Carolina said softly, "Good morning. If you'll come into the study, Xavier will be down momentarily."

Zara followed Carolina slowly.

The house felt emptier than normal. Where were the other servants? Maybe they came later in the day?

"Did you want any tea or coffee?" Carolina's fingers trembled. She squeezed them shut in a fist and tucked her hand by her side.

"No, thank you," Zara said quietly. "I'm good."

She pulled out the updated plan for Xavier and handed Carolina a copy. Zara took off her coat and laid it across the chair.

"What happened there?" She gestured to Carolina's cast.

"Oh, clumsy me. I slipped on the pool deck and when I put my hand out to break my fall, I broke my arm instead."

"Ouch. You poor thing." Zara rubbed her right forearm. She didn't give away that she knew that Xavier had broken her arm. "I had a broken arm in high school, and it hurt like heck."

Xavier walked in a few minutes later. His hair was perfectly styled and he wore a bespoke suit and Italian leather shoes.

"Ready for a big day on the Hill?" Zara smiled brightly.

He frowned at her. "Of course."

He eyed Carolina angrily. "Why didn't you offer our guest anything to drink?"

"Oh, no, I'm fine," Zara said. "I already had a cup of coffee at home." Which if he was listening to her, he would know because she had talked to herself while making the cup, self-consciously thinking about the fact that she was being listened to.

"I trust that you found the information I gave you enlightening."

Zara grimaced, unsure whether she should look sad or upset. How would she feel if the information had been true? "Um, yeah, thank you for that. I had no idea."

"I am happy to hear that Mr. Brown will no longer be a problem."

Carolina's gaze shot to Xavier. Huh. So she knew about Jake?

"Um, yeah, we're taking a break," Zara said.

Xavier barked at Carolina. "Get the tea tray."

Carolina jumped.

Zara was having a hard time ignoring his demeanor. The polish that normally covered him and his actions was non-existent. Worse, he didn't seem to care.

Zara didn't like that he'd completely dropped the charming, suave act.

"As you wish," Carolina said quietly.

After Carolina left, Zara handed Xavier the new schedule. "Spent a lot of time on this looking for things that I think will really help position you well."

Xavier barely glanced at it, watching the door impatiently until Carolina rolled a tea cart in through another door.

"There are strangers in the kitchen." Carolina's brow crimped.

"That's none of your concern."

Carolina said, "They weren't wearing badges. Everyone wears a badge here. Everyone. Even our employees have a badge on so Xavier can track where they've been and where they're going and make sure they don't go into any unauthorized rooms."

Zara needed to remember that if she ever came back. No snooping.

Xavier gestured to the tea cart. "Have some tea."

"Oh, no, thank you. I'm not really a tea drinker," Zara said perkily. "You seem a little on edge." She couldn't pretend any longer that he was acting normally. "Is everything okay?"

She knew that Kita, Jillian, and Marsh were listening in on everything that was happening right now, but she couldn't shake the concern icing her veins. Something was really off.

"I said, drink the tea." His voice was hard, his eyes like chips of brown dirt.

"I'm not sure what's going on here, but I prefer not to drink the tea."

"Drink the fucking tea, or I'll pour it down your throat."

Carolina gasped. "Xavier!"

"You, too, *mi amor*," he snarled.

Holy shit, what was happening right now? Xavier Rodriguez had gone over the edge.

"Look, if it's about the article in today's paper, I haven't had a chance to read it, but I assure you that the other branch of Adams-Larsen has nothing to do with the office that I run."

"I don't give a fuck about the article in the paper."

"Okay," Zara said slowly. "Then I'm very confused."

"Drink your fucking tea."

Zara took a sip, but as soon as he turned his head, she spit most of the liquid back out, hoping that he wouldn't notice.

"You, too, Carolina."

A few things were adding up quickly, and Zara didn't like them. No maid answered the door. The strange catering van in front of the house. The strangers in their kitchen.

"What's in the tea, Congressman Rodriguez?" She couldn't control the trembling that overtook her body.

He ignored her.

"What's your plan here?"

"You know, I get threats all the time."

The non sequitur threw her for a moment. "Okay."

"Threats against me, threats against my family, threats against my lovely wife."

Zara certainly didn't like the direction this conversation was taking. "And?"

"In a very sad day for the Rodriguez family, my darling wife has been kidnapped. I am distraught."

Carolina gasped and ran for the door, except she'd had more of the tea than Zara.

Her movements were clumsy. Before she made it halfway across the room, she fell, her feet tangled up in each other. She put out her arms to catch her fall. Carolina let out a long moan as her casted arm bounced off the hardwood.

Carolina lay on the floor, barely moving, trying to claw her way to the door.

Zara tried to jump up. "Did you drug your wife?" The words came out slowly as if she were talking underwater. The vision of Xavier wavered, her eyes unable to focus, everything blurry and distorted.

Crap, he didn't only drug his wife.

"Help," she whispered, praying the all the tech on her body picked it up and sent out an SOS.

That was the last thing she remembered.

48

———

Jake arrived at the facility, parked illegally in front, and ran into the building. The cops pulled up right behind him. Jake sprinted toward his mother's room. He burst inside. His mother was sitting in her wheelchair, tears running down her face.

Edward Drayton stood between him and his mother, shock on his face.

"What are you doing here?" Jake snarled. Drayton looked small. Prison had not been kind to him.

"Look, don't hurt me. Don't hurt me." He held out his hands up in supplication. "I came to say I'm sorry."

"Then why is she crying?" Jake said.

"I brought up Cia, and she started crying." Drayton looked sincere. "I didn't intend to upset her. I was just trying to say I was sorry."

Jake's shoulders bunched. His hands clenched into fists.

Drayton flinched. "Don't hit me."

"I'm not going to hit you," he said with complete annoyance.

"With your track record, I felt it needed to be said." Drayton appeared to relax.

"Momma, you okay?"

"Jacob, why is he here?"

Jake grimaced. He'd been trying to figure out how to tell his mother that Drayton was out of prison. He would have never imagined that the asshole would go to see his mother. "He was released on good behavior."

"Oh dear Lord, while my baby's in heaven, he's out?"

"Yeah, Momma."

The police burst into the room. "Hands in the air. Lay down on the ground."

Jake held his hands high in the air. "I'm not the one you want. We called about this guy." He pointed to Drayton.

"Weapon," one of the cops said.

"I have a permit to carry."

"Down on the ground! Lay flat! Put your hands behind your head!" They shouted orders at him. At *him*, not Drayton.

Fuck, he didn't have time for this.

In his ear, he'd been listening to Zara chat with Carolina. He could hear Xavier insisting that Zara drink the tea. What the fuck was that about?

"Sir, get down on the ground."

Jake put his hands behind his ears and said again, "Look, this man came into my mother's room without authorization, and we have a restraining order against him."

"Get down on the ground." The cops were yelling at him, and he could hear Zara's voice in his ear insisting that she didn't want tea. What the hell was going on?

"What are you doing to my boy?" his mother cried.

"We got a call about a restraining order."

Jake lay on the ground and gritted his teeth. "Yeah, the

White guy is the one with the restraining order. He killed my sister."

"Stay there while we check out your story."

Jake knew resisting wasn't going to help him. So he very carefully laid down on the floor. "Check with the staff. I told them to call you. She's my mother."

One cop held a gun on him while the other one went to check. Drayton, the asshole, kept quiet.

"Who are you?" the cop finally asked Drayton.

"Look, I don't want any trouble. I…I wanted to apologize."

Jake snorted.

He was barely listening to Drayton babble on about forgiveness and finding Jesus.

Jake knew Drayton couldn't afford to get in any trouble, or he'd be back in jail. At the moment, that was the only silver lining Jake could see. But then he heard Zara fall and her whispered *help*.

Fuck, he needed to get out of here.

49

———

Zara woke up slowly, lying on a cold hard floor, her cheek pressed against frigid metal.

Her head hurt. She went to press her hand to her forehead and realized that her wrists were cuffed together with those plastic zip ties from the hardware store.

What the hell? She was lying on her side, her brain fuzzy as she tried to remember what happened.

She was moving. The van, she was in that stupid catering van. She had known it was weird for it to be at the house so early. Zara's heart rate sped up.

The metal floor was hard, and the van had no actual catering supplies in it. The whole thing had been a ruse. The scent of pepper and honey lingered in the air, as if they'd eaten their breakfast while they were waiting to abduct them.

A soft groan sounded next to her. She turned her head.

Carolina Rodriguez lay next to her, still unconscious, hands also zip tied, a gag in her mouth. That's when Zara realized she had a cloth in her mouth and tape over it.

Shit, they'd been kidnapped.

Zara tried to think, but it was like swimming through sludge. What had happened? Something about tea.

Xavier had insisted that they drink the tea. Zara had barely had any. Crap, it had drugs in it. Must have been a crazy amount.

Don't panic, don't panic. Adams-Larsen would be tracking her. They were probably listening to the whole thing.

Jake would be coming for her.

Wait, no, Jake had left to go take care of his mother.

It was okay, Jillian, Marsh and Kita would be coming. She tried to convince herself.

There was no way Jake would leave her hanging. He would come as soon as he heard. He would be come for her.

She mentally kept repeating that mantra. Jake would be coming for her, for them. They were probably following them right now and as soon as the van stopped, they would storm in and rescue them.

They weren't going to let Xavier get away with this.

But she couldn't stop the worry spiraling in her head. He was a billionaire.

There would be a record of the kidnappers, of her, going in to the Rodriguez house.

She tried to slow her breathing. Panicking would help nothing. She thought about Jake, thought about the last few days.

If something happened to her, he would never forgive himself. Even though there was no way he could have foreseen Xavier kidnapping them.

They were tracking her. Right? They were. They had to be.

Carolina blinked her eyes, waking up in a panic.

Zara tried to transmit to Carolina that it would be okay. But the other woman was beyond consoling. Her wide dark eyes were filled with terror as she frantically tried to pull off the tape.

Zara rubbed her cheek against her shoulder, trying to get the tape off. They had cuffed her hands in front of her. It started to come off, and she was able to use her fingers to peel it the rest of the way.

"Shh," she whispered. "Are you okay?"

Carolina shook her head.

No. Okay. Okay.

"We're going to be okay. It's going to be okay," Zara repeated the words to Carolina.

Carolina finally was able to get her tape off.

"They are going to kill us," Carolina whispered.

Zara reached for her ear and realized the earrings that transmitted what was happening were gone. Shit.

She touched the front of her blouse where they'd attached the button bug. The button was gone, too. She'd lost communication with everyone.

Her shoe!

Zara wiggled her toes, but her shoes were gone, too. "It's going to be okay."

"How?" Carolina cried softly.

Zara said, "I don't know yet. But my team has been looking at ways to get your husband." She tried to reassure the woman.

All the while, her own heart thundered in her chest, because would ALIAS really be able to save them? She didn't know.

"Look, play along, and we'll figure out a plan."

"He's going to have us killed." Carolina whimpered.

"You don't know that."

"He's been threatening me for a while. I've been trying to get an exit plan in place, but it's hard." Tears ran down

Carolina's face. "Yesterday, he found my secret bank account."

"That's why he broke your arm?"

Carolina nodded. "He's been under a lot of stress."

Thank God, Zara had gotten herself out of the relationship with David. She studied Carolina. That could have been Zara in a few years if she hadn't finally put herself first and left David.

"You know that if it wasn't stress, it would be another excuse to abuse you." Zara wanted to sob.

"You don't understand."

"I have a better idea than you might think." That was as close as she could come to admitting her own history with abuse.

"I was trapped." Carolina snuffled. "He threatened to keep me from the girls."

"And he had all the power."

Carolina nodded. "I know you wanted to help me. But he listened in on my phone conversations."

"I would have helped you." Zara couldn't help but feel like she'd failed Carolina. But they had bigger problems at the moment. "So why now?"

"I don't know." Carolina rested her head on the cold metal staring at nothing. "I complied."

Zara, too. And look where that got them.

The van had been moving at a steady pace since Zara woke up, so they must be on the highway, which meant they could be going anywhere. But she had no idea how long she was out. They could be in Virginia, Maryland, or even headed towards New York.

Don't panic, don't panic. She thought about the lessons that Jake had taught her.

"Who are they?" Zara needed information.

"I don't know."

"What did they look like?"

"Dark skin, short curly hair, beards, dark eyes. One guy had a traditional scarf around his head," Carolina said. "They looked angry."

Xavier wouldn't have used the Iranians to abduct them, would he? That was a reach.

"Had you ever seen them before?"

"Yes, they were at the house a few months ago."

"Okay, we need to figure out what his endgame is here."

"His endgame is to kill us." Carolina's lashes clumped together. "My poor babies."

The men up front spoke in low tones, too indistinct to hear the words. Zara leaned closer to Carolina.

"What language are they speaking?"

"I'm not sure. It might be Farsi." Carolina listened, closing her eyes and scrunching up her face. "But I can't make out what they're saying."

"Wait, you speak Farsi?"

Carolina nodded. "I speak five languages, Spanish, English, French, Arabic, and Farsi."

Zara thought for a minute. How could they use this? "So you could actually communicate with them if they will talk to us."

Carolina gave a slow nod.

"All right, we need to think. What else do we know about these people?"

"They work for my husband. They're not going to betray him."

Zara's brain was racing. "We need to see if we can turn that around. We need to spin it so they start to lack faith in Xavier."

"You don't understand his reach, and you don't understand his power if you think that will work."

"All we have to do is create uncertainty." Zara heard Jake's voice in her head, admiring her ability to spin anything. "We can do this. We can at least slow them down."

And then Adams-Larsen could swoop in and rescue them.

"What do you need me to do?"

"Okay, this is our plan." Zara whispered to her quickly and just in time. "We're gonna need to convince them that Xavier is going to double cross them."

The van jerked to a halt.

"I'm gonna need you to translate for me."

Carolina nodded. "Okay."

"Trust me."

Zara knew she needed to trust herself as well.

The men got out and slammed their doors closed. Zara listened intently, heard the squawk of seagulls, the low, mournful blow of a foghorn, various clanging sounds.

"I think we're near the water."

The smell of fish lingered in the air. The crank of a metal door rolling up hit their ears.

The men got back in the van, drove into a dark interior, and killed the engine. The metal clanking indicated they were closing the door of the warehouse or whatever it was.

Hope blossomed in her chest.

Okay this could be it. When Adams-Larsen swooped in and saved them. Right?

Zara waited. But no one came.

They were on their own.

50

H e needed to get out of here!

Jake lost valuable time while the cops confirmed his story, and the nurse convinced them that he wasn't the threat. Damn. Normally their automatic assumption that the Black man in the room was the threat would fuel a rage within him, but all he could think was he needed to get to Zara. Panic jittered through him.

"I need to go. I have an emergency." Jake hugged his mother. "Momma, I'll be back but I've got to go."

He could hear Kita and Jill in his ear. Jill had lost the van. The assumption was they'd taken the sign off the side. Kita was trying to get into traffic cams to see if she could pick it up remotely.

They hadn't heard from Zara in at least thirty minutes. His heart was beating out of his chest.

"How could Xavier be so bold as to kidnap them from his own house?" What in the hell was going on?

"Jake, what's happening on your end?"

"Cops finally let me go. I should be there soon." He

clenched his fists, impotence hollowing out his chest. "Fuck. How could I not be there when she needed me?"

Kita said, "Get your head in the game, Jake. She needs you now."

"It's not a fucking game, Kita," he snarled. "Were you able to comb through any of the data on that iPad? Where are the men from? She said the name District Catering."

Kita said, "Yeah, bad news there. District Catering went out of business, so it was fake."

"Not a surprise," Jill murmured.

"Okay, what other information do you have about drivers from the log on the iPad? Even if they're fake names, we can follow up on that."

Total silence.

"What?" Jake said. "What aren't you telling me?"

"Yeah, when I looked at the log, there's no record of a catering van going into Xavier's compound."

No record. "He doesn't want anyone to know in case the cops impound his logs."

"That would be my guess," Kita said softly.

"What about tracking her? Do we have an approximate location?"

More silence.

"What? You're killing me here, Kita."

"All her comms are offline, and we lost a signal on the tracker we put on the back of her neck. It pings off Bluetooth."

His heart stopped. "You don't think she's..." God, he couldn't even say the words aloud.

"No, we don't think she's dead."

Jake nearly collapsed with relief. He had to hold onto that thought. They didn't think she was dead. She couldn't be dead. He couldn't lose her.

"I think something else is going on here. But clearly, they found our listening devices. I cut off the ones connected to Zara, so they can't hear us if they are somehow monitoring them."

"When they took them off her, they were speaking a foreign language." Jill spoke up.

"Was it Farsi?"

Marsh said, "Not sure. Could have been Dari or Tajik."

So, someone from Iran, Afghanistan or Tajikistan but making assumptions only led to trouble if it was incorrect. "We can't assume it's the Iranians."

"What was her last known position?"

"Right outside of Xavier's compound. That's when we lost the Bluetooth. If they turned off their phones, there wouldn't be anything to transmit the signal." Kita explained.

"If someone near her turns on a phone, it could transmit the signal?"

"It's possible." Kita agreed. "It's also possible that they're blocking the transmission. I don't know. I'm keeping an eye on it."

"I can't…" The words balled in Jake's throat. "I can't let anything happen to her."

"I'll let you know the moment it comes back online," Kita spoke softly.

"Fuck!" Jake screamed the word, throwing back his head and shouting from the pit of his stomach into the void in his car.

Sweat formed on his forehead. "I can't lose her."

"We know," Jill said. "We're working on it. Come back to the office, and we'll go over what we've got."

"Why now? Why today?" Jake said. "He thought we were complying, that Zara was bending to his will."

"You probably haven't looked at the papers, but the FBI announced that they had identified suspects and put BOLOs out for the two Iranians who were responsible for the bomb at Dr. Ghorbani's house."

"What does that have to do with Zara?"

"We haven't put that together," Jillian said. "Maybe he's worried that they will find a link between the Iranians and him? They probably thought they were in the clear since it happened months ago."

"Maybe... but why *today*?"

"Well, the good news is that the article about Adams-Larsen was bumped back to an obscure little spot buried in the middle of the paper because the identification of the Iranians was a bigger deal."

"Did he think the media would be too busy dealing with that to make this a priority? But the kidnapping of a US Congressman's spouse would still be a pretty big fucking deal."

"We'll work on getting Zara back, then we'll figure out why."

Marsh broke into their conversation.

"Xavier's called a press conference."

51

Xavier Rodriguez was an excellent actor.

Jake got to the office as the press conference started. He slid into a chair.

He didn't want to be here. But wandering around D.C. looking for Zara wasn't a logical plan. Fuck.

Maria handed him a cookie and Kita gave him a cup of coffee.

He didn't need any more caffeine. Adrenaline had dumped in his bloodstream, churning around like a whirlpool and pulling him under.

"Anything?"

Kita shook her head.

He'd been in contact the entire ride back to ALIAS, so he knew there was nothing new, but he'd had to ask. As if somehow in his journey between the garage and the conference room, they'd found her.

Jake tossed the cookie on the table. He couldn't eat.

Xavier appeared rattled, his hands shaking, deep grooves on the side of his mouth. If Jake didn't know any better, he would have believed the desperate fear radiating off the man.

He was flanked by several aides and a member of the Capitol Police. "When I arrived on the Hill this morning to start my day, I received a call from the police department that shots were fired at my residence."

Xavier paused, took a breath. "My wife has been kidnapped. As of yet, we have not received a ransom note."

Sweat lined the man's forehead. Jake sat up.

"What about Zara? Why didn't he mention Zara?" Panic thrummed through his body on all frequencies.

Jill's gray eyes were narrowed.

What was happening?

"The perpetrators shot and killed our security guard at the gate. The kidnappers used a white van, but that's all the information we have at this time. Only a partial license plate was captured by security cameras."

Xavier bowed his head for a moment, then looked directly into the camera.

"Please, I'm begging you, whoever took her, return her. Don't destroy my family. Maybe you have an issue with me, but don't take it out on my wife."

Reporters tried to ask questions.

"Don't deprive my children of their mother."

The Capitol Police captain stepped up to the microphone and began speaking. "We have very little details at this time. A white van apparently approached the guard gate, shot and killed the security guard, and then accessed the house. Unfortunately, the kidnappers erased the security tapes after they arrived. No one saw Mrs. Rodriguez get put in the van. However, there were signs of a struggle their home."

"Fortunately, the children were upstairs with their nanny and didn't hear a thing. We have a partial plate number captured from a street camera." He rattled off the letters and numbers. "We are asking anyone with information to call this number, 888-555-1212. Any and all tips would be appreciated. Our goal is to recover Mrs. Rodriguez safely."

The press conference ended, but as Xavier was being led out, he called, "Please don't hurt her."

Jill muted the TV. "Nice performance."

Kita said what they were all thinking. "They didn't make any mention of Zara. Not a good sign."

"What about her car?" She'd driven to Xavier's in one of their Hondas. They had tracking devices like the ones the rental car companies used in all their cars.

Kita pulled up the location of Zara's car. "It's not at the house anymore."

What if they'd killed Zara and left her in the car? What if she was trapped in the trunk? "They wouldn't have left her alive. She can tell the authorities that Xavier was involved."

His chest hollowed out and the numb blankness of static filled his head. Zara couldn't be dead.

"Found the car." Kita rubbed her hand over her mouth. "It's at the Navy Yard."

The Navy Yard was an entertainment complex for the Nationals baseball stadium and the Museum of the US Navy. The park was along the Anacostia Riverwalk Trail and was pretty busy during the summer, but this time of day, it would be deserted.

Jake put his head in his hands. He needed to think. "Is anyone near there?"

"Marsh can go." Jill reached out as if to touch Jake and then pulled back her hand.

She couldn't be dead. She couldn't.

Marsh hadn't come back to the office, so he was closest. "On it."

"We need to get to Xavier. He knows who took them. He

knows where they are." Jake couldn't stop the fear flooding his body. "He's the only one who can help us."

"Xavier is going to be surrounded by security," Jill said.

"I have to operate on the assumption that she is alive and with Carolina Rodriguez. No other option is acceptable." His heart thumped in his chest hard.

Kita said, "Zara may still have her tracker on. We need her to get into range of a Bluetooth, and it should ping."

Jake began to pace with jerky movements.

"I'm monitoring the frequency, and I've got multiple alarms set if it goes off."

"But what do we do in the meantime? I can't just wait around."

"Jake—"

"We need to talk to Xavier."

Jill and Kita looked at each other. "Not a good idea."

"We need to go to his house," Jake said desperately. "And get him to talk."

"Jake," Jill said gently. "You can't go to his house. He thinks you're suspended. And if you go, it's highly likely he'd accuse you of kidnapping his wife to get back at him."

"She's my girlfriend." She was so much more than that. Such a weak word for how he felt about her. He'd dedicated his whole life to protecting people, mostly strangers. When her life was on the line, he couldn't fail the person who meant the most to him. "I can't just sit around and do nothing."

"I understand that, but technically you're a private citizen. You cannot go to his house."

"The security around him will be insane right now," Kita piped up.

"Let me go with you in the car. Let me at least be there in case we get intelligence, please." Jake begged. If they wouldn't let him go, then he'd go on his own.

"He'll just go without us." Marsh got it.

Jake nodded.

"But you can't go running in halfcocked," Marsh finished. "I'm almost at the Navy Yard."

"We know he is willing to kill innocent people," Jake rebutted. *Please let Zara be okay.*

Kita nodded. "That's cold. He killed the security guard who was in on it."

Jake had also put that together. "The van was already there when Zara arrived. The security guard didn't put them in the system and erased their entrance into the compound, which means that he was in on it or that he'd been directed by Rodriguez not to record the van."

Jill had written down the partial license plate number the authorities said they got from the security footage. "Look, that number is different than the one that Zara gave us."

"The security tapes were wiped. No license plate. There are thousands of white delivery vans in the D.C. metro area. Without the full plate, it could take forever to find that van."

"Could we give the police the plate number?" Jake grasped. "Can we say that Zara was at the house?"

"They transposed a couple of the numbers, and one is missing. No plate on the front, so when they left the compound, nothing was visible."

Jake drew in a shaky breath. "We need to find her."

"Ninety-nine percent of all kidnapping victims are returned," Kita said.

"One percent doesn't return. Zara can't be one of the one percent."

"Her odds are good."

"But not guaranteed." Jake didn't want to be that gloom and doom person, but this was Zara. "We need to get to

Xavier, and we need to find out where they are. He knows. He knows what's happening."

Jillian said, "All right. I'll go to his house. Jake, you're with me, but you stay in the car. Kita, stay here and continue to monitor things. Keep combing through those logs so that we can find out any connections, anything that is suspicious."

"Marsh, we'll wait to hear from you."

"Hurry," Jake implored.

Please don't let her be dead.

52

———————

Shit. This was it.

The back of the van squealed opened. The two men grabbed their ankles and yanked, bumping them along the bottom of the hard metal surface. Carolina cried out.

"What are you doing? Where are you taking us? What's happening?" Zara shot questions at the two men—who weren't wearing masks.

Not a good sign. They didn't care if she and Carolina could identify them.

It got even worse when they pulled her into the light, and she saw their faces. She gasped.

The paper this morning had been all about the two men who were wanted in connection with the bombing of the Iranian scientist, Dr. Ghorbani. These two men.

They were in trouble.

"Shut up." The guy backhanded Zara across the face, hitting her mouth.

The shock of the blow immobilized her, as the punch reverberated through her head. Her vision wavered in the dim lighting, as the violence threw her back to when David hit her.

Metallic taste of blood filled her mouth, and her cheek began to swell.

No fucking way was she going to lie down and take this.

She surreptitiously looked around. They were in some sort of single-story warehouse. To the right of the van was a mostly bare office, surrounded by a half wall of bricks and topped with glass windows, presumably so the boss could see what the workers were doing. The building appeared to be deserted. The office had a large wooden desk and an office chair. No phone or computer or file cabinets that she could see, and a single naked fluorescent light bulb that flickered, about to burn out. The rest of the warehouse was empty except for a pair of folding chairs deep in the back. The musty smell of disuse hung in the air.

"Can you please tell us what's happening?"

The two men dragged them toward the chairs.

One guy wore a traditional keffiyeh in black and white check, round cheeks, mouth tilted up in a small smile, and a trimmed beard with threads of grey. The other guy was thinner, his head uncovered, his beard long and scraggly, and his black eyes glittered with anger.

Good soldier, bad soldier. Were they playing them? Her cheek throbbed where the angry guy had hit her.

The good soldier frowned and said something softly to his partner. He gestured to Zara and Carolina. "Come, sit."

They tied her and Carolina to chairs, arms behind their backs and zip tied each ankle to the chair legs.

"Please," Carolina said softly. "Help us."

The angry soldier snorted, said something to the other one in the foreign language. Carolina's face blanched.

"What did he say?" Zara whispered as they walked away.

"You don't want to know."

The good soldier turned on his cell phone, looked to see if

he had any calls and then turned it off. They spoke softly near the van.

"It has to be a good sign that they didn't kill us outright. Yes?" Was she grasping at straws? Maybe.

"I don't know."

"What do you think is happening?" Zara whispered.

"They're waiting for a call."

"Do you think from Xavier?" Zara tried to quell the panic buzzing through her.

"I don't know."

"He clearly had to be in on it. He knew they were in your kitchen."

"Excuse me, excuse me." Zara called to them. She had to do something now.

The angry one turned his evil eye on her. She swallowed, gulped.

Shit, hopefully this didn't backfire. "Can you talk to them in their language?"

Carolina nodded. "Is this a good idea?"

"It's the only one I've got. And we don't want anything lost in translation." Zara said grimly, "Tell them they can't trust Xavier."

She repeated Zara's statement in Farsi.

For a minute they appeared shocked that Carolina knew their language.

"He's setting you up to take the fall." Carolina continued to repeat Zara's words.

The angry one rolled his eyes, but the nicer one studied them.

"I know how he operates. He silences his opponents, then commits violence by using patsies to do it, and then blames the patsy." Carolina continued to translate. "You're going to get caught up in whatever's happening and he's going to get away with it. You're the patsies."

The angry one shot something back.

"What did he say?" Zara said.

"He said, then we will get revenge on him."

"Hard to do if you're in a cell," Zara said. "I bet every cop in D.C. is looking for you right now because of the news."

The angry one just snuffled and stomped away, but the nicer one turned on his phone again. His phone beeped four or five times in a row. The same noise that Zara's phone made when she got a news update.

The guy's eyes widened. He held up his phone and started talking to his partner, fast, furious.

"What's he saying?"

Carolina said, "He's speaking too quickly. Something about the news and their pictures."

Zara's stomach sloshed. Remnants of the drug were making her nauseous, and her face throbbed.

Zara knew she was right about what was going to happen. Part of her was sorry she was right, but once they had started looking at the people who Xavier had exposed in the past, there was a clear pattern. His employees did something that hurt his opponents, he pretended that he had nothing to do with it, pretended to be shocked by their actions, then he silenced them and discredited them. They got all the blame, and he got the benefit of whatever they'd done.

The nice one continued to jabber at his partner.

"Look, you could let us go. Just drive away. We won't tell anyone what you look like."

The nice one shook his head. "We can't do that," he said in accented English.

"Why not?" she asked.

"Because our government will kill us if we don't do what they ask."

"So he is working with your government to kidnap us?" Xavier *was* in bed with the Iranians. Wow, they'd all been conned.

Zara asked Carolina. "Did you have any idea that your husband was a traitor?"

The angry one laughed and stalked toward them. "How do you say? The joke is on him." He leaned close to them. "We were supposed to kill you right away. But now we have leverage."

Was this good or bad for Zara and Carolina?

Zara had no idea.

"Our government wants information from him. If he doesn't give it to them, we are going to let the world know that he was behind your abduction." They laughed as if they had been the engineer of this cluster.

In all the scenarios she could game out, these guys were going to be sacrificed.

"Do you have families?"

They looked at each other, and then at her, nodding slowly.

"You realize that you are the ones who are going to be blamed for everything."

Carolina translated slowly, studying Zara.

"What are you talking about, foolish woman?"

"Once they get what they want, they're going to kill us and you. Then blame you for everything. Deny any knowledge of your actions."

Their precarious position was dawning on them.

"How are you supposed to kill us?" Zara asked urgently.

They looked at each other, and at the van. The nice one made an explosive noise and gesture with his hands.

Bomb? There was a bomb? In this warehouse?

Shit.

"My boss has a contact at the CIA who could help you." Shit, she better hope Jillian could come through on this. "If you kill us, you're either going to be dead or in prison."

Carolina stared at her. "I thought you did public relations."

"I do. But in this town, everyone has contacts. And my boss used to be in law enforcement."

The two Iranians talked between the two of them. Finally, the nice one asked, "How?"

"If you're willing to share with the CIA certain details about Dr. Ghorbani's bomb and why you wanted him dead, they'll help you."

They held up their hands and then went to huddle by the van.

"Do you think they'll listen?"

"I had to try."

"Talking to the CIA won't help our families." The nice one made a slashing gesture with his hand. "You will be dead as soon as we get what we want."

"What is he paying you?" Zara couldn't pull in enough breath, her head spinning and her vision went white. She didn't want to die. She had way too much to live for. "My family has money. They can pay you more." She had no idea if that was true, but she had to try. "Please," she gasped.

The formerly nice one grabbed duct tape and angrily slapped it over her mouth, then Carolina's.

The angry one turned on his phone. He dialed a number and put it on speaker phone.

"What are you doing calling me? I'm in the car heading home." Xavier's voice came over the line. "Luckily, I'm alone."

They listened to him breathe heavily.

"The FBI is going to be monitoring my devices. You can't call this number again. Is it done?"

The angry one spoke. "Not yet."

"What are you waiting for?"

Carolina huddled closer to Zara.

Please, please let ALIAS find them before Xavier did whatever these men wanted. That was all they could hope for now.

"Our bosses have requests."

"You better do what I say, or you're going to go down." Xavier's heavy breathing filled the warehouse. "Do you know who I am?"

The Iranians frowned and looked at each other.

Xavier started yelling. "What's happening?"

Horns blared.

"Fuck. My brakes—"

All the sudden a loud bang rent the air. The screech of metal and the horrible sound of impact filled the airwave, the boom deafening in the silent warehouse.

Zara and Carolina jumped.

Did Xavier just…? The person who wanted them dead was just in a horrendous accident. What did that mean for them?

53

———

God, what if Zara was dead?

And if she wasn't, how was he going to find her?

Jake got in Jillian's passenger seat, put his head in his hands. "We've got to think. We've got to figure out how to get to her."

"I've got everybody in the office ready to go as soon as we find a location. We will get her back."

Jillian reached her hand out and grabbed his and squeezed. The contact should have been reassuring, but Jake was beyond consolation.

"I need to focus." ALIAS wasn't without resources. They needed to employ all of them to get Zara back.

Jillian drove towards Rodriguez's house. The fucker better let them in.

It was taking forever. Traffic was snarled.

"Why the fuck is the traffic so bad?"

Jill turned on the radio.

"Do we have a recording of when Zara was at their house? When he was insisting that they drink the tea?"

"Yes."

"Could we give it to the FBI?" That's who would be coordinating the kidnapping response. Right?

"Not a bad idea." She handed him her phone. "Look up Jo Miner. She's my contact at the FBI."

Before Jake could make the call, a reporter on the radio spoke up. "This just in. Xavier Rodriguez has been in a massive car accident. We're awaiting further details."

"No, no, no, no, no." Static filled Jake's ears. His breath stopped in his throat. He couldn't say anything beyond no.

The radio host continued, "All we know at this time is that Congressman Rodriguez insisted on driving himself back home to await a call from his wife's kidnappers. On his way back, he ran a red light and was hit by two cars coming from opposite directions. The congressman is being life-flighted to the hospital. We believe all three drivers are in critical condition."

Jill said, "That's why traffic's so bad."

"Shit, this cannot be a coincidence. Why was Rodriguez driving himself?"

Jillian tapped her finger against her mouth. "I wish we could get a hold of his cell phone. Maybe he made a call that he didn't want overheard."

"What hospital?" Jake said. "Where would they take him?"

"Jake, even if we went to the hospital, we can't get close to him. It's a security nightmare."

"What about the Marshals? Can we see if Alex and Shep have any connections? Maybe they know what hospital he's at. Maybe they can get close to him." His thoughts were pinging all over the place. He couldn't settle on one idea.

"Okay. We might be able to get some intelligence."

Jillian pressed the display on her dash. *Call Kita.*

"Yo," Kita answered.

"Can you see if Alex has any idea where Rodriguez is or who's protecting him? Is there any way to see if we can get near him?" Jill drummed her fingers against the steering wheel.

Kita sighed. "Yeah, I've got bad news."

Jake was already shaking his head. "No, no, no, no."

"What kind of bad news?"

"I talked to Alex. Rodriguez didn't make it. They're holding off on a press release because they're hoping the kidnappers will try and make contact either at his house or on his cell. But Rodriguez is a dead end, literally."

Fuuuucccckkkk.

Their only credible lead was dead.

Jake wanted to punch the dash.

"What the fuck am I going to do?"

Marsh popped in on the conversation. "I'm at the parking lot of the Yard. Found the car."

Jake's stomach tossed acid, backing up in his throat. *Please don't be dead.* He hadn't prayed since his sister died, but he put his hands together, ready to bargain with God or the devil.

"Car is empty and pretty much undisturbed." The rustling came over their comms. "I see her phone on the dash."

"What about the trunk?" Jake ground out.

He heard the mechanism pop.

"Empty!"

Jake rubbed a trembling hand over his mouth. He couldn't stop shaking. "She isn't dead." Thank God, thank God.

But in the back of his mind, lingered…*Yet.*

"Hey, hey! I got a ping on Zara," Kita said excitedly. "Crap. She disappeared again. But I've got a location."

"She's in an industrial section of D.C. near the Anacostia River." Kita rattled off the address. "It's not too far from where Zara's car is."

Jake punched the location into the GPS. "Go!"

"I'm pulling up more info on it now," Kita continued. "Looks like it's for sale right now so tracing who owns it will likely be a dead end."

"Kita. For the love of God please stop using the word, dead."

"We need backup. You can't just go busting in without a plan," Jill said.

"Let's meet up around the corner from the building." Marsh named an intersection.

"Be there soon."

"Can we go any faster?" he begged Jill.

"There's a security camera on a warehouse across the street." Kita said, "I've got eyes on the building."

"Anything happening?"

"All quiet at the moment."

Jake ran through scenarios in his head, trying to come up with any way to rescue her safely.

Marsh dropped in on the line. "I've got a warrant to enter. The judge came through in a big way."

"Ho ho," Kita interrupted. "One of the guys just stepped out to smoke a cigarette. Trying to get a visual ID."

"Any intelligence would help at this point."

"Wait, I recognize him." Kita didn't say anything else.

"Who is it?" Jake demanded.

"Uh, one of the guys who planted the bomb at Ghorbani's."

Iranians? Could they have kidnapped Xavier's wife? But that would create an international incident. It seemed like a really bad idea. Did that mean that Xavier was working with the Iranians? Or were the Iranians working against Xavier?

"These guys have nothing to lose."

"We need a plan." Jill patiently threw out ideas. Marsh chimed in, and so did Kita.

Jill said, "I need to be the voice of caution. We can't just storm in."

"We can't leave them in that warehouse. Every minute increases the danger." Jake's heart slowed, banging heavy and somber in his chest. "Especially if they find out Xavier is dead."

Everyone was silent.

"What do you want to do?" Marsh asked.

"We need to incentivize them to let the women go." Jake wracked his brain. What could these two want that would help them?

"I know what will work."

54

———

They were going to die.

Zara and Carolina huddled together. She couldn't see any way around it. ALIAS hadn't come, and the two men had gotten increasingly agitated. They'd called Xavier again, but he didn't answer.

That crash had not sounded good. If the men's means to get whatever they wanted was dead, so were they. The men were already wanted by the authorities for the bombing.

I don't want to die. I mean, whoever really ever wanted *to die.* But shit, she had barely lived. She had things she wanted to do. Being close to death put everything in perspective. She wanted Jake.

She wanted a future. She wanted to work hard during the week and then spend Saturday mornings lazing away in bed before they ran together and then got coffee.

She wanted him to meet her family. She wanted kids and a life. She wanted to spend her days working for good and her nights wrapped in his arms.

She had more to do. But she just couldn't see a way out of this.

There was a knock at the exterior door to the office. Both guys were angry now. But at the noise, they flinched, then looked at each other. The angry one came over and held his weapon on Zara and Carolina. He jerked his head towards the door and told the other guy to answer it.

"We're closed. Go away," he said to whoever was outside. He'd opened the door a sliver.

"I know the women are in there."

Zara jerked and sat up straighter. That was Jake!

"I'm willing to trade if you let them go."

What was he doing? No, no. This wasn't right.

The nice one said something too low for Zara to hear. Jake said, "I have something you want. You've got to know you're burned."

They didn't say a word.

"Xavier's dead." Jake kept his voice even.

Zara's heart sank. They were not getting out of here. And now Jake was going to be dead, too.

"Your pictures are all over the news in conjunction with the bomb at Ghorbani's house. But there's one thing you could do that would save you with your government."

The guy made a pffft sound and started to close the door.

Jake said, "Look at me. Do you recognize me?"

The guy took a step back, glanced back at his friend, his eyes wide.

"Yeah, you know who I am. I can tell you where she went."

Zara realized what Jake was doing. *No, no, no, no.* He couldn't do that. He couldn't tell them where Layla was.

Besides, he said he didn't know. She shook her head violently. Jake had his hands in the air, palms facing out. "But the only way you'll get that information is if you let the women go. I am not armed."

He kept his hands up. The guy waved him into the small

office but stayed back so that Jake couldn't disarm him. The other one frisked him, looking for weapons.

Jake was far enough inside now that he could see the interior of the warehouse through the glass wall. He saw Zara.

And for a moment, she saw the relief in his eyes. He hadn't known if she was here.

She tried to transmit to him, *What the hell are you doing?*

Both guys were looking away. He mouthed, "Trust me."

Zara's eyes filled with tears, and she nodded. He had come for her. She hadn't lost faith, but she also hadn't believed that ALIAS would be able to figure out where she and Carolina were.

But he was here. He was insane and going to destroy his life and Layla's if he told them where she was, but he'd come for her.

The two guys spoke to each other in hushed tones.

Jake kept his gaze on the men. Somehow, he shrunk his body, making him seem less intimidating.

It was strange because he wasn't hunched, but somehow his body was just smaller. The angry one held his gun on Jake.

"You tell us where she's at."

"Let the women go."

"If we carry out the FATWA, we will be saved."

Jake nodded.

"We'll be heroes."

Jake said, "I won't tell you a thing until you let them go."

The nice one narrowed his eyes. "This is a trick."

"I would never risk her life—" Jake waved toward Zara, "— on a gamble."

She saw heard it then. Whenever he wanted to say something but didn't want to lie, he was very specific with his words. He didn't say it wasn't a trick. He said he wouldn't gamble.

Something was going to happen.

"Let them go, and I'll tell you what you need to know."

Not where she is, but what you need to know. Hope simmered through her like a drug flowing through her in a cool wave. But the men would be angry when they found out he had no intention of telling them where Layla was.

They were considering it. Zara could see their body language relaxing. They thought this was their way out.

"But if either one of them is hurt, I'll turn you over and you'll both be in prison for the rest of your lives."

The angry one laughed. "You're bluffing."

"No, I'm not."

"Why would you do this?"

Jake pointed to Zara. "Because she's mine…and I'll do anything to protect her."

Zara's eyes welled, emotion balled in her throat. She couldn't talk because of the gag, but she tried to transmit with her eyes that she loved him.

He clearly had a plan, but things could still go horribly wrong. How were they going to get out of this?

"My car is parked right out front. Give them the keys and let them drive away." Jake held up his keys. "Then you'll get what you want."

The two men conferred with each other. The angry one finally said, "Fine."

They pointed their weapons at Zara and Carolina. "You never saw our faces. You say anything differently, we will come after you. Understand?"

They both nodded in terror.

"You need to uncuff them and take off their gags. They can't go outside looking like that."

The men tore off the tape quickly and unchained them.

Jake handed the keys to Zara. "Go."

"I love you." She curled her fingers around the keys. She didn't want to leave him at all.

No way was she leaving without telling him.

His gaze softened, and he reached out.

Zara stepped toward him, and the angry one barked. "No closer."

"Go. Take Carolina home," Jake said. "It'll be okay."

As she stepped out the door, he said one last thing.

"I didn't save my sister, but I am going to save you."

God, that sounded so final.

What if he didn't really have a plan?

Zara and Carolina got in the car. Zara gripped the steering wheel tightly. She didn't want to leave.

"Don't look, but I'm in the backseat," Jillian said. "You need to start the car and head toward the office. Once we're further away, I'll drive."

Zara's hands relaxed. "What's the plan?"

"I can't tell you, but we've got it under control. Hopefully," Jillian muttered the last word, but Zara heard her anyway.

Carolina sat in the passenger seat. "Are we really free?"

"Yes. I'm sorry to inform you that your husband is dead."

Carolina shuddered. "I know." She wiped at her face.

"You're safe."

Zara pressed her palm to her heart. They were safe from Xavier now. But what about Jake?

55

———

She was safe.

Jake breathed a huge sigh and let his head fall back once Zara drove away.

The two men scowled at him. One cuffed his hands, in front, while the other held the weapon on him. He could disarm them right now but that wasn't the plan. He couldn't afford to make any mistakes.

He wasn't out of the woods yet. But he was counting on their desire to kill Layla to rein in their impulse to hurt him.

"We can't take that van. The authorities have the description."

The guy with the keffiyah kicked the wall.

"You still have the keys for the woman's car?"

They nodded.

He pretended not to know where it was. "Is it close?"

They nodded again, quickly getting the picture.

"Okay, let's go get it."

"Where is the girl?" The one without the scarf jabbed him with the Beretta.

"You don't think I'm that stupid, do you? I tell you, I'm

dead." The plan was to lead them to one of their safe houses about an hour away in a fairly rural location where the FBI and CIA would be waiting. Less chance of civilian casualties and better chance of a more controlled take down. There was still plenty that could go wrong. But Zara was safe. "I'll take you."

Jill and Marsh were calling in reinforcements. Everyone was heading out to the rendezvous point as soon as Jake and the two Iranians left this location and as soon as he knew that Zara was far enough away.

He still had his earpiece in. Luckily the two men hadn't noticed. The tech was small and not easily detectable.

"You're a go. We got Zara and Carolina Rodriguez." Jill's gave him the joyous news in his ear.

Now he could take these guys down.

Maybe he could get some intelligence in the meantime.

The men got in the van. The one in the passenger side ordered, "You. Open the garage door."

Jake pulled up the metal door. Scarf guy had his window down and his weapon pointed at Jake. They drove the van out of the warehouse slowly and paused.

"Pull the door down and then get in the back."

Jake opened the back door of the van, but they were too close to the building. "Pull out another foot so I have room to close this garage door."

A cell phone started ringing.

Jake had a split-second realization. Ghorbani had been killed by a car bomb in his garage. Fuck.

The terror on the face of the guy with the gun registered, along with another ring of the cell.

Fuuucckkk.

Jake dove for the doorway of the office, aiming to get under that desk and hoping the flimsy wall offered some protection from what was coming.

Boom.

BOOM. *Boom. Boom.*

"What was that?" Zara cried. She'd gotten a little turned around because she wasn't used to driving in D.C., and she wasn't exactly sure where she was.

Carolina scrunched down in the passenger seat. "I don't know."

"Shit." Jillian cursed in the backseat.

"Jake?" Her heart turned to rock in her chest. Her fingers tingling as she gripped the steering wheel too tightly. "Is Jake okay?"

"Keep going to the office."

"Fuck that."

Zara figured out where she was and turned back.

Jillian swore softly and sat up.

"What's wrong?" Zara looked at Jillian in the rearview mirror.

Jillian took in a deep breath, composed herself. Her eyes hardened. "Keep driving."

"Tell me." Panic fluttered in her chest. Fear whitened her vision, and pure terror flooded her system. "Something exploded."

Zara turned towards the building they'd just left.

"You're going the wrong way," Jillian said tensely.

"No, I'm not. I need to see."

Jillian's face didn't move a muscle.

"How can you be so cold?" Zara accused her. "Was Jake in that building?"

Jillian's face spasmed.

Okay, not cold. "I'm sorry, but I *need to know* if Jake is okay."

"Dwayne, report." Jillian's eyes went flat. "We'll be right there."

Zara sped up until she was going fifty down the streets, racing back to the building they'd just escaped from.

When she turned the corner, she slammed on the brakes, jerking the car to a halt. "It's rubble."

Zara staggered from the car, then froze, unable to move. Jillian hopped out and strode over to Dwayne and Maria.

The warehouse where they'd been held captive had caved in and was little more than a pile of bricks. The white van had blown across the street and flipped over, the open back door swinging wildly. Dwayne and Maria were crouched down, staring into the passenger section.

Dwayne stood and shook his head grimly. "Kidnappers are dead."

"What about Jake?"

"He's not in the van."

They all turned and stared at the destroyed building. The fire department roared up with sirens blaring.

Jake! Zara sprinted for the building.

Dwayne grabbed her, restraining her. "Zara, you can't go in there. Let the fire department do their thing."

"He needs to be okay." She slumped over Dwayne's arm, suddenly unable to hold her body up. *Jake!*

Jillian coordinated with the fire captain. The fire crew set up and began spraying the small flames, but they needed rescue equipment to dig through the damaged building to look for Jake.

Suddenly, Dwayne's arm tightened around Zara's middle. Jillian and Maria jumped up and touched their ears.

"Hold on."

"What's going on?" Zara grabbed Dwayne's arm.

Jillian held up her hand. "You heard it, too?"

Dwayne swung Zara around, squeezing her hard.

Jillian started laughing, complete joy on her face. "Oh, my God. He's alive."

Zara burst into tears.

56

Jake drifted through layers of fog, trying to get a grasp on where he was, like swimming through the watering hole when he was a kid, unable to see, unable to sense anything. Slowly, sounds crept in. The hiss of a machine. A slow, sonorous beep. The sough of his breath.

His lungs tight, he tried to draw in air slowly. Something was over his mouth. That's why he couldn't breathe.

He reached up to grab it and realized…oxygen mask. Consciousness returned in a rush.

Zara! He bolted up in bed. Or tried to; he had wires and tubes attached to his head, chest and arms.

Jake pried his eyes open, trying to compute his surroundings. Sterile walls, linoleum, machines…hospital. The comforting warmth of someone holding his hand filtered in.

Zara sat next to him in the hospital room, her body half resting on his bed, his hand clasped in hers.

She was okay.

Relief washed through him. The beeping slowed.

"Zara." Her name was muffled as he tried to speak through the mask.

She shot up, her hands clasped his and stared at him with a burgeoning hope. "You're awake." She smiled tremulously.

Slowly, memories strobed in his brain. The ring of the cell phone. The panicked look on the kidnapper's face. The realization that if he didn't move, he'd be dead.

The sonic boom, unable to hear, as the building collapsed on top of the desk. Talking to his team.

Hearing Jill say, "Oh, my God, he's alive."

Zara's sobs.

And then nothing.

He lifted his right hand to his forehead. God damn, his head hurt. But he didn't care. He looked at Zara.

"You're okay?"

She nodded and reached out a trembling hand, brushed her fingers over his face, then cupped his jaw. "How do you feel?"

"Like I got blown up." He tried to grin, but smiling did something that made his head hurt more, and he groaned.

"Not funny, Jake."

"Too soon?"

"It will never be okay to joke about." Tears trembled on her lashes. "I thought you were dead."

He'd realized a lot when he'd been walking into that warehouse. "I need to tell you something." He needed to get this out.

She tensed.

"I was protecting myself," he said.

She shook her head. "No, not true. You were protecting everyone but yourself."

"I've been using my need to save people to make shallow connections that I know can't last, because then I won't get hurt." He'd been left behind by both his sister and his mother, and even his father, and he'd erected that protective barrier to keep isolated and safe from pain.

"The first person I really connected to since my sister's death was Layla." Zara squeezed his hand. "And I knew she had to get left behind. So it was still a shallow connection, because in my job, there's no space for any kind of continuing relationship with a client, even if they become a friend."

"I'd say you were wrong about connecting with people. You have a whole family who loves you and is worried about you."

Jake glanced around the empty room.

"Everyone's in the waiting room. The hospital let me stay in here with you."

He knew there were things he should ask. The kidnappers, Xavier, Carolina. But all that could wait. "Waking up to see you is everything."

"I'm so grateful you woke up." Zara squeezed his fingers gently. "Your friends are all here for you. They've been worried sick."

He wanted to see them, but first he needed to tell her. "I realized walking into that warehouse that I want a relationship with you. I want to grow with you and love with you. I'm ready to expand my horizons and learn and love. And that's because of *you*."

There had to be more to life than only sacrifice. And he wanted to find that more with her.

He looked at her uncertainly.

She hadn't said a word.

"I know I didn't protect you. I wasn't there for you. I let you get kidnapped."

She shook her head again. "First of all, you had to go take care of your mother. I knew that. Is she okay?"

"Yeah." Jake realized he was going to have to make amends with his mother. He was half of the equation of perpetuating the distance between them.

"I'm glad she's okay." Zara held tight to his hand. "If you'd been there, you'd be dead. Xavier had no compunction about killing anyone who got in his way. And you came when it mattered. I knew nothing would stop you from coming for me. But you gave me the confidence to trust in myself while I was waiting. What were you thinking, trading yourself?" Her voice was filled with horror. "You matter, Jake."

"I was thinking that I want more time with you."

"Hard to do that if you put yourself in danger like that." Zara frowned at him. "I realized something, too."

"Yeah, what did you realize?" He had hope it was something good.

"I want to move in with you. I want to spend time with you. I want to wake up in the mornings with you."

Emotion balled in his throat.

"I want you to meet my family. I want everything."

Everything sounded about right. "Me, too."

Zara leaned up on the bed and gently pressed her lips to his. It was the tamest, most innocuous, most gentle kiss. And yet, the most intimate.

"I love you."

His heart expanded in his chest, growing until he thought he would burst from happiness. She loved him!

The door to his hospital room swung open. Dr. Mina Patel strode in with a chart.

"Well, you've certainly given everyone a scare." She smiled, her brown eyes sparkling.

"Hey, Mina."

"Glad to see you're awake. There are a lot of people waiting on that news." She did a quick check of his vitals.

"All your scans came back normal. You have a concussion from the blast. But no internal bleeding or punctures. We've been monitoring your heart, and everything seems good. I see you've divested yourself of the oxygen mask." She checked his O2 levels. "I think it's safe to keep it off."

"Your lungs should be clear. You may experience some tinnitus over the next few days, but hopefully it won't last. You're incredibly lucky."

Jake looked at Zara. "Don't have to tell me that, Doc."

She smiled at them again. "If it's all right with you, I'm going to let everybody in. They're literally hovering at the door, waiting to see if you're okay. Technically, they should visit in pairs, but it should be okay for a few minutes."

Jake nodded his assent. "It's fine."

A few seconds later, everyone from ALIAS tumbled into the room, plus a few extras:

Jill and Hamish, Marsh and Ayesha, Alex and Kita, Dwayne and Maria, and Shep.

"Damn glad to see you're okay, man," Dwayne said. Maria smiled softly at him.

"Holy shit, you scared us." Kita patted his hand. "Nice move, trading yourself." She and Alex shared a secret look.

Marsh squeezed his arm gently. "We all do things that are crazy to protect the ones we love." Ayesha tilted her head on Marsh's shoulder, a smear of coral paint on her chin, and smiled. "You certainly made a statement."

Hamish broke the intense moment. "I may have to re-think this job. Seems to be an awful lot of getting blown up."

Jill snorted. "But the perks outweigh the negatives."

"True." Hamish slung his arm around Jill's shoulder and squeezed.

Shep said with wonder, "Damn, son, you must have a guardian angel. Both the kidnappers died in the blast."

Jake couldn't drum up a bit of remorse. The two men had tried to blow up the scientist, tried to kill Layla, kidnapped

Zara and Carolina, and would have killed him the instant that they'd gotten what they wanted.

He took in all the people in the room and realized that Zara was right. His coworkers and their loves were his family. Everyone had paired off, and they were happy. Zara beamed at him. Seeing the joy on her face, his own grew. She'd moved into his heart and planted her flag.

"Wish Viktor was here." Jake missed his old friend.

"He'd be thrilled for you," Jill said softly. "We'll do an in depth debrief when you're out of the hospital, but everyone's safe. Xavier is dead. The reports were true. Turns out my friend at the CIA had been monitoring him for a while. General thought is the Iranians got rid of him by cutting his brakes, but we're not sure. We may never know."

"What about the story in the paper and being investigated by Congress?"

"I talked to some contacts and turns out that Xavier was the one driving the push to investigate ALIAS. We'll still tweak our business model, but for now, we're safe."

Mina popped back in the room. "Everyone out. He needs to rest."

Zara tried to disengage her fingers from his, a strange anguish running through her. He was okay. He needed to rest.

But Jake held on tight. "Stay. Please."

"You need to rest."

"I need *you*."

Gratitude filled her.

"I was lost the night I met you," Jake said. "I thank whatever impulse sent me to *that* bar *that* night."

Zara crawled into his hospital bed, avoiding the tubes, and

rested her head on his shoulder. "Maybe that's why we connected. We were both lost."

"I could have easily taken a different turn, gone down the opposite path, and been wandering forever. Unfulfilled and unable to find my center. I'd protected Layla, but—"

"You're more than a protector." Zara stared into his beautiful topaz eyes. "You're a partner and a supporter. You're amazing."

He shrugged aside her words.

But she'd would make him see. "You gave me the space to be me. To find me. To trust in myself again." Over and over, he'd reminded her why she chose her life. To build things up. To make a difference. To make the world better.

That night in the bar was the beginning of a new story. Their story. *Shit.*

"We're going to have to come up with an origin story."

"What do you mean?"

"We can't tell our kids that we met in a bar as a one-night stand."

"Kids," he said faintly.

She smiled. "Yep. But we'll have time to work out what we're going to say."

"You're good at spinning things." Jake threaded their fingers together. "You'll find a way to make it truthful and real."

"And if I can't, you'll find a way to tell the story without telling the whole story." He was always so careful with his words. A fact she appreciated most of the time.

"There will still be things I can't tell you." He lifted their clasped hands and pressed a kiss to her knuckles.

"I understand." Now that she understood what ALIAS did, she accepted the need for discretion.

"But I'll always tell you the important things, like I love you completely."

"Sometimes you have to lose yourself to find out who you really are." Zara had been drifting along, trying to find her place, trying to make her mark. Losing herself, moving to D.C., falling in love with Jake. Those were all steps in the journey to discovering out what was truly important.

"Everything we did brought us to this moment." Zara listened to the steady beat of his heart. "Meeting in the bar was just the beginning. For both of us."

"We are worth the journey."

57

____

A FEW MONTHS LATER

Zara Cooper woke slowly, warm and cozy, in the luxurious sheets of her bed. The high-thread-count cotton tangled between her legs, and she stretched sore muscles from last night's strenuous workout.

Jake, her absolutely amazing live-in lover, was gone.

But the days of waking up alone were behind her, so she knew he'd be back in a second.

Jake sauntered through the bedroom door with two steaming mugs of coffee. He wore cotton joggers low on his hips, his muscled chest and biceps on display, and her brain blanked at the perfection of his body.

"Morning." He set the coffee on her nightstand and then bent to kiss her.

Zara pushed up to sitting and grabbed the coffee, taking a sip of his delectable brew. She moaned. "My hero."

Jake snorted and slid into bed next to her. "Are you talking about me, or the coffee?"

She leaned back against the headboard, eyes closed, a smile tipping her mouth. "Why can't it be both?"

"If only you loved me the way you love that coffee," he teased.

"I love you more than this coffee."

"Wow, that's really saying something."

He leaned in to kiss her again. Last night had been amazing. Jake continued to be a generous and inventive lover. And that was awesome, but she loved these lazy mornings with soft kisses and conversation as much as their passion.

"We need to get going soon."

Their regular Saturday routine was shelved this week. Normally, they had a lazy morning in bed, then ran in the park. They visited Jake's mom and had lunch with her. The relationship was on the road to repair. Zara had been a bridge between the two when things got awkward. She was thrilled that he and his mom were talking again.

They both needed the connection. And to honor Cia's memory.

"Today's the day." Jake looked nervous, concern crinkling his brow.

"It's going to be fine."

She tried to soothe him but the truth was she was nervous for him.

Her cell phone rang. "It's Allison." Zara answered the call. "Good morning."

"Hey, just wanted to let you know we are set for Carolina Rodriguez's interview Monday morning."

The governor of California had called a special election to replace Xavier Rodriguez, and his grieving widow stepped up and said she was going to run in his place to honor his memory.

She won in a landslide last week. Kidnap victim, widow, immigrant. There was no contest. She'd also begun plans to fund more buildings for "A New Home," the domestic violence shelter that Xavier had eliminated from his schedule.

The public loved her.

"Great. I'll be there as well."

Carolina wanted Zara to work on her media relations and PR, but no hiding this time.

"She's an amazing woman who has been through so much in the past year." Zara was so proud of Carolina.

They had set up her return from being kidnapped without involving ALIAS or the Iranians.

Carolina Rodriguez had cooperated. They'd driven her around the D.C. area, then dropped her at a location where she could make a call. She told the authorities that she had no recollection of what happened and that she'd basically woken up on a bench on the mall in D.C. Zara wasn't positive, but Kita may have erased some surveillance videos to make sure there was no way to tie back to Adams-Larsen.

The authorities didn't have any leads on the kidnappers. Carolina stuck to the story that she hadn't seen them. Or the drugs they'd given her had given her amnesia. Which was very common. Turns out years of hiding her abuse had made it easy for her to hide the truth about her abduction.

The security cameras had been wiped, and Xavier had done an excellent job of making sure there was no evidence when she was taken from their house. The authorities were still looking but so far, the story had held.

The visual everyone remembered was her with her daughters at the internment of her husband. It had been PR gold.

"I'm excited to be able to do a more in-depth piece about our newest congresswoman."

"She's going to do amazing things." Zara had thought Xavier was her dream client. Boy, had she been wrong. But Carolina Rodriguez might just be the perfect candidate. They'd had multiple discussions about the future. A lot of the policies that Xavier had taken credit for in his platform had been researched and suggested by Carolina.

He just hadn't wanted to give her credit.

Allison said, "I appreciate the leads." Because they had never given Allison the information on Xavier—the CIA wanted the Iranian connection dead and buried along with the billionaire—ALIAS had been giving her other stories to pursue.

"The piece on the dangers of sex work is set for tomorrow." The sex worker who'd been beat up in the photos was found safe, and she was fine. They would never know what Xavier had planned for her, but they could rest easy that she was okay, and she had no intention of accusing Jake of beating her up. Instead, Allison interviewed her about the perils of getting caught between trying to make a living and the inevitable desire for their clients to want to keep things quiet and their sometimes violent methods for enforcing a sex worker's silence.

Zara hung up with Allison.

"Time to get going."

Half an hour later, Jake and Zara drove to the ALIAS office in Georgetown in Jake's truck. He held her hand loosely in his. She could feel his fingers trembling.

A stack of well-worn Jessica Jones and Luke Cage comics from the ALIAS series were thrown in the console. Zara loved the symbolism of that. Jake had been coming around to the belief that he deserved love and he deserved to be happy. He could save the world for everyone and still have his own relationships. Zara wanted to be his Jessica Jones to his Luke Cage and he was on board with that.

~

JAKE'S KNEE bobbed up and down.

Nervous energy buzzed through his body.

When they got to the office, Kita and Alex were already in the conference room. They'd set up the laptop and connected to a secure VPN while the laptop screen displayed on a pull-down screen.

The front doorbell rang.

Dwayne was in the booth. "They're here."

Jake was a little jittery. He really hoped this wasn't a mistake. "Go ahead and let them in. Zara will greet them."

"You ready?" Kita asked.

"I think so."

A few minutes later, Zara walked into the conference room with Charlie and Karen Hansen. Jake made the introductions.

"This is Alex Saunders. He's a US Deputy Marshal. And this is Kita, our tech guru who makes sure our communications are secure."

The Hansens looked completely confused. Zara had her hands clasped in front of her. "Would you like some tea or coffee or cookies?" She gestured to the sideboard.

Maria had made some floral sugar cookies in happy spring colors of pink, purple and yellow.

No one took her up on the offer.

"I don't understand why we're here," Charlie Hansen said.

"Please, just have a seat."

The coffee he'd had earlier, usually his favorite, churned in his stomach. This was dangerous, but it had to be done. The Hansens had continued to search and make noise about the disappearance of their son, Ben.

Zara handed Jake a bottle of water and squeezed his elbow. "It'll be okay."

Kita set up the secure line.

Alex was a trooper because he was here somewhat misrepresenting himself. And if the Hansen's ever challenged it, they could all be in trouble.

"We need you to understand that this is necessary. If the situation ever changes, of course we will reassess."

The FATWA had not been lifted. At the moment, the Iranians were very quiet. No one had wanted to let it get out that a US congressman had been conspiring with a foreign government. The CIA released a statement saying that the two Iranians who had bombed Dr. Ghorbani had inadvertently set off a bomb in the warehouse district in D.C. and blown themselves up.

No mention was made of them kidnapping Carolina Rodriguez.

"Situation?" Karen Hansen had lost even more weight. She was skin and bones at this point. Her hands trembled constantly.

Fuck, he didn't know if this was a good idea, but it had to be done. "Give us a second."

The laptop sparked to life and showed two people. Ben Hansen sat in a chair, white background, no identifying objects that would give away where he and Layla were.

Layla sat next to him, her hand clasped in his, but they had put a wig on her and given glasses with blue lenses to conceal her eye color.

Jake wanted her disguised enough that Ben's parents wouldn't be able to recognize her, hopefully, if they saw her again.

Everything about Layla's case had been unusual, and this was no different. You weren't supposed to have contact with family members after you relocated, but usually, those family members had some idea you were in danger. He hoped this would be enough to put the Hansens' hearts at ease.

"Ben!" His father jumped up so fast, the chair tipped over.

"Hey, Mom and Dad, I'm so sorry."

Karen Hansen hadn't said a word. She sat mute, tears streaming down her face. Her throat moved as if she was swallowing, trying to get words out.

"Where are you?" his dad asked.

"I can't tell you."

"What do you mean you can't tell us?"

"My girlfriend is in danger, and we had to go into witness protection."

His father sat back down, slowly, like an old man. "Witness protection?"

"Yeah, I was trying to reassure you by giving you the letter and sending a postcard, but it sounds like that didn't really work."

"You're okay," his mother finally whispered. She had clasped her hands together on top of the mahogany conference table so tightly her knuckles were white.

"Yeah, we're okay. Hopefully one day we'll be able to come home."

Jake watched the relief on his parents' faces turn to sorrow. "When will we be able to see you?"

"I honestly don't know, but we set this up so you would know why I left."

Ben Hansen watched his son.

"This is my girlfriend. I can't tell you her name because that would put us all in danger."

Jake stood behind Ben's parents and studied Layla. She looked good. She caught his gaze, and he gave her a thumbs up. She made a little heart sign with her fingers and smiled at him.

Then she turned to look at Ben. They looked at each other with pure love shining from their eyes.

Jake could see it now. He hadn't understood when Ben and

Layla first insisted that they had to be together, but he got it now.

He glanced at Zara.

She was watching him, not the screen, a big smile on her face. Ben and his parents talked quietly for a few minutes. In some ways, he owed Ben and Layla everything.

If he hadn't been so distraught, he would have never gone to that bar. It wasn't what he did or who he was. But that night, he'd been so out of sorts, and that's when he met Zara.

He was so lucky.

He and Zara had saved each other.

And they deserved happiness. Just like Ben and Layla deserved theirs.

Charlie Hanson put his arm around his wife's shoulder. "We love you, son."

"Love you too, Mom and Dad."

"I hope we can see you soon."

"Unfortunately, we have to keep hiding. And you can't tell anyone about this meeting. It would put everyone in danger."

Karen Hansen stared at the screen hard, as if trying to memorize her son's face. "When did all this happen?"

"We met at a coffee shop." Ben stared into Layla's eyes. "It was love at first sight."

Karen Hansen put a hand to her mouth.

Layla leaned her head against Ben's shoulder.

"I know this is hard, but I knew you would understand because I found the love of my life, and she's where I need to be. She is my home."

That's what it was. Jake finally understood.

Home. Zara was his home. He could be anywhere in the world, doing anything in the world, and she would be his home.

And he would be hers.

***

Wow what a roller coaster ride over the past nine years. I loved creating the found family of the ALIAS group. I got a little teary writing the end. Thank you for reading!

If you'd like to read about the night Jake and Zara met, click here for a link to the free prequel, Duped.

Sign up for Lisa's Confidants and receive updates on books and other fun happenings.

ACKNOWLEDGMENTS

It's been a long road back to writing after several years and I have zillion people to thank.

Many thanks to Tawdra, Mel and Leslie for being my emotional support during the past few years. And Tawdra for her final edits.

Also thanks to the morning writing crew, Page One, for inspiring me to show up every day and work.

Huge thanks to my editor, Becca Hensley Mysoor, for her insight and guidance. I am so grateful for you!

Thank you to Robin Johnson at Florida Girl Designs for the stunning cover.

I started the genesis of this book over three years ago. I plotted and wrote the first third of the story over two years ago. (While some of the elements now mimic today's political landscape, that was not my intention when I came up with the plot for this book)

Thank you most of all for the readers of the ALIAS series who stuck with me to the end. I hope Jake and Zara are a fitting finale!

ALSO BY LISA HUGHEY

ALIAS

Duped (An ALIAS Prequel)

Stalked (ALIAS #1)

Hunted (ALIAS #2)

Vanished (ALIAS #3)

Deceived (ALIAS #4)

Saved (ALIAS Short)

Compromised (ALIAS #5)

Conned (ALIAS #6)

Black Cipher Files Romantic Suspense

The Encounter, A Prequel to Blowback

Blowback

Betrayals

Burned

Dangerous Game

Black Cipher Files Box Set (includes Blowback, Betrayals, and
Burned)

Snow Creek Christmas

Love on Main Street: A Snow Creek Christmas – 7 Author anthology

One Silent Night (from Love on Main Street)

Miracle on Main Street (standalone novella)

Family Stone Romantic Suspense

Stone Cold Heart, (Jess, Family Stone #1)

Carved in Stone (Connor, Family Stone #2)

Heart of Stone (Riley, Family Stone #3)

Still the One (Jack, Family Stone #4)

Jar of Hearts (Keisha & Shane, Family Stone #5)

Queen of Hearts (Shelley, Family Stone #6)

Cold as Stone (John, Family Stone #7)

Family Stone Box Set (Stone Cold Heart, Carved in Stone, Heart of Stone, Still the One, & Jar of Hearts)

The Nostradamus Prophecies

View To A Kill #1

Never Say Never #2

Billionaire Breakfast Club

His Semi-Charmed Life (Camp Firefly Falls #11 and Billionaire Breakfast Club #0)

Everything He Wants (Billionaire Breakfast Club #1 The Jock)

She Feels Like Home (Billionaire Breakfast Club #3)

ABOUT LISA

USA Today Bestselling Author Lisa Hughey started writing romance in the fourth grade. That particular story involved a prince and an engagement. Now, she writes about strong heroines who are perfectly capable of rescuing themselves and the heroes who love both their strength and their vulnerability. She pens romances of all types—suspense, paranormal, and contemporary—but at their heart, all her books celebrate the power of love.

She lives in Cape Ann Massachusetts with her fabulously supportive husband, two out of three awesome mostly-grown kids, and one somewhat grumpy cat.

Beach walks, hiking, and traveling are her favorite ways to pass the time when she isn't plotting new ways to get her characters to fall in love.

Lisa loves to hear from readers and has tons of places you can connect with her. It's a wonder she gets any writing done at all....

Sign Up for Lisa's Confidants
Visit Lisa on the Web

<u>Follow Lisa's Boards on Pinterest</u>
<u>Follow Lisa on Instagram</u>
<u>Email Lisa</u>
<u>Be Lisa's Friend on Goodreads</u>
<u>Like Lisa on Facebook at Lisa Hughey: My Books</u>